Shield from the Heart

Mary K. Norris

CRIMSON
ROMANCE
F+W Media, Inc.

Published by
Crimson Romance
an imprint of F+W Media, Inc.
10151 Carver Road, Suite 200
Blue Ash, Ohio 45242

www.crimsonromance.com

ISBN 10: 1-4405-6187-7
ISBN 13: 978-1-4405-6187-0
eISBN 10: 1-4405-6188-5
eISBN 13: 978-1-4405-6188-7

This is a work of fiction. Names, characters, corporations, institutions, organizations, events, or locales in this novel are either the product of the author's imagination or, if real, used fictitiously. The resemblance of any character to actual persons (living or dead) is entirely coincidental.

Dedication

To my Mom and Dad.
You guys never stop believing in me. You always support me no matter what.
Words cannot express how much I love you. Thank you!

Acknowledgments

A quick thank you to all my family and friends that continue to believe in me. I'd also like to thank everyone at Crimson Romance for helping me make this book the best that it can be.

Chapter 1

Here comes the pain.

Footsteps echoed down the hall to stop outside Merrick's cell door. He tried to roll his shoulders to ease the ache in his joints but there was limited mobility with his arms tied behind his back. His fingers were just starting to lose feeling, which meant he probably had a couple more days like this before they untied him. His hands were always well and truly numb when they released him. The better to keep him incapacitated. After all, he wasn't much of a threat if he couldn't feel his hands to throw a fist.

At least they'd cut back on the drugs.

The door clicked as the lock was disengaged. Stale cologne wafted in to override the scent of Pine-Sol. In walked Vander Donahughe.

Merrick blew at the black hair that hung in front of his face to get a better view. Captivity made it a little difficult to keep up with his barber cuts.

As his hair fell to the sides of his face he knew he hadn't imagined it. Vander Donahughe looked different. Older. Wrinkles stood out along his mouth and eyes. His forehead had permanent creases and his hair was more than eighty percent silver.

Two assistants followed him into the room.

No. Not assistants. Merrick recognized the woman who liked to fondle him. Regina. No last name given. Average height, mid-thirties with brown hair and fake blue contacts. The bulky man who stood at her side was someone Merrick had never seen before. The most likely scenario? The man was there as hired muscle.

That was peculiar. Vander wasn't following his regular MO.

"Merrick Haskell." Vander shook out a sheet of paper in front of him as the muscle man pulled him up a chair. "Age: thirty.

Current occupation: private investigator. And I must say you have quite an impressive success rate."

"Buttering me up isn't going to do you any good," said Merrick.

Vander acted as if he'd never even spoken. "Most would look at that success rate and find it curious, myself included. Tell me, Merrick, how is it that you manage to find all those missing people?"

Vander's dark eyes probed at his blank expression as if trying to glean all the information he wanted from Merrick's face.

Merrick didn't give him an inch. "I'm really good at my job."

Vander leaned back in his chair. Comfortable as could be. Merrick ground his teeth.

"And all the reports from your fellow detectives that you used to work with…?" He scanned the paper until he came across what he wanted. "They talk about eccentricities, like your never ending need to contaminate a scene by touching everything possible. Any reason for that?"

Merrick stared straight ahead.

"I'm really trying to help you, Mr. Haskell. I want you to join the Kratos Guild. You see, I'm looking for something."

Despite his current predicament, he found himself staring Vander in the eye. "Who are you looking for?"

"It's not a who, it's a what. And what I'm looking for is an old employee's journal that contains some valuable information."

"Then why don't you ask the employee?"

Vander gave a forced smile. "I'm afraid he's not very chatty. He's in a coma. Has been for some time."

Merrick returned to staring at the wall. "Sorry, can't help you."

Vander grabbed the front of Merrick's chair and pulled it toward him. Merrick's body flew forward but his tied hands stopped him short. The jarring in his shoulders had him gritting his teeth.

"Don't lie to me." Vander kept him tilted forward on the two front legs of his chair. "I know you have an ability. An ability that allows you to gain some kind of information from an object after someone's touched it."

"No idea what you're talking about," Merrick lied through his teeth. "There's no such thing as powers."

His chair rocked as he was forced back. Vander's hands grabbed his face.

And here it comes.

Pain erupted throughout his whole body. Fire burned through his veins, eating him from the inside out. He refused to shut his eyes and instead stared down the root of his hatred. His heart raced in his chest as if it could outrun the agony. His neck prickled as anger boiled beneath the vicious pull of Vander's power. His muscles started to weaken from the energy drain—

Vander stopped.

Merrick gasped for air.

The blackness that usually danced at the edge of his vision didn't come.

Vander had held back.

During Merrick's other interrogations he'd been drained until the point where his muscles were screaming, his heart fluttering like a caged bird, his vision spotting.

Something had changed since those days. And Merrick had a pretty good idea what. Vander was on the run.

"Trying to keep a disguise, eh Vander?"

The way Vander's face darkened let Merrick know he'd hit the nail right on the head. While Merrick might verbally reject the idea of powers existing, he knew otherwise. Vander's ability allowed him to suck the very life out of a person and somehow manipulate that energy to keep himself young. If he was holding back then he was trying to keep the aged appearance he currently wore. That probably had something to do with the fact that Vander's illegal kidnapping and cage fighting had been alerted to the police. He'd had to evacuate his last facility. Merrick had no idea where he'd been held and he certainly had no idea where he was now. But either way, Vander had to watch his back. Eventually he'd screw up and Merrick would be right there to get out of this hell hole.

Vander's hands returned to his face, his fingers digging into the bone of Merrick's jaw.

If Merrick swung his head fast enough he'd be able to take one of those digits and rip it off with nothing but his teeth.

The opportunity was more than tempting.

"I can feel the difference in your energy," said Vander. "I know you have power and it's only a matter of time before I find out what it is."

Merrick's repressed anger started to surface. The back of his neck tingled.

Vander thought he could manhandle him? Thought he could buddy up or buy him off after kidnapping him and torturing him for months?

Screw this fucker.

Merrick thrust his head forward with everything he had. The scent of copper burst into the air. He hoped like hell it was Vander's blood and not his own.

His hair obscured his view but he could hear Regina cry out as she went to Vander's side. The muscle man's beefy arm came around his neck in a choke hold.

"Drug him," Vander snarled as he wiped blood from his lip.

Merrick smirked.

Vander shoved the bloody sleeve he'd used to mop up his face right in front of Merrick. "You think this symbolizes a win for you? We'll see how gutsy you are after we pull the nails right out of your fingertips."

Merrick's vision went red. He struggled anew as Regina came over with a syringe.

Vander pushed the sleeve into his cheek, smearing the blood there. "Enjoy your feeble smell of victory."

But Merrick hardly heard him.

Vander's clothes…the impression in the fabric…

His own power reared up, and the vision bombarded him before he could stop it.

A woman with dark brown hair stared up at him with disgust. But why? She was his. His Cali. His soul mate. She was the one that would set him free. He leaned in to kiss her. If she didn't see that she was his then he'd make her. Her long, slender hands pushed uselessly against him. She was a fighter. He admired that about her…

Merrick jerked himself back to the present, bile rising in the back of his throat at what he'd seen through Vander's eyes.

That woman…Cali. Merrick had seen her before. The night Vander's corporation had been searched and busted. Vander had fled and Merrick had been transferred, but that woman had been there, staring at him through the cell window along with…the blonde one.

Those green eyes and that blonde hair haunted him in his dreams. He remembered the night of chaos, sitting in his cell waiting for his next visit when the feeling of being watched had him lifting his head and finding her there, watching him. Something had passed between them. Something instant. And he had no idea what it was.

A deep warmth spread through his chest and he had no idea if it was the drug Regina had administered or not.

His vision swam. Regina's hand trailed down his neck and chest until it rested on his inner thigh. She leaned into him, her breasts brushing along his shoulder. The sickly sweet scent of cherries surrounded Merrick. "Until tomorrow," she promised.

Chapter 2

There was no escaping him.

Everywhere Sydney looked, he was there.

The prisoner she'd left behind in the Kratos building.

The ice blue eyes of the Husky she was tending stared at her as if he knew the thoughts his eyes triggered inside of her. Sydney carefully leaned away to jot a few remaining notes into the dog's portfolio.

Andrew, the Husky's owner, clutched his hands nervously. "Well, Doc? Is Shovel going to be all right?"

Shovel was going to be just fine. Andrew was a hypochondriac when it came to his dog's health. "Shovel's in perfect health, nothing to worry about here. He probably started sneezing uncontrollably because he sniffed the wrong plant in your backyard." She closed the folder and stretched out her hand to pat Shovel on the head.

Those ice blue eyes watched her. The burning sensation in her chest intensified.

She pulled her hand back.

"Well, take care. Remember, Shovel is due for his shots next month."

She got to her feet.

Andrew frowned.

Never in her career had she hustled one of her patients out without first chit chatting about their lives. Her parents would be horrified, but she had something else to take care of. Those eyes, so much like the ones that had seared her soul, were a reminder that she had a plan to finish formulating.

Back in her office she logged into her computer and pulled up the copied database from the Kratos computer system that she'd taken from Joel.

It had been a little over three months since the location in Orange County had been shut down. With the exposure of Vander Donahughe's illegal dealings, the entire Kratos Corporation was supposed to crumble and fall. But the large conglomerate had only shut down the one location and while that was supposed to lead to the release of all those captured within, Sydney knew first hand that that wasn't the case.

Vander had been able to get a few of his captives out, her mystery man being one of them. The guilt over that had never truly left her, but it was another deeper fear inside her that urged her toward finding their new location. The fear that her mystery man was her destined Mirror Mate—a soul mate that, once bonded with her, would increase her individual power.

She shook her head.

It wasn't possible.

She clicked on a file folder a little too forcefully.

All she needed to do was find the new location, free the man she'd seen all those months ago, and then her conscience would be clear. She'd be able to celebrate her three year anniversary with Joel without a doubt that he was the man for her.

It was time to take action.

"Come on," she mumbled to her computer as she searched for any address that could be used as an alternative facility.

The harsh clatter of metal hitting the floor made her jump.

"Sorry." Cali Crazar stood in the doorway to her office, two paint cans resting at her feet. "Didn't mean to startle you."

"Liar."

Cali shrugged. "Not my fault you were too absorbed in your computer. What are you looking at?"

"Nothing." Sydney tried to minimize the window but Cali was too fast.

Darn her and her long legs.

Cali had all the makings of a runway model: tall, lean build with dark hair and dark eyes. She was twenty-five, nearly two months older than Sydney. However, with her height, most days Cali made Sydney feel like a child when she stood next to her.

"The Kratos database?"

"Like I said." Sydney exited the window. "Nothing."

Cali leaned against her desk, arms crossed. "That's not nothing. What are you expecting to find?"

As if she didn't know. Cali had been there when they'd found the man with eyes like ice. She'd been there when Sydney had gone to the hospital in hopes of finding him among the other rescuees. But Cali wanted her to say it out loud.

Sydney had a sneaking suspicion that Cali might know what Sydney was too afraid to voice.

Cali had found her Mirror Mate all those months ago in Sydney's best friend, Felix. He'd been sent to rescue Cali from Vander Donahughe—who, at the time, had believed Cali to be his soul mate.

"Well?" Cali prodded. "You were trying to find where they might be keeping *him*, weren't you?"

Sydney avoided her eyes, her heart speeding up.

Her office grew quiet, the faintest *ba-bump, ba-bump* filling the air.

It sounded in time with her heartbeat.

Sydney shot her Shield up.

The sound cut off instantly.

She whirled on Cali. "Don't do that."

Cali narrowed her eyes. "If you'd tell me the truth I wouldn't have to use my powers as a lie detector."

Cali was their guild's Silencer, someone with the ability to manipulate sound, and ever since she became full-forced she'd been experimenting with her powers like crazy—her most recent breakthrough being she could determine if a person was lying by how fast their heart beat.

"Everyone is worried about you, Sydney," Cali continued. "You've been acting different for months now. And don't think I don't know why. What I don't know is why you're so obsessed with finding him."

Sydney dropped her Shield, the prickling at the back of her neck fading with her powers. "I'm not obsessed. I feel guilty. Every time I remember that we had a chance to free him and didn't, it eats at me. We thought he'd be safe with the cops on their way, but all we did was condemn him to more time with Vander. I feel it's my duty to find him."

Cali gave her a look that said she didn't one hundred percent trust her answer. "Duty? That's all you feel?"

"Yes."

No.

"I'm trying not to let it get to me but after so long with no results…"

"It wears on you," Cali finished for her. "I get it. But don't worry, Joel's continually hacking into the system to find new information so it's only a matter of time. Now let's finish painting this room, shall we?"

As well as being a Silencer, Cali was also an amazingly talented artist. She was hard pressed for a job so Sydney had hired her to repaint the office. They both knew it was a waste of her skill but it was the only way Sydney could help her without giving her money outright. Cali wouldn't have accepted it any other way.

*

Joel burst into Sydney's office. "I got something."

Sydney and Cali both looked up from their work.

"What'd you get?" Cali asked as Joel came around Sydney's desk, his midnight blue eyes sparkling.

"I've been keeping tabs on all the e-mails that have been going back and forth to the different Kratos Companies. I have a system in place to alert me if there is any form of address going through the message and today there was a red flag." Joel gave Sydney a quick kiss in greeting.

She hardly felt it.

"You have a new address?" she asked.

He slapped a sheet of paper down in front of her. "Not only an address. Look at what was being shipped to this location."

Cali came up behind him. "Propofol?"

Sydney snatched the document. "It's a sedative, the one that I use in my practice."

Cali caught on instantly. "Which means that there's something at this address that they are trying to contain."

"All in favor that what they're keeping are people?" said Joel while raising his hand.

Sydney shared a look with Cali before they both raised their hands in agreement.

"This is it," said Sydney, staring at the address. San Francisco. Her heart beat rapidly. "We need to get Niella and Felix in here to discuss our next move."

Cali already had her cell phone out. "Felix said he'd be here shortly. He also has a surprise for you."

A surprise for her? The thought gave Sydney pause.

"Come on." Cali beckoned them out of the office to the front lobby where Niella sat at her regular post behind the reception desk.

Niella Souveray was the guild's Dreamer. Her power included visions of the past, present, or future. Unfortunately, she had no control over what or when she Dreamed. She looked up from her work when they entered the room. "So? We learn anything new?" She wheeled herself out into the middle of the lobby.

Sydney handed her the printout of the e-mail.

Niella's hazel eyes scanned the information. "So who's going to

San Francisco?"

"I am."

"I will."

Sydney exchanged a startled look with Cali who had answered at the same time. They both stared at one another until Felix came through the door. Cali's eyes instantly sought him out.

Sydney felt a pang of jealousy—which was ridiculous because she had Joel.

She looked over her shoulder at him and found that he was watching Cali and Felix too, a wistful expression on his face. Her jealousy turned to guilt. Out of everyone in the guild, Joel had suffered the most at her strange behavior. She owed it to him to find this man so that she could return once more to the woman that she was.

He caught her staring at him and offered a warm smile before he came closer and took her hand in his. Sydney waited for the flutter of her heart or the flip of her stomach, but she guessed that after dating for so long it was natural to lose some of the excitement.

She squeezed his scarred fingers, resisting the urge to wince. The scars that ran along Joel's hands and forearms were something that she could never truly accustom herself to. It wasn't that she was shallow and wanted his skin perfect, she just couldn't look at them without thinking about how much pain he'd gone through when he'd been cut or burned working on cars with his father as a teen.

"What'd I miss?" Felix slid one arm around Cali's waist to address the group at large.

Cali gazed up at him. "We're going to San Francisco."

Sydney stepped forward. "Actually, I think it'd be best if I went."

The silence that followed was oppressive. She shifted nervously under everyone's gaze.

Cali found her voice first. "You can't just take off for a week. As much as I hate to admit it, I don't have a steady job like you do. I'm a little more flexible right now."

Sydney's brain understood the reasoning behind Cali's words, but her heart simply wouldn't listen. "I'll take time off, reschedule all my appointments. I'm overdue for a vacation anyway."

"Don't worry about it, Syd," said Felix. "Cali's right, we need you to stay employed to fund our little Guild of Truth." He flashed a grin.

Sydney's temper flared. A normally rare occurrence that she now found happening more and more. "Maybe I don't want to freakin' stay behind this time. Anyone ever think of that? I may not have the most offensive powers but I can still pull my own weight. I don't want to be the guild's sugar momma."

Felix held his hands up. "Whoa, totally not what I meant, Syd."

"I know what you meant and I'm sick of being assigned to the B-team."

"Now you know how I feel," Niella mumbled.

Sydney left that comment alone. She wasn't about to get into it with Niella. "If Vander's at this location then anyone who goes up there is in danger."

"Yeah," Cali butted in, "which is why—"

"Everyone but me," Sydney cut her off. "Vander is powerless with me there. Literally."

Cali wanted to say more. Sydney could see it in her expression. Cali had a vendetta against Vander after he kidnapped and tortured her personally. There was also the small fact that he'd tried to have Felix killed. But she also knew how much Sydney needed to find this mystery man of hers.

Their eyes locked, her green with Cali's obsidian.

"You know, I'm a little overdue on some vacation time too," Joel broke into the conversation.

Sydney gave him a dazzling smile. He was backing her up. After everything she'd put him through he was still sticking with her.

"When are you guys leaving?" Felix kept his hands up in

surrender and Sydney felt a little bad about snapping at him like that.

"As soon as possible, I guess," said Joel.

Sydney straightened her shoulders. "Tomorrow night."

Joel gaped at her. "T-tomorrow night? Syd, I have to request time off. I can't just get up and leave."

"Tell them a relative passed away. They'll understand."

Joel shot a beseeching look at Felix. Felix shrugged his broad shoulders, some of his regular mirth shining in his blue-green eyes. "Oh, before I forget, Syd," said Felix, "I have a surprise for you."

Any more debate about San Francisco was put on hold as Felix led them out into the crisp autumn evening. The wind had kicked up, the sun already setting, the days getting shorter as they neared October. Gone were the days when it was light until eight at night.

"You too, Niella." Felix called as she stopped her wheelchair in the doorway of the clinic.

She waved him off and crossed her arms as the breeze barely disturbed her short pixie hair. "I can see everything I need to from right here."

Cali stuck her tongue out at her. Niella quirked an eyebrow, her lips twitching as if repressing a smile.

"What are we looking for exactly?" asked Sydney with a shiver.

Joel put his arm around her and tucked her into the warmth of his body. She stiffened for a fraction of a second before she forced herself to relax.

"You ready?" Felix's grin widened. He scanned the plaza parking lot but the traffic was slow. He inhaled deeply and focused his eyes on the empty handicap parking spot.

Everyone waited.

They kept waiting.

Sydney looked to Cali to see if she'd give anything away but her attention was riveted to her Mirror Mate. "What—?"

Felix waved his hand. Sydney's Toyota Yaris appeared out of

nowhere.

"Shit," Joel breathed.

Sydney stared at her long lost vehicle. "You brought it back?" Three months ago when Felix had rushed to Cali's rescue, Sydney had followed to offer backup and was rewarded with Felix Erasing her car so that no one could trace her to what had turned into a semi-crime scene. She'd thought the car she'd bought last spring to be lost forever. Felix had never been able to return things once he Erased them. But that was before he bonded with Cali and became full-forced.

She went to the hood of her car. It was hot to the touch. Unnaturally so. There was a faint aroma of sulfur that lingered.

"Where did it go?" She pulled her hand back with a frown. Her fingers were covered in a sticky goo. In fact, the entire car seemed to be coated in the faint pink mucus. Brown dirt clung to the goo-like film and Sydney investigated the side of her car where there were a few dents and scratches.

A frown marred Felix's handsome features. "No idea."

She crouched down to get a better look at the markings. She had to be hanging around Joel and Felix too much, because if she were perfectly honest, the scratch marks didn't look entirely human or animal.

Chapter 3

"When did you learn that you could do this?" Sydney finished wiping the substance off her hand with the towel Niella offered her.

"Cali's not the only one that's been experimenting," said Felix. "I first started with Niella's theory that when I became full-forced it'd increase the distance in which I can use my powers. I tried Erasing something I couldn't see in another room, but that didn't work. So I moved on to something extremely far away that I could still see." He shook his head. "But that was a no-go too. Finally, I tried to bring back something I Erased."

"And still no idea where it went?" Joel pointed to Sydney's car.

The entire guild was a little on edge after they inspected her vehicle.

Felix promised to clean off the "ectoplasmic membrane" by the time she got back. But that wasn't what worried her. What if the substance was toxic? It was highly unlikely, considering that she'd touched it, but what if it was ingested by accident? She almost wanted Felix to Erase it back to wherever it had been.

Felix looked genuinely concerned. "No idea, man," he answered Joel. "Everything else I've Erased and brought back were on a much smaller scale."

"They also weren't Erased for as long as Sydney's car," added Cali.

"So who's going to brave going inside of it?" asked Niella.

Hesitant glances were exchanged all around.

"I think it'd be best if we let it stay here for a while," said Sydney.

"Agreed," said Felix as he ran a hand through his hair. It was a nervous habit of his when he was troubled.

Sydney put her hand on his forearm. She had to crane her head back to look up at him. "Don't worry, okay? We'll figure it out. Thank you for bringing back my car though."

He seemed to relax a bit. "You're welcome."

*

Sydney spent the majority of the evening rearranging appointments and clearing her schedule for the next week. She booked herself and Joel a flight up north to Oakland Airport where they'd stay at a nearby hotel. She couldn't help but think that the further they distanced themselves from San Francisco the safer they'd be from Vander and the Kratos Corporation clutches. Plus it was a little cheaper to stay outside the city.

If this whole rescue went off without a hitch, the first place Vander would look for them would be close-by hotels.

Not *if,* she reminded herself, when. *When* they pulled off the rescue without a hitch…she'd finally be rid of the anxiety that coiled inside of her.

*

"So this is it, huh?" Joel asked.

Sydney stared at the beige two-story building from across the street. Nothing stood out aside from the fact that it looked run down and half empty. The small windows on the bottom floor were all covered. There was no street entrance to the building, only a fenced-in parking lot off to the side.

Joel and Sydney watched as an elderly man got into his BMW and drove away. There was no security guard and no cameras that Sydney could see. But she was far from a trained expert.

"Should we come back later?"

Joel pulled out his laptop and made his way toward the crosswalk.

"Where are you going?" Sydney tailed him.

"I've been updating my hacking and pretty much everything illegal software. I want to walk the perimeter of the building to see if I pick up on anything."

Sydney felt completely exposed, like their intentions were obvious as they walked the outer edges of the building, but no one spared them a second glance.

One their third walk-by Joel stopped. "Got it." He shut his computer. "Let's go plan."

*

"Everything all right, Syd?" Joel kissed the back of her neck.

Sydney jumped. "What?" She'd been completely lost in thought. They'd gone over their plan of action at least a dozen times. Sydney had convinced Joel that they needed to strike that night. She should have been excited, instead she was filled with dread.

He started to massage her shoulders but Sydney couldn't force her muscles to relax. Joel stopped. Sydney braced herself for the inevitable question.

It didn't come. "We still have time before we go out, why don't we take a shower? Calm your nerves?"

"A shower sounds…wonderful." And it did. She'd shared dozens of showers with Joel, why should this one be any different? Everything was fine. She was simply suffering from some pre-rescue mission anxiety. It was natural. Totally and completely understandable.

Joel visibly sighed in relief. He trailed his hand down her arm. "I'll get the water running."

Sydney got up to strip, her hands shaking as she folded her clothes neatly into her dirty laundry bag.

She clenched her fingers into fists to stop the trembles.

What was wrong with her?

It was just a shower.

Just. A. Shower.

Then why was her stomach knotted and her dinner threatening to come up?

"Syd? Are you—?" Joel stopped short when he saw her standing there naked. His Adam's apple bobbed and his navy blue eyes roved over her hungrily.

Sydney felt the ridiculous urge to cover herself.

Joel was only clad in his jeans, his sun tanned chest seeming even darker in the poor hotel room lighting. He drew closer. His hand reached out and rested on her shoulder. "The shower can wait." His voice was rough. His other hand slid along her lower back to bring her closer to his body so that her small breasts pressed firmly into the hard warmth of his chest.

He kissed her. A slow, gentle kiss with a delicate swipe of tongue. His hands started to wander. Sydney pushed back. Her hand shook where it rested on his skin and she snatched it back before he could notice. "Joel." She cleared her throat. "We really should shower."

He stared down at her in confusion, the bulge in his jeans painstakingly obvious. "What's going on, Syd?"

She went to push away but his hands tightened, keeping her close.

"I know this is really going to sound bad, but we haven't had sex in three months. Ever since we helped rescued Felix and Cali from the Kratos building you've been acting differently. You're keeping me at arm's length and I don't fucking know why." His eyes pleaded for her to confide in him.

She looked away.

Joel cursed and dropped his arms from around her. "What's gotten into you? Is it me? Are you getting a three-year itch or something?"

Sydney whirled back to face him. "What? No. Joel, I…I want you." She cupped his cheek and forced herself to kiss him. He clutched her to him as if she'd disappear any second. Their tongues twined; the familiar flavor and feel of him after nearly three years together was like returning to the comfort and safety of home after a long trip away. Joel had been the longest relationship she'd ever had. She didn't want anyone else. No one knew her like he did. Fate had to have missed the memo where Joel was supposed to be her Mirror Mate.

When they broke apart they were both breathing heavily. "Then what's been bothering you?" He tucked a strand of hair behind her ear.

She'd been trying to analyze the answer to that question for months. And the only thing she kept coming back to was her brother. He'd died of cancer at age seven. She'd been able to do nothing but watch as he withered away, as he suffered through treatment after treatment. She had been nine. It had been her job to protect him and there wasn't a single thing she could've done.

No one in the guild knew.

She kept the memory of Aaron locked away like she had his possessions locked away in her closet.

She stared Joel in the eye and answered as honestly as possible. "I can't stand by and do nothing if I know I can prevent someone from dying."

Sometimes she wondered why she never majored as a doctor or oncologist to deal with her brother's loss. It would have made more sense than becoming a veterinarian, but she'd never forget the proud look on Aaron's face when she told him that she wanted to take care of animals. He'd always wanted a ton of pets but with his disease they were never allowed to have them. Sydney had promised that when she became a vet and when he got better, she'd take care of all the animals he could fit into his house. She'd pinky promised him.

Joel brought her back to the present. "You're too good of a person, you know that."

She shook away the melancholy thoughts. "I'm not *that* good of a person, trust me. So…are we okay?"

He trailed a finger down the side of her face affectionately. "We're golden."

"How're we on time?"

Joel glanced over at the alarm clock. His face fell.

"Not enough time for sex and a shower?" she guessed.

Joel flashed her a bright smile. "We can always kill two birds with one stone."

Sydney scrunched up her nose. "You know how much I hate that saying. Besides, in the shower? I don't think so. Sex wasn't meant for the shower." His face grew crestfallen. She kissed him on the nose. "After," she promised. "After we get back home we'll spend the rest of our vacation together. In bed."

Joel perked up instantly. "Then what the hell are we waiting for?"

*

"Not much security, is there?" Sydney surveyed the area for what was probably the seventh time. She wrapped her arms tighter around her body as another breeze swept through the streets. She didn't know if it was just her, but the San Francisco wind seemed so much colder than the breeze that blew off the Newport ocean back home.

Joel was busy on his laptop. Somehow he had hacked into the building's well-concealed security system and deactivated the feed and alarms. He had some kind of loop playing that would make them invisible in the building as long as they didn't encounter anyone.

"Only a handful of guards on duty," he answered.

And they had no idea if those guards had powers or not. Which made their plan extra tricky. Back in their hotel they'd come up with a roughly put together plan. If they came across someone with powers, Sydney would Shield until Joel could get close enough, then she'd drop her Shield and he'd use his ability to Lock anyone to anything, including a person's shoes to the floor. One their prey was stalled with nowhere to move, Joel would knock them out. Because once she put her Shield back up his Lock would be negated.

She patted the side pocket of her cargo pants. And if all else failed then it was a good thing she'd brought her own supply of Propofol.

Joel shoved his laptop into his backpack and slung it over his shoulder. "Ready?" He looked positively delighted. Sydney couldn't understand how he and Felix could get so excited about playing super hero. It was downright terrifying.

Maybe you should *have let Cali come instead.*

She could hardly keep the water in her stomach down.

"Syd?" Joel asked when she hesitated.

No backing out now. You can do it.

"I'm ready."

He gave her an encouraging squeeze on the arm.

They crept out from the bus stop when there was a lull in traffic. This late at night on a weekday there weren't many cars on the street. They reached the chain-link fence and Joel pulled out a master key that he'd programmed to open the gate. He slid it past the sensor. She held her breath. The gate rattled open on its rusty wheels.

They slipped inside the parking lot and made their way along the wall of the building to remain unseen to those driving along the street.

Any minute she expected a car to drive in and spot them.

Did her heart always sound this loud?

She shook herself. *Stay focused.*

A loud burst of laughter came from down the street. Sydney spun.

Joel got to work on the entrance lock. "Don't worry." He

seemed to sense her nervousness. "No one from the street can see us."

The gate started to rattle closed.

"Joel—" she started.

"It's supposed to do that," he reassured her. "It's set on a timer as if a car was driving in."

Right.

Stop being so childish. Remember why you're doing this.

She recalled to mind the way her mystery man had been drugged, sitting all alone in that cell, suffering.

The image bolstered her confidence.

Joel cracked the lock on the front door. "Go in easy," he whispered as she passed by him to enter the dim lit lobby.

She hovered near the door while he propped the door open an inch for an easy escape. He turned around to survey the area.

It was like any other office building, Sydney supposed: empty lobby, two hallways leading in opposite directions to lead up behind the main wall. There were no decorations whatsoever. Along the ceiling was the impression of inverted stairs, which meant that they were above them behind the wall they were facing.

She pointed to the ceiling. "Do you think they're being held upstairs?"

Joel tilted his head as if listening for something. "I don't know. Maybe. I'm a little more worried about where the workers on duty are at."

Neither one of them spoke the one doubt that she was sure they were both thinking: What if no one was being held here at all?

Footsteps came from down one of the hallways.

Joel flew to the opposite hall and motioned her over.

They slipped behind the cover of the front wall just as a man came around the other end. He was average height with dark hair, but with the poor lighting she couldn't tell if it was black or brown.

She exchanged a glance with Joel. They were both thinking the same thing.

The man was too thin to be a hired guard. That left only one other option. He was hired because he had powers.

Joel motioned for her to use her ability. She nodded.

The man strolled through the lobby, his gaze catching on the ajar door.

Joel crept out from behind their hideaway and carefully made his way over.

The back of Sydney's neck gave the appropriate tingle, letting her know that her Shield was up.

Joel tapped the man on the shoulder. He spun. "You picked the wrong place to rob, buddy," the man said as he grabbed Joel roughly around his neck.

Joel wasn't the least bit concerned. The man stared at Joel, his arrogant smile slipping when he realized his powers, whatever they were, were useless.

"Something the matter?" asked Joel before he clocked him.

The man went down.

Sydney lowered her Shield. Not that Joel really needed his powers. That right hook took his opponent down. But just to be on the cautious side she ran over and injected him with her sedative.

"Questioning my fighting ability, Syd?" Joel asked as they propped the man up in a dark corner.

"Not at all," she huffed. "Simply covering all possible means for interference."

"How much did you give him?"

"Not too much, he should be out for a good half hour."

There was the scrape of a chair being moved upstairs, followed shortly by footsteps.

Joel eyed their unconscious friend. "Coming to check on him?"

Sydney strained her ears. What she wouldn't give to be able to use Cali's powers right about then to hear better. "I don't think so." The steps were getting further away.

"We should move slowly then. There's still two more up there."

She followed Joel as he took the stairs two at a time. The second floor opened up to a long hallway with doors on both sides. Some were open, others closed. The footsteps they heard could have gone into any number of those rooms.

A chill slid down her spine. Were they being expected?

Joel cursed under his breath.

She joined him down the hall. "What?"

"I think we found where they're holding their captives."

He jerked his thumb at the sideways folder that rested in the holder that was mounted to the door. It was the same type of paperwork a doctor would have for their patients.

Sydney's stomach twisted. Was this it? Was her mystery man inside?

Joel already had one of his gadgets out that would hack into the electronic lock on the door. "You should watch this," he told her.

"Why?"

"Because we have no idea where the other two guards are and I'll be a better look out. You can get everyone out of their cells."

He didn't give her time to argue. Not that she would have. "See this?" He held up some kind of card that was connected to a small device he held in his hands. "Jam it into the slot here." He motioned to the designated spot on the lock. "When the card's in, it'll scan the proper code and unlock the door. When you're all done pull the card out and open the door. Simple."

He handed her the stuff as he opened the door he'd been working on.

Sydney's heart leapt into her throat.

A young man lifted his head.

She exhaled. It wasn't her man.

"Who're you?"

Joel pointed to himself. "I'm Joel, this here is Sydney. We're here to bust your ass out."

She rushed over to the kid. The lighting was poor in the cells, more so than out in the hall. "What's your name?"

"Luke. Luke Teagan."

Luke had hair that was either a sandy blonde or a mousy brown. His sky blue eyes watched her carefully as she worked on the ties at his hands. He had the smallest cleft in his chin.

"Nice to meet you, Luke." Sydney ripped at the knots until they came undone. His fingers were nearly purple and swollen from poor circulation. She cringed inwardly. "Can you stand?"

He got slowly to his feet. He towered over her.

Kid must still be growing.

"This way." She ushered him out. "Stay with Joel, all right?"

He nodded.

She rushed down the hall past an open conference room and stopped outside the next locked door. She shoved Joel's key card into the slot and waited as the machine ran through its algorithms.

There was a faint click and she pulled the key from the slot and opened the door.

Peering up out of a face shrouded in ink black hair, ice blue eyes locked with hers.

Sydney's heart hiccupped.

Chapter 4

Regina must have gotten bored, Merrick thought as the lock disengaged. He went to straighten his posture then thought better of it.

Screw it.

What good was showing defiance, anyway? Regina just seemed to enjoy it more.

The door opened. Merrick felt a kick to the gut when *she* walked in.

It couldn't be…

Yet his eyes told him a different story. Dressed in a black shirt, green cargo pants, and black…Sketchers? His blonde beauty stood in front of him like a dream come to life. For a handful of heartbeats she stood in the doorway watching him, as if afraid to breathe.

There was a hiss from down the hall. A male voice. It snapped her into action.

She raced around his chair, her soft fingers working at the knots binding his hands, brushing against his skin every now and again. Merrick repressed a shiver. The warm scent of vanilla wafted over from her. His cock stirred.

"Who the hell are you?" he finally found his voice. It was a little rough.

There was a hard tug on his wrists before the bindings fell away.

"Sydney Spencer."

He massaged feeling back into his hands. She watched him openly with a mix of curiosity and fear.

He stood, for the first time realizing how tiny she was. She didn't even reach his shoulder. "I'm Merrick."

She stared up at him, swallowing visibly. She forced a smile. "Nice to meet you."

She booked it for the door.

"Where are you going?" He took a step and had to reach out for the wall as a sudden surge of vertigo hit him. Damn drugs, malnutrition, and dehydration.

"I have to free anyone else," she threw over her shoulder.

He followed her into the hall. At one end there stood two men. One was dressed in scrubs like him. Another prisoner. The other man motioned for Merrick to join them but he followed Sydney.

She was busy deactivating another lock.

He came up behind her. "Where did you get that?"

She stiffened fractionally. It was a small tightening in the shoulders, but Merrick saw it. Did his presence upset her?

"I got it from Joel, the man over there. He's really good with electronics."

"And what do you do?" he found himself asking, wanting to know the answer. Who was this woman that looked so incredibly young and why was he so drawn to her?

She pulled a wired card from the slot in the door and twisted the handle. She turned to face him and his gut clenched as their eyes locked. His whole body prickled with awareness.

There was a flash in her green eyes, gone before he could identify it. "I'm a vet," she said before disappearing into the room.

He decided to stay outside the cell. He heard Sydney introduce herself and ask the girl's name.

"Hazel Benedict," came the answer.

A girl a little taller than Sydney came out of the room. She had thick, straight black hair, with a full set of bangs that brushed into a pair of deep forest green eyes. Hazel eyed him hesitantly before she noticed he was dressed in scrubs. Same as her.

"Right that way." He pointed down the hall where the man named Joel stood with the other freed captive.

Hazel went to join the others. Merrick continued to follow his blonde.

"Who do you work for? Why are you doing this?" he asked as she worked on the last locked room.

She shot him a frustrated glare. "Can't I say I'm doing this out of the goodness of my heart and be done with the interrogation?"

She vanished into the last cell where another girl named Juliet Arden was being kept. She had long, wavy brown hair and deep blue eyes. She was nearly the same height as Sydney, but unlike Sydney, Juliet was gifted with curves and an ample chest.

Any further questions Merrick would have asked were put on hold as Juliet conducted her own interrogation. "What's going on? Why am I here? Those people kept asking if I have any powers. I don't! Who are you really?"

Sydney looked like she was holding back an eye roll. She gave Merrick an annoyed look as if the girl's curiosity had been his fault.

"No more questions," she hissed to shut Juliet up. "We need to get out of here first."

Juliet's blue eyes widened as she realized they weren't out of the woods just yet.

Merrick held his finger up to his lips to signal her to be quiet then pointed to the group forming at the other end of the hall.

Juliet scurried to meet them.

"Where are you going?" Merrick whispered.

Sydney continued down the hall investigating all other rooms. "I thought I said no more questions." She sighed. "I'm looking for the other guards on duty. We only took down one. There's supposed to be three." She paused when she came to the end of the hall.

"What is it?" He followed her gaze. It was another set of stairs. "You think it leads somewhere else?"

She shook her head, blonde hair flaring out to brush his arm. He inhaled sharply. How long had it been since he'd been with a woman? Fisted her hair? Obviously too long if he was this riled up over a woman he just met.

"The building is too small for those stairs to lead anywhere else but the bottom floor," Sydney answered. "The only problem is that we left an unconscious man on the bottom floor."

That was certainly going to give them away.

"Maybe they're in a break room," he offered optimistically though he highly doubted it.

She nodded absently. "Come on." She went back the way they'd came to join the others.

"Joel," the man with rich brown hair and midnight blue eyes introduced himself. His hands and forearms were covered with scars. Now wasn't the time to ask questions, though Merrick did catalogue it for later.

"This is how it'll go down." Joel rallied them into a small circle. Merrick noticed with some discomfort that Sydney positioned herself at Joel's side. "Syd and I will go down first and make sure the coast is clear. You guys follow after, okay?" There was a collective nod. "Only after we give the all clear," he stressed.

More nods.

They made their way to the stairs. Merrick slid to the front to speak with Joel who seemed to be the obvious leader. "I can help," he whispered.

"I appreciate it, man," said Joel, "but—"

Merrick cut him off. "Look around you, the others are just kids. I'm not. I'm trained."

Joel studied him. Merrick didn't back down. Finally Joel leaned into him and lowered his voice. "Do you have powers?"

Merrick froze.

Joel waited with a "no bullshit" expression on his face.

Could it be possible that these people were like him? His first instinct was to lie. Self-preservation and all. But then his eyes slid to Sydney. His heart quivered in his chest and he rubbed at it absently.

He forced his gaze back to Joel's. "I do," he said just as quietly.

Joel nodded. "Stay close and don't do anything stupid. My power allows me to Lock a person if I touch them. That means if I can get my hand on their feet they won't be able to move from wherever it is they're standing. It'll be a lot easier to take down an opponent that can't move. You feel me?"

Merrick couldn't believe he'd been found by more people with abilities. "I understand."

They proceeded down the steps. The building was in dire need of repair. Cracks lined the walls, dirt marred the floor. Where the hell had they been keeping him? He was tempted to ask but they reached the bottom floor. Joel and Sydney split off in opposite directions to search for their two missing targets.

Merrick trailed Sydney. There was no way she'd be able to take on another person. She barely looked like she'd be able to fight off a twelve-year-old.

"Why do you keep following me?" She raised her hand as if to shove him away but stopped herself before her hand could make contact.

For some reason that bothered him, he wanted her hand to touch him. He wanted her skin on his again.

He shook himself.

"You look like you could use some help," he said.

Anger sparked in her eyes. "Because I'm small?"

Merrick was smart enough to know wounded pride when he heard it. He refrained from answering.

They came across no one in the few hallways that eventually connected to the second set of stairs. They rejoined Joel and the others by the first set. Joel's eyes flickered from him to Sydney and back again, a frown forming.

Shit.

Were they together?

As if in answer, Sydney crossed to Joel and laced their fingers together.

Fuck.

Merrick's lungs constricted, an unwanted burst of anger bubbling up inside of him.

"No one," Sydney reported.

It's better this way, he told himself, unable to tear his gaze away from their clasped hands. It may have been a while since he'd been with a woman, but he reminded himself that there had been a damn good reason behind why he avoided them.

"All right then," said Joel. "Let's go."

They circled around to the front.

An unconscious man lay off to the side. A small noise from his right caught Merrick's attention. Hazel's eyes were locked on the male, burning bright with hatred.

Merrick took a closer look at the slumped over figure and balled his hands into fists. He'd endured a lot of pain at the hands of that man. He had some kind of ability to cause excruciating pain on contact. The idea that that man's hands had been on someone as young as Hazel made Merrick see red. He was pretty sure if he had seen any kind of fear or tears in her eyes he would have gone over and broken the fucker's unconscious neck. As it was, Hazel's bottom lip didn't so much as tremble. She simply glared.

Joel came to an abrupt stop.

Sydney dropped his hand. "What is it?"

"I left that open." He gestured to the front door.

It was closed, the electronic lock engaged.

Joel pulled his backpack off and rummaged through it.

A shadow shifted in the corner.

Merrick took a step forward to warn them but it was too late.

"Stop right there." Regina cocked a gun right at Joel's chest.

Joel froze, the device Merrick had seen Sydney using clutched in his hand.

Regina motioned with her gun. "Drop it."

Joel carefully set his equipment back in his pack and placed it at his feet.

"Push it away from you," instructed Regina. Another shadow detached itself from the wall. Dennis. Again, no last name given.

The young man in their group shivered as Dennis walked forward to relieve Joel of his belongings.

Regina smiled at them. "I knew I smelled intruders." She tapped her nose with her free hand.

Joel and Sydney exchanged confused glances. But Merrick realized what they didn't with a sinking sensation: Regina had a power. He recalled all those visits from her, some of her words making more sense to him now. The off-hand comments about his scent and how it drove her wild, how she couldn't get the smell of him out of her nose. She must be some type of blood hound with the olfactory ability to track others by their scents.

He scanned Dennis but found no weapons on him, concealed or otherwise.

If he could figure out some way to disarm Regina they'd have a chance. Dennis's abilities required physical contact. As long as he was in contact with another he could take away a person's sight. They'd done it enough to Merrick in the past. It was a scare tactic: blind the captive so they wouldn't know when the pain was coming. It was a sick sort of amusement that left the captive in constant anticipation.

Dennis started to shift through Joel's bag.

"Hands up," Regina commanded.

Merrick found his gaze drawn to Sydney. She was watching him.

Have to protect her…

He couldn't stand the thought of Sydney going through what he had for the past however many months of his life.

He tore his eyes away. "You're not going to stop us from leaving," he told Regina.

Dennis paused in his ransacking. Regina's lips curled further. "Is that so?" She aimed the gun at him.

Merrick could feel the group around him tense. He braced himself for the pain he was about to unleash upon himself. His leg muscles bunched. He readied his hands. He sprang—

"No!"

Movement on his left.

A shot fired.

Merrick slapped at his chest. No wound. He lunged for Regina. Cries erupted from all over.

He caught Regina's wrists and forced them up. Another shot rang out. Plaster sprinkled down on them.

"You know there's no escape," Regina whispered to him as she fought his hold. "Wherever you go, I'll find you."

Before he could break his rule of not hitting women, Joel was at his side. He dropped to the ground and covered Regina's feet with his hands. "Leave her," said Joel. "We don't have much time—I heard someone mention reinforcements."

Merrick tore the gun from Regina and threw it down the hall. He stepped away from her. She went to follow and tipped forward.

"What the fuck is this?" she shrieked. She clasped her ankles and heaved. They didn't move from the floor.

The others were huddled around the front door. Merrick scanned Sydney for injury but it was the young man with blue eyes and a cleft in his chin that took the shot. The sleeve of his scrubs was wet with blood.

"Joel," Sydney cried. "We need the code."

Joel reversed direction back to Dennis who must've been knocked out during the chaos. He was starting to stir, Joel's pack tucked between his feet.

"No time." Merrick forced his way through. He inhaled deeply and put his palm flat over the keypad.

The back of his neck tingled. He shut his eyes as he was

bombarded with visions. Different people, tons of emotions, but they all typed in the same code.

He pulled his hand back and punched in the five digit password. The lock clicked free. He threw the door open and held it. The others stared at him. "Out," he ordered.

Sydney hustled the injured man out.

Joel clapped him on the shoulder. "Nice."

They ran out into the parking lot.

"Where's your van?" asked Juliet.

Joel ran to the gate. "Don't have one."

"You don't have a van?"

"Look," said Joel. "We had no idea how many of you we were going to find, if any. Not to mention finding parking would have been a bitch."

"We're in a parking lot," countered Juliet. "You could have parked here!"

Joel grumbled under his breath.

"So, what?" Juliet continued. "You thought you'd get us out nice and smoothly, no problems whatsoever, and we could just walk away?" Juliet laughed humorlessly. "You guys overestimated your skills."

"You know, you're about as optimistic as Niella," Joel mumbled.

Sydney shared a secretive smile with him.

"So how'd you get here?" asked Juliet.

"The BART."

BART. Bay Area Rapid Transit. Merrick inhaled, catching the faint sea breeze. If he had to guess he'd bet his money on them being in San Francisco. Shit. He was over three hundred miles from home.

"The what?" cried Juliet.

Joel ignored her to address Merrick. "Can you open this gate like you did the front door?"

Merrick put his hand on the metal box. "This isn't the same. There's no password."

Joel cursed.

"Isn't there some way to overload the system with a jolt or a kick or something?" asked Sydney.

Hazel perked up from where she hovered at the injured man's side. Without a word she ran to the box and put both hands over it. She took a deep breath and held it. Her whole body shook. Electricity surged from her hands into the box. Smoke rose, the system blown. The gate rattled.

There was no time to stare. Joel raced over and manually opened the gate. Merrick went to help.

"Now where?" asked Juliet.

Two cars came speeding around the bend of a nearby corner.

"Backup," said Sydney.

They all huddled behind a bus stop poster board.

"Should we make a run for it?" Sydney said to Joel.

"No need." Merrick peered out around their hideout. A bus pulled up and stopped.

"Everyone on," commanded Joel.

They packed in. It was deserted, which was good. Joel ran to the front to pay their fare while the rest circled around their injured comrade to hide the blood.

Joel returned a second later to claim a seat behind Sydney and the injured one. He leaned over the seat to take a look and cursed. "How're you holding up, Luke?"

Luke.

Merrick filed the name away.

"I'll be fine." The sweat beading on Luke's forehead indicated otherwise. "I'd rather die than go back there."

"Well, you didn't have to get so close to dying to prove your point," said Joel dryly.

Luke tried to grin but it looked more like a grimace. "I'll try to remember that next time."

"Hopefully there won't be a next time." Sydney tried to take a look at the wound but he kept shifting away from her. "Don't worry, I'm a doctor," she said when Luke continued to evade her advances.

He quit squirming. "Really?"

Sydney scrunched up her nose. "Well…I'm a vet. And we're going to need supplies."

Luke shook his head. "No you don't. I told you, I'll be fine."

"You were shot," Merrick reminded him, wondering if Luke was going into shock.

Hazel squeezed in at Merrick's side. He stepped aside to give her room. "You were really brave back there," she told Luke.

Luke ducked his head, his neck growing red.

Juliet leaned in around Hazel. "You know, whoever saw us get on this bus is going to be able to track us. Shouldn't we have a destination in mind?"

"Why don't you and Hazel check the routes up on the wall and find us a way back to the BART station?" said Joel.

Juliet's chest puffed up at being given an important task. "Come on, Hazel," she said warmly and led the other girl to the middle of the bus.

Sydney worked at Luke's sleeve and pulled it up to reveal his wound.

Merrick stood in front of Luke to block the bus driver's view. "That's not too bad. I thought it was a lot worse from the amount of blood."

"It was a lot worse," said Luke. "But I told you I'd be fine. I heal rapidly. That's my power."

"That's why you took the shot," Sydney mused out loud.

Luke nodded. "I saw you," he jerked his head at Merrick, "get ready to jump the woman with the gun but I lunged for her first so she'd take me down, giving you time to tackle her."

Merrick's admiration for the kid grew. "I have to agree with Hazel, that was really brave. Thank you."

"We're still going to need to stop," said Sydney. "He's going to need another shirt. He'll draw too much attention with all this blood. All of you are going to draw enough attention as it is in those scrubs."

Merrick looked down at his feet. They were all barefoot too. Luckily the bus driver didn't give them shit about that.

Joel leaned back in his seat. "I don't think anything's open this late, Syd. It's late and dark out—as long as we keep Skywalker here in the shadows we should be fine."

Luke turned around in his seat to face Joel. "Skywalker?"

Joel shrugged. "You have to admit, you're a striking resemblance of him."

"I guess." Luke hunched down in his seat to rest his head back.

"Any idea what Juliet can do?" Joel asked Luke.

Luke opened his eyes. "No idea."

"Juliet said she didn't have any powers." Sydney dug around in her pockets and pulled out a small tissue that she used to push against Luke's wound. He hissed in pain.

Joel made a thoughtful noise in the back of his throat. "I have to say I was a little surprised to find Static Shock on our team."

Merrick frowned. "Who?"

Joel pointed to the girls. "I'm talking about Hazel and her electrokinesis ability. Out of the two of them I would have thought she was the one that didn't have powers."

"Electrokinesis," Merrick repeated, still unable to believe what his life had turned into. "And I thought my clairsentience was odd."

"Clairsentience, is that what you call your power?" asked Joel.

"I looked it up on the internet one day."

"Well." Joel leaned forward and put a hand on Sydney's shoulder. She jumped. "Let me tell you, if you join our group back home we'll find you a much better title."

Merrick wondered if Joel's offer would still stand if he knew Merrick was secretly lusting after his girlfriend.

Juliet cleared her throat, announcing her and Hazel's return. "We're going in the wrong direction. We need to get off this bus as soon as possible. At the next stop we'll have to walk about a mile, if I estimated correctly, to another pickup. That new bus will then arrive close enough for us to walk to the Montgomery station."

"Luke?" Sydney asked tentatively.

He opened his eyes. The poor kid looked absolutely exhausted. Merrick knew the feeling but he had to keep it together. He'd be able to rest when they were all well and truly free.

"Are you going to be able to walk all that?" Sydney relayed Juliet's instructions in case he had dozed off.

"Think so," Luke mumbled.

"We're about to find out." Joel got to his feet. "Because here comes our stop."

*

Luke ended up making it. His injury slowed the entire group down but no one said anything about it. It was because of him that they were able to get away at all and Merrick wasn't going to knock the kid when he took a bullet for him.

However, Merrick could feel their head start slipping away as they wove through the tight streets. Once they were back on the bus it wasn't too bad, but he kept himself on high alert. There was no telling how far Regina would be able to track them. The whole group might already be watching all the stations. He sincerely hoped that wasn't the case.

He took a seat across from Sydney. "It was a good thing you guys didn't stay at a nearby hotel."

She kept her expression carefully guarded. "We figured that would be the first place anyone would start looking."

"Smart."

By the time they arrived on Market Street the young ones were fading fast.

Luke had rolled his shirt sleeve up to cover the blood. His wound still bled, but they figured it was better to have a small amount of blood instead of a large stain that drew the unwanted eye.

"Come on," Joel tried to rally them. "We have to make the last train."

Joel took the down escalator at a run. Merrick waited for the others to go before he followed. Brown hair caught his eye but when he turned there was no one there.

Was he imagining things?

He scanned the street one last time before heading below ground.

Stale air greeted him. It was mixed with the scent of machinery and unwashed bodies. He could hear the approaching transport. The platform was nearly empty. Juliet, Hazel, and Luke all stood near the bright yellow marker at the edge of the platform, eager to board. Joel and Sydney were not far behind them.

"Are you going to take us home with you?" asked Hazel.

Merrick joined them.

"Only if you want," said Joel. "Our main goal was to get you guys back where you belong. But if you don't have anywhere you're more than welcome to join our Guild of Truth."

Juliet perked up. "You mean there's more of you?"

Sydney nodded. "Not too many more, only three."

"We'll tell you more about it on the way to Oakland." Joel motioned to the oncoming transport.

Merrick's stomach clenched.

Nerves?

No. He felt an itch at the back of his neck as if he were being watched.

The BART pulled up, doors opening. The others started to board. Merrick scanned the platform. Nothing. But he knew better than to doubt his instincts. He studied every person whether sitting, standing, or walking.

Sydney went to board.

Regina stepped out from behind a scheduling board, something raised in her hand.

Merrick didn't think. He reacted.

He grabbed Sydney by the shoulders and a jolt went through him at the contact. He wrenched her away from the doors. Sydney yelped in surprise.

Joel jumped to his feet. "What the fuck are you—"

A shot *pinged* off the transport cart.

Joel ducked inside with a curse.

The doors shut.

"Joel!" Sydney cried out.

Joel banged on the glass but the BART was already moving.

Chapter 5

Sydney watched their only chance at escape leaving without them.

Merrick grabbed her hand. "We need to get out of here."

Her heart skipped as his warm hand enveloped hers.

To emphasize his point another silenced shot went off three feet from where she was standing.

They booked it for the escalators. Sydney tried to keep up with Merrick's longer stride. She started to fall behind, her hand tugging him back. He slowed his pace and gave her a reassuring squeeze. Her stomach flipped.

"How'd they find us so fast?" she huffed.

"Regina is a tracker."

The man they'd knocked out with Propofol stepped out from behind a pillar.

They skid to a stop. Sydney threw her Shield up.

The man grabbed her, purposely going for skin to skin contact.

"No," Merrick roared, unaware that her power would negate whatever the man's ability would have done to her.

Merrick's fist flew. Their attacker flew into another scheduling board. Another shot rang out. Cries of alarm burst into the air. A security guard was racing toward them.

"Merrick." Sydney tugged his arm to alert him.

"I know." His jaw bulged.

They sprinted for the escalator and made it top side, shouts ringing out behind them.

Sydney had to stop and catch her breath. "Now where?"

Merrick's black hair whipped out as he looked up and down the streets. "Do you have cash on you?"

Sydney patted her cargo pockets. "Yeah, why? Where can we go with you in scrubs that won't draw attention?"

He hailed a taxi. He held the door open for her. "The obvious choice, of course." He climbed in after her. "To the hospital," he told the driver. "Stay low," he whispered and pushed her head down as the taxi took off.

She sunk lower into her seat, her heart racing a mile a minute. The taxi smelled like cheap incense. She tried to breathe through her mouth to lessen the smell but it wasn't helping.

"A hospital?" she asked to distract herself from her body's reaction to Merrick's close proximity.

He looked out the back windshield for perhaps the third time. "Like you said, scrubs are going to make it a little difficult to blend, but not at a hospital. Not to mention the ER has people there at all hours of the night so no one will think twice of us staying there."

The idea of staying in one place all night didn't sit well with her, but they didn't really have any other options. They could try a hotel but what if Vander was watching them? She had no idea how far his wealth and power reached.

Was he even in San Francisco? The location of Vander had eluded her guild for the past three months.

The hospital wasn't very far from the BART station. Sydney paid the driver and Merrick led her into the ER. It was about half full, ranging from bed wrangled individuals to snot nosed little children.

Sydney shivered as she was reminded of all the time she'd spent in the hospital with Aaron, staying by his side as he went through his treatments.

A nurse behind the front desk eyed them. Well, she eyed Merrick. She didn't give Sydney the time of day.

A stab of possessiveness went through her. She instantly shoved it away as Merrick went over to a far corner.

She took a seat in one of the stiff-backed chairs. "We're going to stay here and wait out the night?"

Merrick didn't take his eyes off the entrance. "We can take shifts sleeping. I'll take first watch."

Something told her that she wouldn't be able to fall asleep. It wasn't the constant noise or hushed voices, it was the atmosphere that put her on edge.

"You can relax," Merrick said after a few minutes of silence, startling her. "I'll keep watch for Regina or anyone else that looks suspicious."

"Regina was the woman who shot at us?"

Merrick nodded.

"No offense, but I don't think I'm going to be able to sleep. My brain is a little overwhelmed right about now." That was an understatement. She'd gone in knowing that they might have to fight more of Vander's employees. But the escape she had imagined had been nothing like the chaotic run for their lives that she was currently experiencing. Not to mention being shot at was never a pleasant feeling. "I hope Luke's okay," she mumbled aloud.

"That kid is resilient. I'm sure he's fine." He took his eyes off the front entrance to give her a small smile.

Her heart did that stupid flip thingy again, her cheeks heating.

She shifted in her seat, her mind going back to that moment where she thought Regina was going to shoot Merrick. She'd cried out before she'd even knew what was happening, the fear for Merrick's life overwhelming her.

Could it be possible that he was her Mirror Mate?

Her stomach knotted with both dread and excitement.

Joel's anguished expression as the BART pulled away haunted her. He'd be so worried. She pulled out her phone before she realized that Joel wouldn't get reception while the transit was traveling underground. She tucked her phone back into her pants and readjusted herself in her seat.

"Are you going to tell me why you're so fidgety or am I going to have to guess?" said Merrick.

She crossed then re-crossed her legs, caught herself, and then glared at him.

Amusement touched his face. "So I'm to guess? In that case I'd say it's the hospital that's got you uncomfortable and not our situation, which is curious considering that you told me you were a vet. Don't you work in a clinical setting?"

Sydney didn't like his astuteness. "How did you get so good at reading people?"

"I'm a PI. It comes with the territory." He went back to watching the room at large. Sydney was just starting to relax when he spoke again. "So are you going to tell me why you don't like hospitals?"

So much for avoiding the question.

She got the feeling that Merrick could wait out any question. Her fingers curled into fists. "They bring back old memories I'd rather not think about," she confessed. Memories of Aaron with no hair being pushed in a wheelchair, his little bones sticking out against his skin, and the scent of sickness that seemed to permeate the air.

"What happened?"

"That's none of your business," she said curtly, though something inside of her said she could tell him—trust him. Still, she refused. She'd never even told Joel about her brother and now she was supposed to just open up to Merrick because she *felt* like it?

She studied Merrick's profile determined to find what it was that was drawing her in. There had to be some logical reasoning. His black hair was straggly, so that couldn't be it, his face gaunt from his time as a prisoner—that most definitely couldn't be it. Yet…he had a strong jaw line and the most captivating eyes she'd ever seen. Heat pooled in her belly. He was also brave and protective, a quick thinker too. Her gaze dropped to his hands. She remembered how warm they were around her own. Her breasts ached as if eager for his touch.

Merrick stiffened.

Sydney mentally slapped herself. *What am I doing?*

"What is it?" she asked, glad her voice didn't come out husky. She tried to ignore the throbbing of her body.

Merrick gave the smallest nod to the far end of the ER. "See the janitor over there? This is his second time in here and his second time watching us."

Sydney instantly tensed. "You think he works for Vander?"

"I don't know." Merrick's head whipped around. "How do you know Vander?"

Something like disappointment settled in her chest. He didn't remember her?

Come on, Sydney, that was three months ago and he was drugged up.

She cleared her throat. "Three months ago my guild exposed the underground illegal fighting matches he held at his facility. We tried to bust the prisoners out but we didn't have enough time. I…I saw you in one of the cells. You probably don't remember me but—"

"I remember you."

Their eyes locked. Sydney's breath caught. Everything she had been denying was right there staring back at her. Suddenly she couldn't get enough air into her lungs. Her heart beat wildly in her chest, her stomach filled with butterflies. Her gaze dipped to Merrick's mouth. What would he taste like? She desperately wanted to know.

She licked her lips.

His eyes snagged on the movement. Lust sparked in his ice blue gaze. Sydney felt an answering spark inside her very center.

If I just move a little closer…

Merrick tore himself away.

Sydney blinked. She was leaning heavily over the side of her seat. Mortification set in and she jerked back.

Merrick's face was carefully neutral. "So," his voice was gruff, "how long have you and Joel…uh…been together?"

Embarrassment and shame flooded her. He knew they were dating? She wanted to melt into a puddle right then and there. "Our three-year anniversary is coming up in a little over a week," she said meekly, feeling even worse.

Merrick's knuckles briefly flashed white. "That's a long time."

She picked at invisible lint on her pants. "It is."

A brief quiet settled over them.

"You know, you're really going to need to get some sleep. If you don't you're going to be too exhausted tomorrow to do anything."

"I know," she sighed. "I just have to calm myself first, then I should be all right."

He glanced at her out of the corner of his eye. "It might help if you focused on something else other than whatever is bothering you."

The trouble was there were too many things bothering her. Her memories of Aaron, her relationship with Joel…him.

"Why don't you tell me about what kind of powers you have?" Merrick said. "You already know mine."

She smiled at the much-needed distraction. They were in a corner far enough away from the other patients that they wouldn't be overheard. "I'm a Shielder. My power negates everyone else's around me when I use them."

He looked mildly impressed. "So when that man grabbed you at the station you didn't feel anything?"

"No. What does he do anyway?"

"He causes pain."

She swallowed thickly. "How long did Vander have you for before he moved you?"

He shrugged. "There's no way to keep track of time, but I'd guess a month give or take."

She processed that for a minute. Four months total. "I'm sorry we didn't get to you," she voiced the one regret that had been haunting her all summer. "We wanted to free you, the woman I was with and I, but we thought for sure you'd be rescued by the police. We never knew Vander moved you until we couldn't find you in the hospital."

"You searched for me?"

Her cheeks flamed. "Yeah."

He started to reach for her, then stopped. He stuffed his hands into the pockets of his scrub pants. "Thank you."

She didn't know what to think of his small slip. Did he want to touch her like she did him? "Where are you from?"

"Anaheim."

Her body traitorously perked up at the realization that he didn't live very far from her. "Were you working on any big cases before Vander took you?"

That half smirk was back on his face. "Are you interrogating me?"

"It's only fair after you questioned me *during* a rescue mission."

"In all fairness you didn't answer all my questions."

"I did too," she protested.

"You told me you were rescuing me 'out of the goodness of your heart,' when really it sounds like you were doing it for your 'guild.'"

"Technically it's both. The Guild of Truth has vowed to stop Vander at every turn, plus we wanted to save those that we let down back in Irvine."

"The Guild of Truth? As opposed to Vander's Kratos Guild?"

She stiffened in genuine surprise. "How do you know the name of Vander's Guild?"

He watched a nurse wheel a patient through the swinging double doors. "Because he wanted me to join it."

She gripped the arm of her chair. "And what did you say?"

He gave her a flat stare. "What do you think I said? I denied him."

Sydney sagged in relief, the wheels in her brain turning. "Did he say why he wanted you to join?" If he was building another facility to run illegal fights then the guild needed to know about it. They needed to cut him off before he could even start.

"He wanted me to find something for him—a journal from an old employee that's in a coma."

Her stomach turned to ice.

Her feelings must have shown on her face because Merrick turned his full attention to her. "What is it?"

What were the odds? "I think I know which employee Vander is referring to."

"Who is it?"

"His name is Kevin Bauer. He's been in a coma for a few years now because my best friend, Felix, put him there. He was a full-forced Dreamer, someone with the ability to see the past, present, or future," she explained at his puzzled expression. "Kevin's Mirror Mate was a woman named Collette—she had a sick obsession with Felix and wanted him to love her. He didn't and to punish him, Collette tried to have Kevin kill him. Felix fought back and nailed him in the head with a chair as he ran for his life. That's why he's in a coma."

Merrick cursed. "That's some life your friend's got there."

"That's not the half of it. Three months ago Vander went after Felix's Mirror Mate, Cali, because he thought she was his. He later found that he was mistaken, that Kevin had lied to him, but still he sent Collette after both of them. It was through this whole mix up that we formed the Guild of Truth. We learned of Vander's dealings and vowed to stop him. Cali put a stop to Collette but Vander got away."

"Collette…" Merrick frowned. "I know that name."

"She was Vander's right-hand woman for a while. She could create Illusions with nothing but a thought and a wave of her hand."

The muscles in his neck strained as he clenched his jaw. "Now I remember that bitch. She was the one that lured me to her with a false case. She had all the documentation but when I touched the paperwork I couldn't get a reading from it."

She nodded. "Probably because it wasn't real."

He inhaled deeply as if to calm himself. "So Vander is looking for this journal that was written by a…Dreamer? Why?"

"I wish I knew. We have a Dreamer in our guild, her name is Niella. She keeps a little notepad on her because I think it helps keep her sane. She's never told me but I think she writes down everything she Dreams so she can differentiate between what she Dreamed and what is real. I can only imagine that Kevin did the same thing, writing down everything he was asked to Dream about." That's when it clicked. "He hasn't given up on finding his Mirror Mate," she whispered.

"What?"

She grabbed his arm. A flare of desire shot through her. Merrick's eyes flashed. She released her hold. "Vander hasn't given up looking for his Mirror Mate," she repeated, trying to sort it out through her jumbled brain. "He went after Cali because he thought she was his Mirror Mate but when he found out she wasn't, the guild and I thought he'd simply drop the issue. Now he's looking for Kevin's journal because I bet you anything he's looking for any clue as to her whereabouts."

Merrick pinched the bridge of his nose. "I'm trying to follow you but I'm a little confused about what a Mirror Mate is."

"A Mirror Mate is a destined soul mate of sorts. When the two individuals find each other and bond completely they increase each other's power. That's why Vander wants to find his so badly. He wants to expand his power." She needed to tell the guild as soon as possible. If Felix's theory proved true, then the whole reason Kevin lied to Vander about Cali was not only to get back at Felix, but to protect humanity from Vander ever becoming full-forced.

"And how do you know who your Mirror Mate is?"

Sydney's mind was going a mile a minute. "Hm? Oh, usually there's an instant connection. A deep awareness of each other after you set eyes on one another or touch."

His expression turned guarded. "What kind of connection?"

As if against his will he trailed the back of his fingers along her forearm.

Sydney repressed a shiver but she could tell he felt it.

Those intelligent eyes watched her, taking in too much, putting together the pieces.

Uh-oh.

Did he know?

Did he suspect, like she did, that they...

She swallowed thickly.

Chapter 6

The tension between them was broken as the janitor wheeled over his cart.

Merrick snatched his hand away and shot to his feet.

Sydney could only sit there in a daze, her body humming beneath her skin.

The janitor put his hands up, clearly startled at Merrick's aggressiveness. He was an older man with graying hair and dark brown eyes. "I didn't mean to startle you, son. I just thought that you'd want a more private room to rest between your shifts is all."

He gestured to Merrick's scrubs.

Sydney felt her eyebrows rise. Merrick shot her a "what do I do?" look and she had to hide her smile behind her fist.

The janitor didn't notice their hesitancy. "There's a room in the back currently empty. It's got a cot. I know it's not much but it sure beats these piece of shit seats. Pardon my language." He nodded in Sydney's direction.

She waved him off. She was more than used to Cali's and Felix's cursing. In fact, everyone in the guild had a pretty colorful vocabulary except her.

She watched as Merrick mulled over the janitor's offer.

A few minutes later they were led back to a secluded room with dim lights and a scantily dressed cot. There were a few chairs and side tables, and a small TV mounted in one corner.

Merrick moved a chair in front of the door. "I figured the further away from prying eyes, the better."

The cot was a little stiff. Sydney gave it an experimental bounce. "That sounds reasonable to me. I have to admit I'm a little surprised the janitor didn't question you about working here—he just saw the scrubs and instantly assumed."

He took a seat across the room from her, near the door. "I know, he didn't even say anything about my bare feet. In fact, look what he gave me." He held up the blue coverings for shoes and slipped them over his feet.

At least now it wouldn't look so obvious that he wasn't wearing shoes. And the whole ensemble did make him look like a surgeon, or at the very least a nurse.

"You should probably get some sleep now," he told her as he rested his ankle across his knee.

She leaned back and tried to get comfortable. She wanted to bring up Vander again but didn't know how to breach the subject without including Mirror Mates. They had to find that journal first. If there was any clue in it as to where Vander's soul mate would be, then they needed to get to it before he did.

Sydney spent the next hour or so attempting to fall asleep. No such luck. Every time a nurse wheeled past their room she thought it was Vander's people looking for them.

A warm hand on her shoulder nearly had her jumping out of her skin.

"Hey, it's just me," said Merrick.

She sat up. "Is it my turn to watch?"

He took a seat next to her on the cot, his body so close she could feel the heat from him. "No, it's not your turn. You haven't slept a wink."

"How did you know I wasn't sleeping?"

"Your breathing," he said as if it were obvious.

"If it's not my turn to watch then why did you come over here?" Did her voice sound a tad nervous?

"To try to help you fall asleep. Now, lie back down."

Her heart started to pound.

"Don't worry," he said, seeing her terrified expression. "I'm not going to jump you."

Was that a stab of disappointment she just felt?

Despite herself she looked at his crotch where there was obvious evidence that he did want to jump her.

"You know, your staring at it isn't going to make it any better."

Horrified, and with her cheeks burning, she went to scramble away.

"Hey." He caught her easily. "You don't have to run." He put a pillow in his lap and patted it. "Try resting your head against me."

She stared at him incredulously. Was he kidding?

He smirked. "I'm serious. Give it a chance, for five minutes at least. If you can't fall asleep then I'll go back to my side of the room. Fair?"

She kept eyeing his lap.

Why are you so scared? You've cuddled with Felix tons of times. This is no different.

Then why did it feel like she was betraying Joel?

"Five minutes," she conceded and curled up on the cot. She hesitated before letting her head rest against the pillow. Her shoulder pressed against the side of his thigh, the heat of him calming a tension deep inside of her.

She focused on his steady breathing and found her eyelids drooping.

Fingers sifted through her hair. She tensed. Merrick's hand froze.

She wanted to tell him to keep going but the words were lodged in her throat. Her emotions were in such turmoil. She forced her eyes closed.

She was just starting to drift when she felt Merrick's hand return to her hair. She smiled sleepily before sleep claimed her.

*

Vander watched the security footage off the commandeered laptop Regina and Dennis had offered up to him. All four of his prisoners had been taken. *Rescued.* He sneered at the word. And by whom?

He zoomed in on the blonde and her brown-haired companion. Sydney Spencer and Joel Kegler. He knew them, recognized them from their last attempt at destroying his work.

It seemed like Cali's little Guild of Truth was following him.

He'd underestimated them, but not anymore. He learned from his mistakes and now more than ever he'd keep his eye on them. After all, they did have something that he wanted.

"There." He paused the video: Merrick was holding his hand over the security panel, eyes closed. He was using his powers. Vander had been right; he could learn information from touching an object.

His phone went off. "What?"

"Sir, they're on the move." Regina's voice came through the other end.

Vander resumed the video. "Good, don't lose them." They had been smart to go to a public location, a hospital no less. It was a lot harder to apprehend a person there. It was also the perfect destination to lose Regina—with all those different scents even someone as powerful as she would be slowed down. Fortunately for him, his form of motivation kept her performing at her best. There was no room for failure. All he needed to do now was find the proper motivation for Mr. Haskell.

"And what about the others, sir? They've arrived in Oakland and are staying in a hotel."

He didn't have to be quite so tolerant of them. "Pursue them at any cost. Keep tabs on Mr. Haskell and Miss Spencer—you'll get further instruction on them later. Am I clear?"

"Yes, sir."

He ended the call and debated whether or not to fly Jente up to assist with Regina. Jente Mitchell was an invaluable asset. With the ability to go invisible he could tail anyone and learn valuable information.

He thumbed through his contacts.

*

"So I was thinking that if Vander is so set on finding this journal that we should get to it first. You live in Anaheim, which is close to where my guild functions out of my clinic. Kevin lived down there too so his things should be somewhere close by. We could pool resources and find this thing. You'd be a great asset if you wanted to help us."

"You were thinking all this while you slept?" Merrick asked as they walked Market Street. Ever since they woke up Sydney had kept up a constant chatter. Her bubbly personality was so at odds with the doom and gloom he'd been subjected to for the past four months. It was a welcome change.

He snuck a glance at her and his cock stiffened. She was so beautiful when she was relaxed and smiling. Waking up with her golden hair spread across his lap that morning had him seeking a private bathroom stall very quickly.

She's taken.

He knew. Hell, he was probably only attracted to her because she was the first woman besides Regina that he'd really been in contact with. His past celibacy before being kidnapped probably wasn't helping matters either.

But what about those Mirror Mates she kept referring to?

He could have sworn that when he asked her about them there had been a flash of fear in her eyes. But why would she fear finding her soul mate?

Shit, was he really buying into this?

Obviously she was afraid that he'd jump to the conclusion that they were Mirror Mates when they clearly weren't. Which he was. She was right to be wary.

"I do some of my best thinking while I sleep," she said happily. She checked her phone.

Waiting for a text message from Joel? Again?

He'd called earlier that morning to check on Sydney. As if Merrick would have let anything happen to her. His hands balled into fists.

They were supposed to meet up that day and eventually fly back to So Cal.

Merrick prowled the streets as he searched for some way to disguise their scent. Joel might think they were in the clear but Merrick knew better. Regina would find them and they had to be ready.

"Where are you going?" Merrick asked when Sydney stopped at a set of doors.

"In here." She disappeared inside, forcing him to follow.

"Why?"

Sydney stopped and put her hands on her hips. "You need clothes, remember?" She gestured around the store.

In his haste to find some way to escape Regina's tracking ability he'd forgotten about his state of dress. A few employees eyed him, clearly appalled.

"Can you even afford to buy clothing in a place like this?" he whispered to her.

"Please." She waved him off. "I'm not buying you a new wardrobe. We only need an outfit."

That didn't mean he was going to let her spend a fortune on him. He searched for the cheapest clothing available: one pair of jeans, a black v-neck sweater, and a pair of shoes. Simple, affordable, and essential.

He stepped out of the fitting room, not bothering with his reflection. The clothing fit, he didn't care how it made him look. He already knew a lot of his body had withered away from his captivity, no need to reinforce the fact. As soon as he returned home he was going to hit the gym and gain back all the muscle that he'd lost.

"Let's get out of here." He approached Sydney where she sat in a waiting chair.

Her bright green eyes widened. They raked his body from head to toe.

That really wasn't helping his situation. When she looked at him like that he wanted to force her back onto a flat surface and take her, driving any thoughts of Joel clear from her head as he drove himself into her body.

His erection strained against his new jeans. He clenched his jaw, forcing any and all images of her from his mind. He needed to focus on more important things. Like Vander. He'd be damned if he was going to let that fucker get away with what he'd done to him. Four months of his life were gone. His business was probably bankrupt, his bills long overdue. Had anyone gone looking for him? Was there a missing persons out for him?

He doubted it. No one at the station where he used to work truly cared about him. All those friendships had withered when he'd started succeeding on cases that others had failed at.

He followed Sydney to the cashier. She paid for his clothes with a card. "I appreciate the clothes. I'll pay you back as soon as I can."

She collected her receipt. "You don't have to. I like helping others."

He held the door open for her as they exited the store. "If you won't let me pay you back with cash I can at least help you find that journal Vander is looking for."

She stopped right in the middle of the sidewalk. "Seriously?"

He grabbed her arm and kept her moving. The longer they stayed in one spot the easier it'd be for Regina to find them. "Seriously," he told her. "He fucked with the wrong PI."

She pried his fingers from her arm, the touch stirring his blood even more. "So all you want is revenge?"

"Four months, Sydney. That's how long I was isolated and tortured."

She was quiet for a moment before she stared up at him. "You called me Sydney."

He frowned.

"That's the first time you've used my name…Merrick."

He didn't understand the big deal until she spoke his name. His gut clenched. It was like an intimate caress. Lust seized him but he wrestled it back.

His gaze caught on a store to his right.

"Where are you going?" asked Sydney.

Merrick held the door open and ushered her in. He scanned the crowds before following her but didn't see any brunettes with fake blue eyes.

Sydney's nose instantly scrunched in that adorable way of hers. "Bath and Body Works?"

The smell hit Merrick a second later and his own nose screwed up as the sickly sweet scents bombarded him. "We need to disguise our scents," he told her and started for the tester sprays.

"You mean to hide from Regina?" Her eyes grew distant as she thought. "You said she was a Tracker."

He glanced at her in surprise. She had a good memory.

She shook her head, her lips curling. "Man, you'd definitely fit in with the rest of the guild."

"Why do you say that?"

"Because you made up a title for Regina." At his blank expression she elaborated. "You called her a Tracker. Everyone in the guild has come up with at least one title for someone with a power."

"What title did you come up with?"

Her chin rose just a little higher. "My own."

"You came up with the term Shielder?"

"Yup. So far our list of titles include: Shielder, Eraser, Dreamer, Silencer, LockSmith, Veiler, Diverter, and Illusionist."

Merrick tried to commit all those to memory. He'd have to ask about each one. Later. "You can explain that after we conceal our scent." He picked up a spray. Twilight Woods. He gave an experimental sniff.

He pulled the bottle away from him. Well, it was definitely strong enough.

Sydney picked up some kind of vanilla fruit blend. He took it from her hand. "You already smell like vanilla. You need a *different* scent."

She studied him. It didn't take him very long before he realized that he'd admitted to smelling her.

Shit.

He thrust the Twilight Woods at her. "Try this." He spun on his heel to go look for other sprays.

"Hey." She trailed after him. "You never explained what a Tracker is." She doused herself in spray before picking up another stronger smelling one and misting him with it.

He jumped.

She grinned.

He snatched the bottle and squirted her right in the face. "Imagine for a moment that werewolves existed. Their sense of smell? That's what Regina has."

Her smile faded. "Do you think she'll be able to Track us?"

Merrick continued to spray himself. A female employee stared openly at him. "She might," he said at last. "She's well acquainted with my scent. She was always assigned to bathe me." Sydney's knuckles went white around the new bottle she held. "She used to tell me she bought my soap specifically for me. It was Irish Spring. She thought Haskell was Irish. I felt like telling the bitch that my last name was Welsh." The old anger started to rise, the back of his neck prickling. He recognized the sensation and quickly stuffed his hands into his pockets.

Sydney's body was turned away from him, making it hard to get a read off of her.

He wanted to reach out and touch her shoulder, to turn her around to face him. But he didn't trust himself to touch anything at that moment. Every time his neck tingled the way it was now it meant his powers were lingering, waiting to read the next thing that touched his skin.

The clothes he wore had been specifically chosen from the bottom of their piles in the store. It meant fewer people had come into contact with them, which meant there were fewer impressions left for Merrick to pick up. He caught glimpses of bored employees, but nothing too distracting.

No matter how much he wanted to touch Sydney, he couldn't. He didn't want to pick up on her pity or worse…any lingering thoughts about Joel.

A low growl started in his throat when a flash of brown hair caught his eye. Merrick spun to gaze out the window.

"Is it Regina?"

He shifted at the last minute to avoid brushing shoulders with Sydney. He might have his clothes as a barrier but one could never be too careful. "We need to keep moving. What time is our train at?" They were going to take the BART out of San Francisco to meet up with Joel and the rest of the escapees.

She pulled out her phone. "We still have plenty of time."

"In that case," he made his way toward the exit, "we should switch stations. We can't afford to linger here any longer."

Merrick started making his way up Market Street. There was little time for conversation as Sydney huffed next to him to try to keep up. She was stronger than she looked. Not once did she complain that he was going too fast or ask him to slow down.

A glimpse of brown hair up ahead had him slipping up the next street they came across.

"Why are we going this way?" Sydney gasped.

Merrick double checked over his shoulder. "Regina was up ahead. We can circle around this block to bypass her."

A lone man with his hair tied back in a ponytail caught Merrick's gaze and held it. Merrick's instincts went into high gear. That man worked with Regina. He just knew it.

He deviated off course again. Before Sydney could ask he spoke out of the side of his mouth. "There's more of them."

Her postured stiffened. "Is it the man who caught me at the station?"

"No." He hoped like hell that fucker wasn't near. He'd kill him if he laid another hand on Sydney. In fact, he hadn't caught sight of Dennis either.

He paused, another suspicious man up ahead.

Sydney stopped next to him.

Merrick glanced over his shoulder, his mind realizing what was happening too late.

More men were behind them.

Regina stepped out from around a corner.

"Shit, they herded us."

Chapter 7

Joel paced the hotel room as the sound of Juliet, Luke, and Hazel playing cards lingered in the background of his mind.

"Joel, you can stop pacing," said Juliet. "You're going to wear a path into the carpet. Besides, Sydney will be fine. Merrick's with her."

His nails bit into the palm of his hand. It was that very reason why he was so wired. If Syd had been trapped with anyone else he wouldn't have been as worried. But he'd seen the way Merrick had looked at her. Fuck, he even had to admit that Syd had looked at Merrick a few times with some kind of emotion in her eye.

You're overreacting.

Was he? He didn't fucking know anymore.

More than once he'd wished with every fiber of his being that he and Sydney were Mirror Mates. Then he wouldn't have these niggling doubts. He'd know for sure that she was the one for him.

He forced himself to sit with the others.

Hazel quietly passed him a hand of cards. He picked them up. "Thanks."

Three games later Joel was convinced Juliet was cheating.

She planted her fists on her curvaceous hips. "I am not," she protested.

Joel leaned toward her. "Oh yeah?" he challenged. "Then let someone else deal."

Luke and Hazel exchanged a smile.

A knock at the door interrupted Juliet's stammering.

Joel's head whipped around. "Syd?" Had they caught an earlier train?

The others got to their feet.

He pulled open the door.

"Your girlfriend is a little busy, I heard." A hand grasped Joel's hand.

He wrenched back but it was too late. His vision went black. "What the fuck?" He blinked, flailing his free arm. He couldn't fucking see!

Juliet and Hazel cried out behind him. He heard shuffling followed by a crash.

He dropped to the ground and reached out blindly with his hand. He connected with a shoe. His neck prickled and he Locked it.

"Bastard," the man growled before Joel was kicked in the chest. He reeled back. The connection between him and his attacker was broken. His vision slowly started coming back into focus. He glanced around the room.

Vander's men had found them.

*

"Nice trick." Regina strolled toward them, tapping her nose. "Would have worked too if we hadn't been watching you since the hospital."

Merrick pushed Sydney behind him.

"What do you mean they herded us?" she whispered up to him.

He took in their surroundings. "They manipulated me into thinking I was escaping them when really they led me right where they wanted me." He waved his hand around. "To somewhere much less crowded."

They started to close rank around them.

The man with the ponytail pulled out a long piece of fabric.

Merrick tensed. "I'm not going back with you."

Regina smiled like she used to when he resisted her in his cell. She always found his defiance amusing.

Her smile was all the warning they got. The men pounced.

Merrick was far from his peak performance but he wasn't starved and sleep deprived anymore either. He knocked a man with a buzz cut right off his feet. He could hear another attacker coming up behind him but the man with the ponytail came at him at the same time.

They locked grips. Merrick could hear the struggle behind him. Every instinct raged at him to help Sydney, but if he didn't take care of the man he was fighting he'd be no help to her.

Anger fueled his strength and he kicked out, taking his attacker by surprise. The man's leg buckled and he dropped to one knee.

Sydney cried out.

Merrick whirled.

Cloth wrapped around his nose and mouth.

"You shouldn't have taken your eyes off me," Ponytail said. He tightened the fabric around Merrick's face making it difficult to breathe.

A kick to the backs of his legs had him dropping to his knees. He struggled to get a grip on the hands behind his head. The cloth tightened further.

Sydney cried out, struggling against the man holding her. Regina walked over to the two of them but didn't pay Sydney the least bit of attention. Her eyes were for Merrick. She watched him, as if waiting for something.

What the fuck? What was she waiting for?

He'd ask, but the bastard behind him was slowly suffocating him.

"Leave him alone." Sydney kicked out behind her. The man winced as her heel made contact with his shin.

A few more seconds ticked by. Merrick started to get lightheaded, his heart pounding.

Regina's brows drew together in confusion. "Why isn't it working?" Her nostrils flared. Her expression went blank as she finally turned to Sydney. "You," Regina hissed. She sniffed the air again. "What are you doing? Why can't I smell him from here?"

Beneath the cloth Merrick smirked. Sydney was using her powers.

Sydney feigned ignorance and shrugged.

Regina's face darkened. She struck Sydney across the face.

Merrick saw red. The back of his neck suddenly prickled. The sensation cut off as abruptly as it had come.

Regina inhaled through her nose. "Stop it," she yelled at Sydney before she hit her again, this time dropping her to her knees.

Merrick roared behind the fabric. The back of his neck was pins and needles again. The cloth around his face cut into his skin. He didn't care, he—

He saw a woman with the most beautiful blue and gray eyes. His Collette. He was the luckiest man in the world. He'd do anything to keep her. Anything. He finished the last of his journal entry. He'd put it away later. Right now all he wanted to do was watch Collette as she danced. All he wanted was to follow her to their bed like he did every night she beckoned him. He'd follow her to the ends of the earth. He clutched his heart, the feelings inside of him nearly bursting with how much he cared for her.

He hesitantly approached her. "Would you like a partner?" he asked.

She assessed him from head to toe. He knew he was lacking. He would never be worthy of someone like Collette, yet she allowed him to remain by her side.

"Did you finish your silly writing?"

He stared over his shoulder at his beat-up notebook with the warped spirals. "It's not silly," he mumbled. She didn't understand. Didn't understand what it was like to see so much, to feel so much. He rubbed his aching temple. He was trying his best, but Vander asked the impossible.

He rubbed his head harder.

Too much. They demanded too much!

His nails bit into his skin.

Gentle fingers curled around his hands, pulling them from his temples. "Shh," Collette soothed. She smiled seductively at him. "Dance with me?"

The pressure in his head eased. "Always," he breathed.

Merrick gasped as he was hurled from the vision.

"Merrick," Sydney cried out. She glared at Regina. "What'd you do to him?"

Regina released her hold around Sydney's throat.

Merrick heard the faint pounding of feet coming their way.

Regina lifted her nose to the air. "Perfect timing," she said softly. "Gentlemen," she raised her voice. "The authorities are on their way. Let us depart."

The rag around Merrick's face disappeared, though he knew now that it wasn't a rag. It had once been a shirt.

"Merrick, are you all right?" Sydney rushed to his side.

"Hey." An officer ran over from one of the side streets. "I heard shouts. Are you two all right?"

The officer helped Sydney get Merrick to his feet. His head was pounding and his legs were a little shaky, but other than that he was fine.

"We're okay, officer," Merrick said politely. "Just a little roughed up." He pretended to feel around in his pockets. "Bastards got my wallet."

"I'll call it in." The officer stepped back to give them space as he pulled his radio from his belt.

Sydney ran her hands along his arms and torso worriedly. "Are you sure you're okay?"

Her touch set his pulse racing. His cock hardened as a wave of hunger and want flooded him. Their eyes locked and he saw an answering flash of desire swirling in her green gaze.

Fuckin' A.

His hand reached for her face.

The officer returned.

Merrick dropped his hand. Sydney glanced away, but not before he saw the disappointment. His lungs constricted.

"I called it in to the station. They'll keep a look out. I didn't get much of a look at your attackers. I'd be happy to take you back to the station so you can give a full report."

Merrick shook his head. They needed to make their train. "That's much appreciated but we'd rather be on our way. Could we leave the report with you?"

The officer took notes as Merrick described Regina and her goons down to the very last detail. He even dropped her name to give her a little extra hell.

"And how did you learn her name?" the officer asked.

"One of the men let it slip when they were talking to her," he supplied helpfully.

The officer nodded and wrote it down on his pad before flipping it shut and tucking it away. "I'm really sorry this had to happen to you two. You seem like good people." He offered Merrick a card. "You can check in with the station to see if they get your wallet back. We'd be happy to mail it to you."

"Thanks."

The officer disappeared the way he'd come.

Merrick headed back to Market Street, Sydney at his side. She worked her jaw, reminding him that she had been hit. His temper flared. "Come on." He led her into a drugstore and bought a frozen bag of peas from the food section with the card she handed him.

"What're those for?"

He crunched the bag in his hands. "It's for your face."

They made it to the Montgomery station without incident. Merrick sought out a deserted part of the platform and took a bench. He turned to Sydney and cupped the side of her face in his hand. She shivered. He pretended not to notice as he placed the frozen peas on her jaw.

She jerked away from the cold. "Ow. Don't you need your own bag of peas?"

"I wasn't hit in the face," he said, though the backs of his legs and his knees were aching fiercely.

"I don't get it," she said. "Why'd they attack us to just run off?"

Merrick scanned the crowd. No one was within hearing range. "I don't think they were trying to capture us."

"Then what were they doing?"

He shifted the bag against her face. "The fabric they used to cover my nose and mouth, I'm pretty sure it belonged to that Dreamer you told me about. Kevin."

She didn't need any more prompting. He could all but hear the wheels in her mind turning. "That's why they roughed you up. They wanted your emotions running high so you'd use your powers without meaning to."

"Roughing me up wasn't what pushed me over the edge."

She blinked up at him, her head tilted slightly. "Then what'd they…oh." Pink flushed her cheeks and she looked away. "You got upset because they were hurting me?"

With his free hand he cupped the other side of her face so that she'd look him in the eyes. His blood rushed through his veins, his cock throbbing with repressed need. "When they touched you, I wanted to kill them," he confessed.

Her lips parted but nothing came out.

He couldn't explain why he felt this need inside of him to protect her. To claim her. All he knew was that he had to have her. That she was his. And he had to taste her.

He dipped his head to capture her mouth with his.

She gasped against his lips.

He pushed harder against her, half afraid that she'd pull away.

Fingers gently slid through his hair to grasp the back of his head. Excitement and desire spiked through him. Her lips moved under his, carefully at first before gaining more and more confidence.

Merrick dropped the peas on their bench so he could reach around her waist and draw her closer.

She slid willingly into his lap, her mouth hot on his. Merrick groaned low in his throat as some kind of deep tension within him eased.

He couldn't even begin to explain the rightness of Sydney in his arms. It was as if she was fashioned for him. Her petite body pressed tight against him, her perky little breasts brushing against his chest.

His cock pulsed against her thigh.

He slid his tongue deep into her mouth. She opened wide for him, moaning as she fisted his hair.

Merrick's control was slipping.

Everything about her was intoxicating: her touch, her scent, her taste. He wanted to sink himself so deep inside her body that he shook with the force of it.

The platform rumbled.

In the distance a child shrieked in glee.

Sydney's hold tightened in his hair, her tongue stealing deep into his mouth, as if she couldn't get enough of him.

Merrick growled in frustration as he regretfully pulled away. The platform was filling as their departure time drew closer. They were both breathing heavily.

Sydney blinked as if waking from a dream.

Thirty feet away a young man with a Mohawk gave Merrick a thumbs-up.

Merrick glowered at the kid. He scampered away.

"Our train is coming," Merrick said gruffly.

Sydney's emerald green eyes went wide. She instantly released her hold on his hair. He'd been thinking of getting it cut as soon as he could but suddenly thought better of it. He liked the feel of her hands in his hair. She stared down at where she sat and scrambled off his lap.

She brushed at her clothes as if to smooth out any stray wrinkles.

He picked up the abandoned bag of peas and joined her by the yellow safety line. "You're going to have to wait until you wash your clothes to get out those creases. You slept in that outfit, remember?"

She blushed.

He handed her the bag of peas. "How's the jaw?"

She took the frozen food from his hand without touching his skin. "Better." She pressed it to her slightly swollen cheek and winced.

Merrick shoved his hands into his pockets to keep from touching her.

"So," Sydney said after a few seconds of silence. "You never finished telling me about that piece of clothing that they wrapped around your face. You said it belonged to Kevin?"

A group of giggling girls came to stand next to him. Merrick shifted closer to Sydney, uneasy. He stuffed his hands deeper into his pockets.

Sydney watched him.

He dropped his voice. "I know it belonged to Kevin because when I got a reading off of it there was a woman in the vision. Collette. That was Kevin's Mirror Mate, right?"

She nodded eagerly, all ears now. "What else did you see?"

"I don't just see things. I pick up impressions: thoughts, feelings, sights, sounds, everything really. Kevin was writing in his journal. If Vander's expecting some leather bound encyclopedia then he's clearly mistaken. It's a beat up blue notebook that you'd buy at any office supply store. The spirals are warped and the coloring on the cover is cracked and faded. I couldn't tell what he was writing because his thoughts kept drifting to Collette. He kept obsessing on how lucky he was to have her and how she didn't understand how hard it was for him to sort through all the information he has obtained. I'm guessing he's talking about his Dreams?"

Sydney shifted the peas to the other side of her face. "It has to be. If Vander was trying to find his Mirror Mate along with a whole bunch of people with powers then he'd have been demanding Kevin to be Dreaming quite a bit. That much information would be like sensory overload."

"That would explain why Kevin seemed to be going mad," Merrick muttered aloud. He elaborated when she tilted her head askance. "It's hard to explain but his thoughts were…erratic. He kept grabbing his head as if it was driving him crazy. Which I guess it was."

Could that ever happen to him?

Would he reach a point in time when he used his powers so much that he'd no longer be able to keep track of reality anymore?

The group of girls next to him started getting louder. A few even shuffled closer to where he stood.

He shoved his hands as deep as they'd go into his pockets. He couldn't read them if he didn't touch them with his skin. Yet he still felt that underlying fear of accidentally absorbing something that he didn't want to see.

Maybe he would be driven to insanity.

Chapter 8

Sydney followed Merrick's lean frame through the train cars. She watched with rapt attention as he avoided brushing up against anyone. There were a few close encounters but all he did was push his hands further into his jeans—jeans that hugged his narrow hips and surprisingly still muscled legs.

When he'd stepped out of that fitting room Sydney's stomach had flipped. The clothing had fit him as if tailored for his body. The black of his sweater had brought out the ice blue of his eyes and emphasized the darkness of his hair. Sydney had expected him to be lanky from his captivity but Merrick had surprisingly held on to his muscled frame. He wasn't as big as Felix but he wasn't too far from Joel either. She was sure that with a few visits to the gym he'd make a very impressive male specimen.

Unbidden, her mind drifted to the kiss they'd shared. Her body grew both hot and cold. She could still feel his lips against hers, the addicting taste of his tongue and lips, her body throbbing with want, her breasts aching, her sex pulsing.

She'd never experienced a desire so fierce before. And the worst part of all was that she didn't even feel guilty about it.

You should! You just cheated on Joel.

She had a whole list of excuses ready in the back of her mind but she wouldn't do that to Joel. She had cheated on him. Plain and simple. And the fear and dread churning inside her only intensified when she thought about telling him.

Joel had been all she'd known for the past three years. He was her first real love. The thought of hurting him tore at her. What if he never wanted to speak to her again? What would that do to the guild? Would they fracture and drift apart?

The idea made her sick. They were her family. How could she have been so stupid to jeopardize that?

She stared at Merrick's back, the muscles rippling beneath his black sweater as he moved through the train cars like a panther moved through the forest. Her heart fluttered.

Merrick made her feel things that, if she were truly being honest with herself, she hadn't felt with Joel in months.

She rested her hand against her pants where her cell phone resided. She longed to call Cali or Niella. But what if they found her act of kissing Merrick as a betrayal to Joel?

She snatched her hand back. She couldn't tell them. There were too many of them invested into the guild. She would have to reason it out herself.

That was fine. She could do it.

Merrick wouldn't tell anyone. She had to trust that he wouldn't tell anyone.

He finally stopped when they reached an abandoned car. He took a seat at the furthest end in a corner.

She hesitantly took the seat next to him. They both still smelled like those ridiculous fragrant sprays. If they wanted to gain any chance of losing Regina they needed to shower and re-disguise their scent again.

She turned to Merrick. "I think it's fishy that Regina just let us go."

"I agree."

"They wanted you to get a reading off Kevin's shirt." That much was obvious. "I think it was a setup."

"I know. I figured as much when they fled. Regina would have been able to smell the cop; she would have known there was only one. They could have easily taken him down but they didn't. They used that officer as an excuse."

She tried to ignore the heat of his body next to hers as she thought.

"How did they know you'd be able to read the shirt? Did you confess to Vander that you had a power?"

His face darkened. "I didn't confess shit. I'm assuming he had suspicions long before he captured me. He had my business records. He was putting the pieces together and I probably cemented those suspicions when I pulled that stunt on the entrance of the facility you broke me out of."

"I wonder what he thought you'd gleam from that shirt," she mused aloud.

He leaned back in his chair. "Like I said, I saw Kevin writing in a journal but his thoughts and emotions weren't focused on it. I'd probably be able to distinguish the notebook however if it was in a stack of books."

"Maybe that's what he wants. Both Kevin and Collette are in a coma, which means that their possessions are probably in some kind of storage somewhere."

"How'd Collette end up in a coma?" he asked.

She lurched in her seat as the BART came to the next stop. They lucked out. No one entered their cart. That wasn't likely to happen again.

"Felix's Mirror Mate, Cali, knocked her out with a fire extinguisher to the back of the head," she answered.

Merrick cursed under his breath. "You hang out with some violent people."

Sydney's smile was bittersweet as she thought about losing her guild. "They really grow on you." Even Cali, who she'd had a rough start with, was a dear friend to her now. She wouldn't trade any of them.

"Like a fungus?" His voice was serious, but Sydney saw the glitter of amusement in his eyes.

"Just like a fungus," she agreed with a grin. "You'll be able to meet them when we get a flight back home."

"We have to make it to an airport first." The brightness in his gaze dimmed. "If you're right and Vander wants me to pick the journal out of a group of books then that means he won't quit looking for me."

She put her hand on his thigh before she even knew what she was doing. The muscles under her palm stiffened. Desire flared in his eyes. She snatched her hand back. "Look, I'm not going to abandon you because Vander is after you. I've dealt with that before, trust me. We have a plan, remember? We're going to find this journal before him and we'll destroy it. Together."

"And what if I want to destroy more than just a silly journal?"

She refused to drop his gaze. "If you want a piece of Vander then I suggest you get in line."

"What did he do to you?"

"He came after my friends, that's enough in my book."

There was a brief flash of emotion in his face but it was gone too fast for her to catch.

At the next stop people started trickling into their cart.

She noticed that Merrick still had his hands tucked safely away in his pockets.

"Why were you avoiding touching anyone?" she asked.

He exhaled slowly. "It's a habit. I know better than anyone that people aren't what they seem and I don't want to 'pick up' anything if I don't have to."

Had he picked up anything on her when they'd touched? There were so many emotions running rampant inside her that he probably wouldn't have been able to differentiate between them. The thought gave her some peace of mind. She didn't want him to see the fear inside her over whether or not they were really Mirror Mates, or the more embarrassing, all-consuming lust she had felt as she ran her hands through his silky black hair.

"Do you accidentally read people a lot?" she asked as inconspicuously as possible. Would he tell her if he'd ever read her?

A man in a black leather coat walked into their compartment. Merrick sat up a little straighter. The man spotted an older woman, his face splitting into the biggest grin.

Merrick relaxed. "Sometimes I can't control it." He spoke softly from the corner of his mouth. "Mostly my control slips when I'm angered or—" He cut off, his eyes darting to her.

"Or what?"

He stared at her for a few seconds before answering. "If I'm aroused."

Sydney felt the blood rush to her face. He had read her then!

He must have caught sight of the sudden fear in her expression. "I haven't read you," he said fiercely.

"Are you lying?" she shot back.

"No."

How did she know if he was telling the truth?

Oh, what she wouldn't give to have Cali's powers right about now.

Merrick turned to face her more fully. "I wouldn't do that to you, okay? Believe me, I've learned my lesson. I never want to know what's inside someone's head. It's not meant to be known. It gives you nothing but pain, horror, or disappointment."

Something in his voice had her believing him. "Why do you say that?"

His stare was level. "Do you really want to know?"

She nodded.

"There was a high school teacher I took out to dinner once. My powers were still relatively new. I didn't fully understand the consequences of having them or what they'd expose me to, but I got my first glimpse that night. The whole date went off without a hitch until I took her home."

Sydney didn't know if she wanted to hear the rest of this story.

"I kissed her outside her apartment. She was wearing this scarf around her neck and when I touched it..." He paused. "When I touched it I saw her using that same scarf to tie one of her students to her bed as she had sex with them."

Sydney's heart stopped.

"She slept with her senior students. No one knew about it."

"Except you," she said softly.

"Except me," he said, disgusted.

"Did you report her?"

Merrick nodded. "Not at first. I was too sick to my stomach. Eventually I realized what I needed to do so I gave an anonymous tip. I stopped dating for a while after that. Then I met this woman who was a friend of a client of mine. I decided to give dating another try and took her out for coffee. I made sure not to touch her clothes but that didn't matter. I bought her a scone and accidentally touched the cloth napkin while she went to the bathroom." His jaw bulged. "I got a full view into her mind when she first laid eyes on me in the café. She found me lacking and entertained thoughts about how I'd look so much better if I adopted her ex-boyfriend's fashion sense and body language."

"Did you ever date after that?"

He shook his head. "I gave up on finding comfort from another human being. One way or another I'd eventually see something that I wasn't supposed to."

"That must be very lonely," Sydney mumbled. Her heart constricted in her chest. Did he think she was harboring ill thoughts and feelings about him? She wanted to touch him, to let him read her so that she could prove him wrong.

She swallowed the lump in her throat. "When did your powers first start manifesting?"

"I noticed things when I started working as a detective. I'd touch something and get glimpses of things, things I knew no one else would know. I researched my ability on the internet and then started practicing at work. Sometimes I could get my powers to work when I wanted, other times they didn't. As my control grew I started solving more and more cases. My co-workers didn't like that." He gave a forced laugh. "They started to alienate me. Eventually I got the hint and left. I started my own PI agency."

"And that's when Vander found you?" she guessed.

He focused his ice blue eyes on her. She felt the touch all the way to her soul. Heat bloomed in her lower abdomen. "Not Vander," he corrected. "Collette."

*

Sydney tried Joel's phone for the fifth time.

Straight to voicemail.

Again.

Unease wormed its way into her thoughts.

"Still no answer?" asked Merrick. He stood at the curb on the lookout for a taxi.

She pocketed her phone. "That's not like him. He always picks up."

A yellow cab made its way toward them. Merrick dropped his arm. "We'll go see for ourselves why he's not answering his phone. Don't worry too much until we know all the facts." He rested his hand briefly on her shoulder before opening the car door for her.

She missed the heat from his skin instantly.

She gave the cab driver directions to the hotel and tried to refrain from fidgeting in her seat.

Why wouldn't Joel answer his phone? There'd be no reason for him to have it switched off.

It could have died.

She considered the idea. It was feasible that it had died and he was simply charging it.

When they arrived at the hotel she felt a little more reassured. There were no cops, no ambulances, which meant that nothing of import had happened.

She approached the main desk. Their check-out time had long since passed and she hadn't discussed with Joel if they were going to prolong their stay or not. She'd imagine, given the circumstances, that he would have rebooked their room, but she needed to make sure.

"Excuse me." She offered up her best smile to the woman behind the counter.

The woman held up her finger as she finished giving directions to the person on the other end of the phone. Merrick came up behind Sydney. The back of her body grew warm from his nearness.

The woman hung up the phone and turned to give them her full attention. Her eyes stuck to Merrick and her smile instantly grew.

Sydney had to tamper down the jealousy that surged inside of her. "I was wondering if you could tell me if the occupants in room 436 renewed their stay," she said through clenched teeth.

Merrick glanced at her out of the corner of his eye. Was that a smirk she saw tugging at his lips?

At the mention of room 436, the woman instantly snapped out of her doe-eyed daze. "I'm afraid the occupants of room 436 were asked to leave after the disturbance they caused. If you're looking for some kind of refund, I'm sorry but the credit card given has already been charged with the damages done to the room."

"What?"

The woman flinched. "There's no need to yell." She held her hands out in front of her. In any other situation Sydney would have found the idea of a woman nearly five inches taller than herself cowering from her in fear laughable.

"What happened?" she demanded.

At her side, Merrick was already scouting the area.

Sydney slammed her hands down on the counter. "Did anyone get hurt? Where did they go after you kicked them out?"

Had Vander gotten to them? How had he found them? Did they have more than one Tracker?

Sydney's mind was awhirl with possibilities. She focused her thoughts. She had to concentrate on finding Joel and the others. What about Luke and his injury? Was he healed? Had he been reinjured?

"Well?" she snapped when the woman didn't answer her in a timely fashion.

The woman still held her hands out in front of her as if that would protect her from Sydney's wrath. "There was a noise complaint. When the staff was sent up to give them a warning they found the room in shambles."

"You mean you didn't find anyone there?" Sydney's blood turned to ice.

"I wasn't working at the time and only heard from a co-worker. I'm not sure whether the occupants were there or not. All I was told was that they destroyed the room and that there had been a noise complaint."

"So what you're telling me is that what you heard could have been embellished and you would have no idea?" That gave Sydney nothing to go on. That left too many options and she didn't like it. She liked order, simplicity.

"Thanks very much," she managed to ground out before she stomped down to the elevators.

The woman didn't even bother asking if she was a paying resident.

Merrick waited until they were alone in the elevator to speak. "I've never seen you go bat shit crazy before," he said idly.

She turned on him. "I did not go bat shit crazy. You want to see bat shit crazy?" She floundered for something else to say or do that would demonstrate bat shit crazy and came up blank.

Merrick laughed. "Behold, she curses." As if her cussing was some remarkable feat.

She crossed her arms over her chest and huffed in silence.

Merrick eventually sobered. "Want to tell me why we're going to the fourth floor?"

She avoided looking at him. How dare he make fun of her! "I want to see the damage for myself if they haven't cleaned it up already."

"You think they were ambushed by Vander?"

"What other option is there?"

He shrugged. "But if you already know they were ambushed then why go visit the room? What are you hoping to find out?"

Some of her anger diminished. "I don't know. Maybe there's a clue they left that would let me know they got away?"

He nodded. "Good thing you have your 'clue' right here." He pointed to himself.

Sydney's anger faded completely as she perked up. "I forgot. You can read the objects around the room, right? You'll be able to tell if they were taken again?"

"In theory. I can't promise anything, Sydney."

She didn't care. She threw her arms around his neck.

He stumbled from the unexpected weight, his arms instantly banding around her as his back connected with the wall of the elevator.

For a split second Sydney reveled in his embrace. The hard planes of his body, the feeling of protection and security…she could stay in his arms forever.

She pressed harder against him, her heart hammering in her chest. The tingles of desire only increased when she felt his erection press against her lower abdomen. She clenched her legs together as a throb of want went through her.

She pulled back. Merrick held her at arm's length, those intense light blue eyes of his searching her face.

She could no longer deny that there was something here between them. How deep that connection ran, she didn't know. But she needed to.

She recalled the first time she'd met Cali and how the Silencer had thought Sydney and Joel were Mirror Mates. Cali had asked if

Sydney had felt a jolt the first time she'd touched Joel. She hadn't, but with Merrick she had.

She swallowed the lump in her throat. "Did you feel a shock the first time we touched?"

"I felt something." His voice came out low, rough. His fingers tightened around her hips.

Her breathing grew shallow as she imagined his fingers digging into her flesh as he pounded himself into her. As she imagined his powerful body atop hers covered in a thin sheen of sweat, nothing but raw passion reflected in his eyes.

The force of her desire shamed and embarrassed her.

Merrick's erection twitched against her.

Oh, what are you doing, Sydney?

She didn't know. She was spiraling out of control and she hated herself for it.

She was trapped in his icy gaze.

Would he kiss her again?

Would she let him?

Her body was suddenly too hot. The elevator too small.

Merrick cupped the side of her face. That fiery passion she'd been imagining seconds ago was now present in his eyes.

He wants you.

It should have scared her. She should have been appalled. But all she felt was a giddy excitement and an answering burn in her breasts and between her legs.

For the first time in her life she entertained thoughts of having sex with a man somewhere other than in a bed.

Merrick leaned toward her, his chest rising and falling just as fast as hers.

She wanted his tongue in her mouth again.

The realization slammed into her.

Chapter 9

No. This is wrong.

The elevator doors dinged. Sydney used them as an excuse to jump away from Merrick before he could kiss her. She practically ran into the awaiting hallway. The temperature was frigid compared to the stifling heat in the elevator. She wrapped her arms around herself as goose bumps erupted along her skin.

Joel. Think of Joel, she chanted over and over again in her mind.

That's why she was here. That's who she should be thinking of at a time like this. He was missing. She had no idea if he was safe or injured or captured.

Merrick was a silent sentinel behind her as she made her way to room 436. She didn't want to turn around and see his face. She was too afraid of what she might find there.

Would he be angry? Relieved? Her stomach knotted.

Or would he be hurt? Her heart constricted.

She kept her eyes straight ahead as the room came into view. She tried the handle. Locked. She tried her keycard. Didn't work. She stomped her foot in frustration.

"Stay here," Merrick said. He continued down the hall toward the distant sound of vacuuming.

She waited, hoping no one would open their doors and find her standing there like an idiot.

A few minutes later Merrick returned holding the housekeeper's master key.

She blanched at him. "You stole that? What if we get caught?"

He unlocked the door and propped it open for her. "Get in," he ordered.

She stepped into the room. The receptionist had been right. It was in shambles. The door slammed shut behind her. She jumped and turned to find Merrick not in the room with her.

He wasn't in the hallway either.

A few seconds later there was a knock followed shortly by, "It's me. Let me in."

"Where did you go?" she asked him as she stepped back to give him room.

His stare was flat. "I had to go return the key. Don't want to tarnish your perfect little record, now do we?"

So he was angry? Heat flooded her cheeks. "What's that supposed to mean?" she snapped.

"Let's not do this," he said, his voice still frustratingly emotionless.

"Do what?"

"Argue. We have a mission to do."

"Well, if you didn't want to argue then why did you make that dig at me? Are you angry at me for not kissing you back there in the elevator? Is that it? Because—"

"I know," he cut her off. "You have a fucking boyfriend, you don't have to keep repeating it. Shit." He stuffed his hands into his pockets.

Sydney's temper started to rise. "Well, sorry for trying to remain loyal to my boyfriend."

She could read in his eyes that he wanted to call her out on their kiss earlier. On everything they'd done that would raise eyebrows. "When you throw yourself on a man who hasn't been with a woman in well over four months you shouldn't be surprised with his reaction."

The comment cut deeper than she thought it would. "So you're saying the only reason you wanted to kiss me was because I was the only available female to you?" Her hands itched to slap him clean across the face.

He leaned closer to her. "That's exactly what I'm saying."

And to think she'd thought he was her destined soul mate.

Tears burned the back of her throat but she rather choke on them than let them fall in front of Merrick. "Then why did you tell me you felt something the first time we touched?"

The question caught him off guard. For a moment his impeccable mask slipped, she glimpsed a flash of hope before his face settled into a harsh, unfeeling expression. "We need to get to work."

Sydney didn't know which was worse—his non-answer or if he would have answered. She decided it didn't matter.

"Agreed," she said as aloof as possible.

*

Merrick's neck tingled as anger rode him. He kicked a coffee table leg out of his way.

Sydney sat silently on one of the beds.

He should be focused on finding an object to read but all he found himself thinking about was Sydney and Joel fucking under those sheets. Had she and Joel had a quick fuck before they'd busted him out? Had she moaned his name as she climaxed?

He wanted to hate her, but he couldn't muster the feeling with her sitting there looking so miserable.

He felt like the biggest asshole. He shouldn't want her. She had been absolutely right to pull away from him. Shit, he could only dream of having a woman as loyal as her. She was a good person.

Too good for you.

He didn't deserve someone like Sydney. She was honest and true, while he scammed people with his powers when he was crunched for money. He could only imagine what she'd think of him if she ever learned about that.

His thoughts circled back to her question in the elevator. It was the only thing that didn't make sense to him. Why would she ask if he'd felt anything when they first touched? Had she been trying to figure out how he felt about her?

His mind flipped through the possibilities.

Why would she be asking about an obvious sign of chemistry between them if she had no plan on exploring it?

His frustration grew.

He paused near the fallen cards that littered the floor. He picked up a handful and received a hurricane of different impressions. Juliet's smugness at her sleight of hand, Hazel's feelings of contentment as she sat surrounded by the closest thing to friends she had, Luke's hesitant thoughts about having a future where he wouldn't have to be afraid all the time, and finally Joel's worry over Sydney.

He let the cards fall to the floor.

He picked up the coffee table leg and found himself inside the head of the man who'd been knocked out. He dropped the leg.

Merrick systematically made his way around the room until he found what he was looking for. He stumbled upon the impression by accident. After gleaming nothing for so long he started to run his hands along every surface, skimming the surfaces faintly to see if they held what he was looking for. It was next to the mini fridge that Merrick came across a section of the side table where Joel had rested his hand.

"They got away," he told Sydney. He ran his fingers over the wood again. "Joel stood here, surveying the others, amazed that they'd fought so fiercely. He was also worried about you. Us," he corrected when he realized Joel had thought of Merrick's safety. And didn't that feel like a punch to the gut? *You repay the man who saved you and is worried for you by making attempts on his girlfriend?* Fucking asshole. That's what he was.

Sydney got to her feet. "Anything else?"

Merrick pulled his thoughts back to where they needed to be. "They made a run for it, somewhere public where they can hide in plain sight. He'll try to contact you as soon as possible."

"Maybe that's why his phone is turned off," she thought aloud. "He wants to conserve battery power because he didn't have sufficient time to charge it."

"Could be," he ceded. He listened for the sound of vacuuming. It was closer but they still had time. "You should shower," he told her. "We need to wash as much of the fragrance off our skin as possible. We'll probably need new clothes too if we want to stay one step ahead of Regina."

"I have just the thing," Sydney said brightly as if remembering something. She dove over the second bed and pulled out two luggage containers from beneath. "I forgot about these. Joel wouldn't have had time to take our things with him." She pulled out a nice pair of khaki pants and a white shirt that she laid a green sweater over.

A few seconds later she was digging through Joel's things. She threw Merrick a pair of jeans and a long sleeve button-up that was dark blue. She tossed him a black jacket as well.

"The shirt and jacket should fit you okay but if the pants are too big there's a belt in here too." She pulled out said belt before disappearing into the bathroom where Merrick distinctly heard the lock being engaged.

He forced his eyes back to the clothing that had been laid out for him and refused to let his mind wander to where it wanted: specifically the shower, where Sydney would be wet and naked.

His cock stiffened painfully. He groaned and dropped down onto the edge of the bed, his head in his hands.

Why did his thoughts always come back to her?

The water started in the bathroom.

Merrick steeled himself. *You will not think about another man's woman,* he ordered himself.

He owed it to Joel. The man had done nothing to warrant this kind of treatment. If the man was a rat bastard then this would be easier, but from everything Merrick had seen, Joel was nothing but an upstanding citizen with a super hero complex and a love of all things nerdy.

By the time Sydney finished with her shower Merrick had a raging hard-on that he was desperate to relieve.

Once in the privacy of the bathroom he took care of business, all the while convincing himself the blonde that he envisioned was *not* Sydney.

He came with a muffled groan and put his hand out in front of him to brace himself against the side of the shower. The back of his neck tingled. His palm touched the smooth imitation marble and he found himself inside Sydney's head.

She was running her hands over her soapy body.

Merrick's mouth instantly went dry, he grew erect once again.

Pull away, he commanded himself.

In a second…

Her hands circled her breasts, a fleeting thought of how small they were. She gently squeezed them. Her thoughts swirled with worry over the others but in the forefront were thoughts about…him.

Merrick could hardly breathe.

She squeezed her breasts again, wondering if Merrick would find them too small, wondering what his hands would feel like on them…

"Fucking hell," he muttered harshly.

He ripped his hand away from the wall. Arousal rode him so hard he thought he might die from it.

There was a tentative knock on the door. "Merrick," her beautiful voice called through the wood. "Are you almost done? The vacuuming is getting closer."

He cleared his throat. "I'll be out in a second." He thrust the shower knob all the way over to cold. Freezing water pelted him. He forced his head under the spray.

She wants you just as much as you want her.

He shook the thought away.

He curled his hands into fists, cursing his powers. He hadn't asked to see inside of Sydney's head.

But you did. Now what are you going to do?

Nothing, he thought vehemently.

Sydney's inner thoughts meant nothing. They didn't change

their current circumstances; all his knowledge did was torment him. Now he knew that she harbored feelings for him—feelings that she would never act on.

She'd never be his.

Chapter 10

"Is everything all right?" Sydney asked Merrick as they made their way out of the hotel.

He'd been more tense and silent than usual. She was willing to move past their argument, but maybe he was still upset about it?

His hands sank deeper into Joel's jean pockets. "I'm fine," he said.

She'd been surprised at how well Joel's clothing had fit him. The entire outfit gave him a rugged, hard edged look that she found very distracting.

"I'm sorry for trying to spray you with Joel's cologne," she said. She had been trying to help disguise his scent but Merrick growled when she caught him on the arm with the stuff. She didn't know what the big deal was. Joel's cologne smelled good, but if that's what was upsetting him then she wanted to make amends. They were all each other had right now—they needed to clear the air so they could go back to the way things were before.

"I already told you that you don't have to apologize. It was a good idea but Regina might already have that scent memorized."

Her phone went off in her back pocket. She fumbled for it. "H-hello? Joel?"

"Syd! You're all right."

Sydney's shoulders sagged in relief. "I'm fine. Are you okay? What about the others? How's Luke holding up?"

Joel chuckled. "Easy, Syd, they're all fine. Damn strong bunch of kids if you ask me. We were like the Fantastic Four."

Sydney rolled her eyes even though he couldn't see her. "Where are you now?"

"We're at a library. I got in contact with an old hacker friend of mine who is getting us some fake IDs for our little refugees and then I'm booking us flights home. We need to get the hell out of dodge, or in this case Nor Cal."

"Are there any open flights that leave today?" The sooner they got back home the better. Not only would they be further away from Regina, but they'd be able to start looking for Kevin's journal.

The sound of a keyboard clicking traveled through the phone. "There's a flight to John Wayne that leaves in an hour but there are only four vacancies."

"You should take it."

"What?"

Sydney pulled the phone away from her ear at his outburst. "Merrick and I can catch the next flight after you. But you need to get the others out of here. Every second we spend up here is more time for Regina to find us."

"How am I going to give you Merrick's fake ID?"

"You can leave it with someone."

Joel grumbled something under his breath. "You know I hate leaving you, right?"

Her heart twisted in her chest. Unable to help herself, her eyes flickered to Merrick. "I know," she said.

"Hey, I have an idea. What if you met up with us and then we could send Merrick along with the others. You and I can stay behind and catch the next flight."

There was absolutely no reason for her to argue with his logic. It was doable. It made perfect sense. And yet...

She wanted Joel to travel with the others.

She felt like the world's biggest heel.

"We might not make it to you in time." She found the excuse slipping off her tongue. "We'll meet you at the airport and see what happens, okay?"

"Copy that, Gold Leader," he said.

She hung up with him and put her phone away.

Merrick came up next to her. The heat and masculine smell of him tantalized her. "So we're off to the airport?"

She couldn't look him in the eye. She nodded.

*

"I can't believe you went back for this stuff." Merrick nudged his elbow into the back of the car seat to signal the trunk where Sydney and Joel's luggage was safely stored.

Sydney shrugged. "We're just going to the airport and it seemed foolish to leave all that clothes behind."

"You know," Merrick leaned over to say to her. "Whoever is left behind could drive down."

She gave him an incredulous look. "That's like an eight hour drive."

"It goes fast if you keep changing drivers. It beats waiting in an airport where we can be Tracked and trapped."

"You really think Regina would attack at an airport?"

His gaze was level. "I think Regina will do whatever Vander orders her to do. And Vander sure as fuck is crazy enough to attack in a public place if he really wants me, which I'm guessing he does."

She shook her head. "We'll fly. It's faster." Something nagged at the back of her mind. "Did you see Vander here, in San Francisco?"

"He was there a few days ago when he interrogated me. It could have been the same day you came and broke us out."

Sydney digested that bit of information. "What did he look like?" She knew the authorities were still on the lookout for him, but did that mean they'd informed all the police stations across the nation?

"Older. He's been holding back with his powers, hasn't sucked the life out of many people lately which is causing him to age quickly. If I had to guess I'd say he looked around late fifties."

Sydney suppressed a shiver at the mention of Vander's ability. She'd heard about it from Cali and was eternally grateful she hadn't experienced it firsthand. "That's at least a twenty-five year difference than what the media images portray him as. He'd be able to go out in broad daylight and no one would know the difference."

"Don't worry," said Merrick. "I doubt he's going to be in the thick of things. He can't risk using his powers and becoming younger. We'll be safe from him personally, at least for a little bit."

*

Jente Mitchell watched, invisible, from the backyard as Cali fussed around the kitchen.

Something was bothering her. She kept pacing, her dark hair pulled back. Her tall, lean build was encased in black tights and an off the shoulder sweater. She looked absolutely stunning.

He hadn't been able to visit her for a while due to the busy schedule Vander had him on. Now he'd have to watch from afar with no idea as to why she was agitated. Was it because of her "soul mate," Felix?

Trouble in paradise? One could only hope.

Through the glass back door he saw the front door open. Felix entered, running a hand through his hair.

Cali rushed over to him.

Jente felt a pang of jealousy. Would there ever be a time when a woman would run to be by his side?

They stood together talking.

Boring.

He could sneak closer and try to hear what they were saying but he didn't risk it. Cali had developed the uncanny ability to sense when someone else was near and now that her powers were at their maximum she'd be able to hear his heartbeat a mile away. It didn't matter if he was invisible or not.

His pants pocket vibrated.

He pulled out his phone and glanced at the caller ID.

He sighed and picked up. "What?"

"There's been a change of plans." Vander's voice was tight with irritation. Good. Bastard deserved it. "You won't be flying up. In fact, I need you to monitor the John Wayne airport and keep a look out. I'm sending you an e-mail with pictures of the targets. I need you to follow them." Vander hung up on him.

Jente growled low in his throat and a second later his phone *pinged,* alerting him of a new e-mail. He opened the attachment and flipped through the pictures.

Well, well, well…

It looked like Cali's little guild just kept digging themselves deeper and deeper into Vander's business. No wonder the man was so pissed off.

*

Sydney spotted Cali waiting for them by the baggage claim. She waved, the silver bracelets on her wrists clinking together with the movement. She was dressed in regular Cali fashion: dark blue jeggings, black boots, and a white t-shirt. Her dark hair was pulled back, her side bangs framing the side of her face.

Sydney gazed out of the corner of her eye at Merrick and she couldn't help but wonder, did he prefer his women tall and leggy?

His expression gave nothing away, leaving her to ponder the idea.

They'd missed Joel and the others at the airport but were able to catch the next available flight. Merrick had insisted on walking around the airport the entire time they'd waited for their flight. Sydney's legs had wanted to fall off.

The plane ride had been heaven. She'd never wanted to sit more in her life. She'd even dozed off and woke up with her head propped against Merrick's shoulder. She had apologized profusely but he hadn't seemed to mind.

"Hey," Cali said when they reached her. "Everyone else is waiting."

"They made it okay?" Sydney asked.

"Of course," she said to Sydney before she turned her attention to Merrick. She eyed him up and down with her obsidian gaze. "It's nice to finally see you out of that hell hole," Cali said.

Merrick did his own head to toe evaluation. "I know you," he said. "You're the one that Vander tried to get to love him."

Cali stiffened. Her head whipped to Sydney as if to ask if she had told him about her time with Vander.

Sydney shook her head. *It wasn't me.*

"You know," Cali said at last, "it seriously creeps me out when you guys seem to already know me without actually knowing me."

Merrick's lips curled into a small smile. "Tell me about it."

They followed Cali out of the airport to Felix's white Hummer.

"Where is everyone else?" Sydney asked.

Merrick climbed into the back seat and Sydney nearly followed him. She stopped herself at the last second and hurriedly made her way over to the passenger seat.

Cali started up the behemoth of a car. "Everyone is at Felix's. We didn't realize it was going to be such a slumber party. A little warning would have been nice."

"Didn't Joel tell you we were bringing back some people?"

Cali gave her an arched look. "He said people, not kids. You know that Hazel girl is only nineteen?"

Sydney winced. "Was she taken from her house?"

Cali shrugged as she merged onto the freeway. "She doesn't really talk all that much. Unlike Juliet." She shuddered.

Sydney laughed.

"So what's your story?" Cali asked as she stared Merrick down through the rearview mirror.

"Well, I'm not a kid if that's what you're asking. I'm thirty, a PI, and want to crush Vander like a fucking cockroach."

Cali nodded. "I like it. You got a name, Mr. PI slash Vander killer?"

"Merrick Haskell."

"Cali Crazar." She flipped the blinker to exit the freeway. "Nice to meet you. I think we'll get along swimmingly."

They pulled into Felix's driveway. It was well into the evening. All the lights inside were blazing.

When Sydney entered the house she realized Cali had been right. It looked exactly like a slumber party. Sleeping bags were thrown on the floor of Felix's living room. There were bowls of popcorn, chips, and pretzels everywhere and the distinct smell of pizza wafted from the adjoined kitchen.

Sydney made a beeline for the kitchen. Now that she knew Joel was safe she could take care of some more basic urges. Like hunger. Felix was behind the counter, a piece of pizza in his hand. Felix was the only guy in the world that she knew of who looked good with a five o'clock shadow. He smiled when he caught sight of her, but she noticed the small bags under his blue and green eyes. His bronze skin was looking a little pale too.

She frowned. "Everything okay?"

He saluted her with his pizza slice. "Busy week."

She nodded and moved closer to the open pizza box. "Tom's?" she asked hopefully. Tom's Pizzeria was a few stores down from her clinic and offered the best pizza around.

He closed the lid so she could read the fast food chain name. "Sorry," he said around a mouthful of pizza. "We tried to get Niella to order us one but she refused to go over there."

One day Sydney was going to unearth the reason behind why Niella avoided Tom's like the plague.

That day wasn't today.

She snatched a piece of pizza and turned, nearly running face first into Merrick's chest. His warm hands settled on her shoulders, steadying her. She gazed up into those ice blue eyes, her mouth dry. "Sorry," she managed to squeak out.

"It was my fault, I was too busy following my nose to watch where I was going."

"Help yourself." Felix held out the pizza box to him. "We ordered plenty. I'm Felix, by the way, Felix Del Valle."

Merrick released Sydney but he still remained where he was, which meant he was only a few inches away from her. She could feel the heat from him, her body hyperaware of his.

Merrick introduced himself and Felix started the whole friendly chit chat thing.

Sydney could have gone and mingled, left the boys to their manly talk, but she stayed where she was.

Merrick settled against one counter while Felix faced off on the other. Every now and again Merrick would reach for another piece of pizza, his arm brushing against her side or her stomach. He apologized each time, but she noticed that as it went on the touches became bolder, the pressure of his touch firmer.

Sydney's stomach was flipping so frequently she had to stop eating for fear that she wouldn't be able to keep her pizza down.

Felix gave her a curious look when she continued to remain in the way of the pizza. She could easily tell he was wondering why she didn't just hand it to Merrick.

Because I want to steal as many touches from him as possible.

Of course she'd never tell Felix that.

"Here you are." Joel's arm slid around her shoulders and he planted a firm kiss on her cheek.

She tensed. Felix's eyebrows shot up. She forced herself to relax. Beside her Merrick's body went stiff.

"I should have known you'd be by the pizza." Joel reached around to grab a slice. "So what are we talking about?"

Sydney ducked out from under his arm. "I better go find Cali and Niella."

As she passed Merrick she could have sworn she felt his hand reach out and slide against her arm.

She shivered.

Chapter 11

Merrick watched Sydney leave out of the corner of his eye. He hadn't been able to resist stealing one last touch. And when she shivered? His entire body clenched.

He directed his attention back to Joel and Felix. Both men were watching him.

Shit, caught red handed.

Joel looked like he was barely holding on to his temper.

Felix's expression was carefully neutral, almost contemplative. He glanced between Merrick and Joel. "Come on, Merrick." Felix hustled him out of the kitchen. "Let's introduce you to Niella."

The name tickled something in the back of his memory and Merrick allowed himself to be led over to a woman in a wheelchair. Cali was at her side. Joel had pulled Sydney back into the kitchen where they were talking near a small circular table. He didn't like the way Joel was invading Sydney's space. The urge to go over there was fierce, but he shoved it down.

"Ladies," Felix interrupted the two women. "I wanted to bring Merrick over here to introduce him to Niella."

Merrick tore his eyes away from the kitchen. Niella had light brown hair that was cut in a short pixie style. She had intelligent hazel eyes and an attitude that Merrick could feel from two feet away. This was a woman who didn't like to let people get close to her. Again he felt the tug of familiarity. Like he'd seen her before. But where?

"So you're the one I've been Dreaming about the past few days." Niella held out her hand politely.

Merrick drew back.

"Told you," Cali said smugly. "Creepy as fuck."

After being introduced to Niella, Merrick migrated over to where the "kids" were sitting around their own pizza box. The fact that they were closer to where Joel and Sydney were standing had nothing to do with his sudden interest in them—or so he told himself.

Hazel smiled at him and offered him a piece of pizza. He was beyond full but he accepted the food anyway and took a bite to keep from having to talk. He sat down on the couch and listened.

"—Felix can take care of them. We're on vacation. I thought you said we were going to spend the rest of the time together." He could barely make out Joel's voice.

"I know." Sydney sounded genuinely conflicted. "But I feel bad just leaving them behind. We're kind of all they know. I don't want to abandon them."

Joel grumbled in frustration. "It's only for the night. They'll be fine."

"Exactly, it'll just be for tonight," Sydney bargained. "Once I know they're taken care of, then we'll spend some real time together."

"You're killing me, Syd," Joel said in defeat. "Trust me, after three months of celibacy every day is like an eternity."

Three months of celibacy?

Sydney hadn't slept with Joel for three months?

Merrick's mind whirled.

Three months…

He realized with a start that it was three months ago that Sydney had seen him in his cell.

Surely that was nothing but a coincidence…

You don't know that. She could have stopped sleeping with him because of you.

He threw the thought away. It was impossible.

Wasn't it?

His mind circled back to the question she'd asked him in the elevator.

What if she'd asked him if he'd felt something between them because she had too?

What if, like him, she thought they were Mirror Mates?

He shook his head. Too many "what ifs."

He spent the rest of the night in a thoughtful stupor.

Cali drove Niella home but the rest of them bunkered down at Felix's. Joel and Sydney retreated to the guest bedroom. Juliet and Hazel each took a couch in the living room while Merrick and Luke toughed it out on the floor.

"I'm really sorry I don't have anything more comfortable for you to sleep on," said Felix. "I used to have an air mattress but I accidentally Erased it."

Merrick was still trying to get used to all the new terminology Sydney's guild seemed to use. Felix was an Eraser and caused things to vanish. Cali was a Silencer—she could manipulate sound. Niella was the Dreamer. He'd even learned the proper name for Joel—a LockSmith with the power to Lock anyone to anything with a single touch.

Merrick, Hazel, and Luke had all confessed to their abilities and Joel had promised to think them up titles. Juliet had seemed very interested with the entire ordeal. She'd even taken down notes. When she was questioned about her own powers she admitted that she didn't have any. It turned out that she had been a little too close to another woman that Vander had taken and because Juliet was seen so close they instantly assumed the two were friends and that Juliet had powers as well.

Merrick didn't know if he bought the story. Why would Juliet be seen hanging around another person with powers? How would she even know that person had powers?

Had it all simply been bad luck?

Merrick focused himself back to the present.

Sydney walked in behind Felix. "I thought you could bring back anything you Erased? Why not bring back the air mattress?"

She continued into the kitchen, which meant she missed Felix's reaction. But Merrick didn't.

Felix instantly tensed, something like unease flickering behind his eyes before disappearing. "Remember how your car came back, Syd?" Felix's voice held a hint of forced cheer.

"Don't remind me," Sydney said as she filled a glass with water.

Felix grinned. "I rest my case. I don't think I'll be bringing back anything I've Erased for a little while."

"Well, goodnight." Sydney waved to them before disappearing down the hall. A few seconds later Merrick heard a door click shut.

Felix stood there for a few awkward moments before he stepped back. "I have an early start so I better turn in. The others all gave me their orders but I didn't catch yours, Merrick—do you want anything in particular from the bakery?"

Merrick shrugged. "Anything, really. I'm a man of simple tastes."

Felix excused himself and Merrick tried to get comfortable on the floor.

He slept a solid four hours before Hazel started making noises in her sleep. The others were too exhausted to be bothered by the small mewling but Merrick couldn't ignore the sound. He decided to head to the bathroom and come back in a few minutes to see if the nightmare would pass. He didn't want to wake Hazel up. The kid deserved all the rest she could get.

He finished drying his hands in the bathroom and stepped out into the darkened hall where he collided with something small and soft.

A quick gasp.

Merrick's body instantly stiffened as the person shifted against him. He inhaled deeply and caught the faint scent of vanilla.

Sydney.

She tried to step back but he wrapped his arms around her, keeping her flush against him. She didn't resist.

He ground his teeth and forced himself to speak. "What are you doing up?"

"I heard someone in the bathroom."

She heard someone and had wanted to investigate? Or had she gone to investigate because she had been hoping it was him?

You're delusional. Stop making something out of nothing; you're only going to hurt yourself in the end.

His hands trailed down the sides of her body. He hissed when his fingers reached the end of her oversized t-shirt. It was all she wore.

Here he was shirtless and she was in nothing *but* a shirt.

"What are you doing?" she whispered and knocked his hands away. He noticed that her voice was shaking.

He invaded her space until she was pushed up against the wall. "Why haven't you slept with Joel in three months?"

Her mouth gapped. "How did you—? That's none of your business."

"Was it before or after you saw me in that cell?"

Please say before, please say before.

She avoided his gaze. "Before."

Fuck.

She was lying.

Merrick's emotions were in turmoil, his cock swollen and aching. "Why did you ask if I felt anything the first time we touched?"

Even in the dim lighting he could make out her eyes widening. "N-no reason."

His finger trailed the outside of her exposed thigh. She trembled beneath his hand but didn't knock it away.

He leaned in to speak into her ear. "Stop lying."

He needed to pull away. He needed to stop. He was obviously sleep deprived. But everything in his body was telling him that this was so right. He brushed her hair away from her neck and kissed her there.

She gasped and he barely stifled a groan. He ground himself against her, unable to help himself. Every instinct inside of him said to claim her.

Her fingers traveled over his skin, feather light touches that set his blood racing.

He snaked his hand behind her head and kissed her. Her mouth opened for him instantly, her hands getting lost in his hair.

Desire flared white hot.

He slid his hand beneath her t-shirt to cup her hip. He brushed the material of her panties with his thumb. It would be so easy to hook his finger through and pull them down.

Would she be wet for him?

He followed the hem until he reached her center. Sydney jerked. Merrick bit down on his tongue, hard, to keep from cursing.

She *was* wet.

He drew his hand away before he went too far.

Sydney kissed him harder and her tongue twined against his, driving him crazy.

The hall light flickered on.

Chapter 12

One second Merrick's body was pressed deliciously against hers, the next it was gone.

The hall light burned Sydney's eyes and she blinked to give them time to adjust. Hazel stood a few feet away, face flushed.

Heat crept up Sydney's neck. She'd been caught kissing Merrick less than ten feet away from where she was sharing a bed with her boyfriend.

Hazel shut the light off and turned to retreat.

Would she tell anyone?

Sydney's body went cold.

Merrick looked conflicted, as if he didn't know whether or not to go after Hazel or to stay with her.

She made the choice for him. She raced back to her room and shut the door. She climbed back into bed, her heart racing.

Coward.

Joel was still asleep.

She tried to do the same but all she kept thinking about was if Joel would be able to smell Merrick on her.

*

"Are you sure you'll be all right?" Sydney asked Juliet for perhaps the fourth time.

Juliet placed her hands on her hips. "Of course I'll be fine. It's my family. I've been away from them long enough."

"And you want to go with her?" Merrick asked Hazel.

She kept her eyes downcast, her thick black hair obscuring her face. "I don't really have anywhere else to go and Juliet said they wouldn't mind. They seem nice too."

As stupid as it sounded, Sydney was going to miss Juliet and Hazel. She'd grown attached to them, or at least felt responsible for them. But Juliet had insisted that she get back to her family. Apparently she'd even invited Luke to come with her and Hazel, but Luke had declined. Instead he'd asked Sydney if he could join The Guild of Aletheia. Joel would be ecstatic over hearing Luke use the "real" name of their guild. Most of them just referred to it as the Guild of Truth. However, Joel had been called into work for some kind of emergency.

"We'll be happy to provide as much money as you need to get wherever you're going," Sydney told the two girls. Even though Juliet wasn't even a year younger than Sydney she still thought of her as a girl. She'd helped rescue her after all.

"It shouldn't cost us too much," said Juliet. "We're only going to Thousand Oaks."

Which was quite a ways from where they lived, at least an hour and a half.

"And you're sure you want to go?" Sydney asked Hazel.

Juliet looked put out by all the questions but Sydney wanted to make sure this was something Hazel wanted and not just Juliet.

Hazel looked her in the eye. Cali must've provided her with some make-up because the black eyeliner she wore made the forest green of her eyes pop.

"I'm sure," she said. "I really appreciate everything you've done for me. I'd like to stay but I don't want to get involved with Vander anymore. I'd rather stay away from the super hero life. At least for a little bit."

Sydney couldn't fault her for that. Hazel was young and obviously scared. As their guild dug deeper and deeper into Vander's business they were constantly putting themselves in danger, a danger Hazel didn't want.

Sydney pulled her into a hug and Hazel tensed, reminding Sydney of Cali before she got used to regular human contact. "We'll miss you," she whispered into Hazel's ear.

When she pulled back, Hazel was smiling at her. It made her look both beautiful and young. "I hope you and Merrick make it," she whispered to Sydney. "I think he really likes you."

Sydney blushed.

Hazel moved on to hug Merrick. From afar the two could pass for siblings. She noticed that Merrick even embraced Hazel like a sister.

"If you ever need anything," she heard him tell Hazel, "you call here and they'll find me. Okay?"

Hazel nodded. "Okay."

Merrick ruffled her hair affectionately.

Sydney's heart tightened in her chest.

Hazel moved on to Luke. He was shifting nervously. She looked like she didn't know whether or not to hug him. Finally Luke gave her a quick embrace.

"How're you guys getting to Thousand Oaks?" Sydney asked Juliet after she gave polite handshakes to everyone. There was no hugging from Juliet. She briefly wondered if it was a defense mechanism so she wouldn't become attached.

"Cali and Felix are going to drive us to a metrolink station."

Sydney checked the time. Felix still wasn't back from the bakery but she could hear Cali grumbling about the early hour all the way from her bedroom. It was just past ten o'clock in the morning. Sydney shook her head. How Cali dealt with Felix's early morning schedule, she had no idea.

*

Sydney watched Felix's Hummer disappear down the street, leaving her and Merrick in the front yard.

They made their way back into the house. Sydney's eyes slid to the hallway where they'd made out. Her body grew warm at the idea of being alone with Merrick in Felix's house. It was like the first time she found herself alone with a boy in high school all over again. A giddy nervousness that she wished she could make go away.

Merrick did a good job at masking his emotions. He'd been coolly detached all morning. The smile he bestowed on Hazel was the only warmth she'd seen from him. Was he just going to forget last night even happened? Was he going to wait until she brought it up?

Like that's really going to happen.

She wasn't going to put her heart on her sleeve and tell Merrick her fear about their "destiny." What if he laughed at her?

Or worse, rejected her.

He wasn't making it any easier either. When she told Merrick about Mirror Mates she hadn't been able to tell if the idea frightened him or excited him.

Felix had been downright ecstatic when he'd learned about Cali being his Mirror Mate. He'd done everything in his power to win her over and keep her in his life.

But Merrick…

Merrick had confessed to being afraid of ever getting close to a woman for fear of learning her inner thoughts and feelings. Did that mean that if she told him they were Mirror Mates he'd keep her at a distance?

He had been very receptive when everyone told him their powers but it was a lot harder for someone to believe in soul mates when there was no tangible proof.

Sydney rubbed her chest where she felt a small ache. Cali used to tell her that the further she was from Felix the more her chest felt empty, but was this feeling Sydney had really solid evidence?

And what if Merrick didn't feel it?

Had she ever seen him rub his chest? She tried to remember but the last few days were one big blur of activity. She was more than ready to go back to her day to day life at the clinic. She didn't know if she was cut out for this adventure stuff like Cali and Felix and Joel.

But you're not done yet. You still have to find Kevin's journal.

She thought about handing that torch off to Cali and then berated herself for it. She could do this. She was going to see out the rest of her vacation and she was going to hinder Vander anyway she could because everyone who was hurt by him deserved some kind of peace of mind.

She straightened her shoulders and turned her attention to Merrick. He'd had to borrow more of Joel's clothing. Today he wore snug jeans and a black turtleneck that Joel had forgotten he owned. He looked downright sinful, especially with his black hair flaring out over the collar of his shirt. Felix had offered to take him in for a haircut, but to Sydney's delight Merrick had declined. It'd be a shame to cut off all that silky hair.

She found her thoughts wandering and instantly reeled them back in. "So," she broke the silence. "Did you have something in mind to do today?"

Felix had washed off her Yaris, and it waited in the driveway for her.

"Actually, if you don't mind, I'd like to see the damage Collette has done to my life."

"Then let's go."

*

Sydney wrinkled her nose as she slipped into the driver's seat of her car.

Merrick hesitated with the door open. "What is that?" he asked. "It smells something like sulfur."

She turned around to survey the back seats and found small claw marks in the fabric. Had a cat gotten into her car?

As Merrick got in she briefly explained the fate of her poor Toyota.

Merrick swore. "Strange goo and foreign scratch marks? There's never a dull moment in your life, is there?"

"That's not true." She exited the freeway. "Last week the most exciting thing that I did was give a puppy a flea bath. While seeing Niella soaking wet and miserable was very entertaining it was otherwise very dull."

Merrick stared at her as if he didn't know whether or not she was joking. When she returned his stare he started to laugh. The sound caught her off guard, as did how handsome he was when he laughed.

The light she was stopped at turned green. She barely noticed.

The car behind her honked. Merrick sobered. Sydney stomped on the gas.

When they arrived at Merrick's apartment he left Sydney in the car to go talk to his landlord. She didn't know why he wanted to exclude her, but she tried to tell herself it wasn't personal.

He returned twenty minutes later with a key dangling from his finger. He opened her door for her.

"And?" she asked him.

"It was a good thing I was never late with my payments. When I started missing rent he decided to give me a break the first two months, after that he realized that my mail was piling up. When he found me missing he called the cops. He said he didn't touch any of my things and left it just in case I turned up dead and my apartment would need to be investigated."

"So what'd you end up telling him happened to you?"

"I said there was a family emergency overseas that came out of nowhere. I apologized and said I'd get him the missing rent as soon as possible. He didn't seem too beat up about it but he did give me his sympathy for whatever happened overseas."

He walked her up a flight of stairs that led to a single door. He ushered her into a utilitarian room. Sydney really hadn't expected anything less from someone like Merrick. There was one sofa, one

TV, and a large bookshelf surrounding the TV. Everything was so tidy. It was sparsely decorated too. Though Merrick wore a lot of black, his home was done in rich browns and touches of green or blue depending on the room. The kitchen was green and brown, the living room blue and brown.

Sydney walked over to the tall bookcase. She smiled and pulled out one of many books. "John Grisham?" She waved the paperback around.

Merrick snatched the novel from her hand and gently put it back in its designated slot.

She wanted to tease him more but one look from him had her mouth snapping shut.

She continued her inspection in the kitchen. She half expected to find empty beer cans and old pizza boxes, but the place was immaculate. The only thing that told of Merrick's absence was the thin layer of dust collecting on all the surfaces.

She spotted a food and water dish near the refrigerator. She smiled. "You have a pet?"

Merrick's face darkened.

She felt her smile fading. "Oh no." She looked around, realizing that if he had a pet it would have had to survive on its own for the past four months. "I'm so sorry, is it…?"

He shook his head. "Not what you think. I did have a pet. A black lab. The best kind of running buddy. I got a visit from Vander when they took me. He didn't appreciate Marshal barking at him so he decided to make an example out of him while I was held captive."

Sydney felt bile rise in her throat. "Oh Merrick…" She didn't know what else to say.

"It's fine." He turned his back on her. "I guess it worked out for the best. He would have starved anyway."

It was far from fine but she didn't press him. "Is everything here? Vander didn't take anything?"

He looked grateful for the distraction and slipped into his bedroom that branched off of the living room.

She followed at a respectful distance, curious to see what this room would look like. It wasn't very different from the rest of his place. There was a king sized bed, a work desk covered with neatly organized stacks of paper, and a few photographs.

Sydney made her way over to the pictures while Merrick checked out his closet. When she took a quick glance she noticed the majority of the shirts hanging up were—surprise, surprise—black.

There was a picture of Merrick graduating from the police academy, another of him in uniform with his parents, and finally an older photo of Merrick when he was younger with his arm wrapped protectively around a girl that looked remarkably like a younger version of Hazel. Sydney picked up the frame to get a better look.

It was obvious that this was Merrick's younger sister, but why wasn't she in any of the other photos? Had she been the one taking the pictures? Or maybe there had been a falling out between them?

Merrick came up beside her. He froze when he caught sight of what she was holding.

"How come there aren't any more pictures of you two together?"

His face shuttered closed. He took the photo and put it back on his desk. "They didn't take anything. I'd like to head over to the station now, if you don't mind. I want to find out what happened to the cases I was working, if anyone took them over." He didn't wait for an answer. He just left the room.

Sydney watched him go. She glanced back at the picture. The little girl smiled back at her, reminding her painstakingly of her brother Aaron. She swallowed the lump in her throat and left the room.

Merrick was waiting by the front door.

He gave her directions to the station, even told her to stay inside the car when they got there, but this time she refused.

They argued for a good two minutes before Merrick gave up and said she could do whatever the fuck she wanted.

She didn't understand what the big deal was, but as soon as they entered the station she knew why Merrick had wanted her to stay in the car. He didn't want her to see how the others treated him.

"Well, well, well," a man with a straining belly said as soon as they walked in. He smelled of coffee and looked like he was a few days overdue on his shower. "Look who came back from Camelot, Merrick the magical. Or was it Merrick the mad?"

"Nice to see you too, Russell," Merrick bit out.

Russell's oily dark gaze slithered over Sydney, making her skin crawl. "Nice piece of tail," he said with a nod in her direction. "Where'd you find her? The high school bleachers?"

Sydney flushed, her hands fisting.

Merrick moved in the blink of an eye.

Sydney heard the sound of flesh impacting flesh. Russell swore. He staggered back a few steps before he lost his footing and went down on his ass.

She bit back the smug smile that tugged at her lips.

Another officer came over after the commotion. He stared down at Russell who was now cupping his jaw and trying to mop up his split lip.

"Jesus, Russell," the newcomer said. "Can't you go ten minutes without opening your mouth?"

Russell got to his feet with a baleful glare directed at Merrick. He swiped at his lip again before storming off.

The man watched him go with a shake of his head. "Sorry about that," he said, turning to them. "Russell's a piece of work, always has been and always will be." He shook hands with Merrick. "It's good to see you again, Merrick. Word was that you'd moved on to greener pastures." The man's gaze darted to Sydney and he gave Merrick a quick smile. "I see the rumors are true?"

Merrick shook his head. "Family emergency. This is Sydney, a colleague of mine helping me on a new case."

Sydney tried not to wince at the term colleague. Was that all he thought of her as?

"Sydney," Merrick said, "This is Detective Stokes. Steven Stokes."

"Please," Steven held out his hand to her, "call me Steve."

He had a firm grip. "It's very nice to meet you, Steve."

His blue eyes sparkled. "Likewise. So, what brings you back here, Haskell?"

Merrick tucked his hands into his pockets. "Did you hear anything in regards to my cases? The ones I was working before…I had to take off?"

Steve scratched at his chin. "Now that I think about it, I'm pretty sure someone came by and dropped off your files and notes. You had an arrangement made, right?"

Merrick nodded slowly. "You said you'd take care of my cases in the event that I couldn't finish them."

Steve snapped his fingers. "That's right. Now I remember, it was a few months ago when I got a huge box delivered to me. You had quite the handful of cases. I was able to solve most of them. Some weren't very difficult at all. I don't know why you even took on some of the customers you did."

"I have to make my rent somehow."

Steve nodded. "True enough. Come on back to my office and I'll show you the cases."

Sydney followed behind Merrick. She couldn't help but notice how everyone looked and pointed at him before whispering to their co-workers.

Merrick kept his gaze forward but Sydney knew he could hear what was being said, the major give away being his back was ramrod straight.

He tried to act indifferent, but Sydney knew what it was like to be the center of unwanted attention. She'd been the only twelve-year-old at her high school. If people thought she looked young now they had no idea how young she looked when she was twelve. Super small and childlike, she'd been the constant source of whispers down the hallways. Most would make fun of her size, but there were a few others who would attack her with more scathing comments. She knew they only envied her academic skill. It wasn't her fault that she'd excelled in her classes and had been able to skip grades.

Steve led them into a private office and excused himself while he went to get Merrick's box full of cases.

"Don't let them get to you," she said as soon as the door shut.

Merrick jerked around to look at her.

She gestured to the door. "All those people out there whispering? They're not worth your notice."

"And you have experience in this department, how?"

She told him about her high school. "The most embarrassing moment of my life was when the school threw the Backwards Dance. It's like Sadie Hawkins except for some reason my school liked to use a different name. Anyway, I had the biggest crush on the star quarterback. Brandon Archer. He was a senior but I didn't care. I went up to him one day after our advanced algebra class. He was already surrounded by his group of friends but I went over anyway and asked him to the dance. I figured I better get to him first before any other girls."

"What happened?" Merrick's muscles were tense. Was he still on edge from earlier? Or was that menacing glint in his eyes on behalf of her?

When they locked gazes she got her answer. Her stomach fluttered and she looked away. She cleared her throat. "I asked him and his whole group got really silent. Brandon studied me for the longest time, probably unsure if it was a prank or not. Either way he turned me down flat, said he didn't date twelve-year-olds and if he ever wanted to rob the cradle he'd go after a more developed child."

The tendons and veins in Merrick's neck stood out. "Fucking bastard," he hissed.

"He was," she said. She wasn't going to disagree with him. "But the point is that I didn't let it get in my way. I was the talk of the school for a month straight after that little stunt, especially when everyone thought I didn't go to the dance because I was rejected. In reality I was too busy helping my parents at the vet clinic to make it to the dance. I'm getting off subject again, but Merrick, don't let what those people out there say about you get to you. They're probably just jealous. I'm guessing that Russell guy is one of the ones that got upset when you started succeeding in solving all your cases?"

Merrick gave a humorless laugh. "Russell was the tip of the iceberg. He was also the most outspoken, as you got to experience firsthand. You saw everyone out there whispering, that's what it was like. Russell wasn't one of few or one of many; he was one out of everyone. They all held some kind of animosity toward me."

"Steve didn't seem so bad."

Something like sadness washed through his expression. "Steve's better at hiding it. I think he tries harder because we were best friends in the academy. He was a great detective and when I started to one-up him…I think he felt more angered than any of the others but he didn't want to admit it. He hid his jealousy well but I still heard others talking, mentioning things Steve had said about me behind my back."

"You mean he pretended to be your friend while he talked about you behind your back? What a jerk. What an ass."

Merrick's brows arched.

"You heard me. He's an ass." She glared at the door where Steve had exited a few minutes ago.

When Steve returned carrying a cardboard box, Sydney continued to glare at him. He paused in the doorway, startled by her sudden hostility.

Merrick leaned back in his chair, smiling.

Chapter 13

Merrick watched in amusement as Steve slowly tiptoed around Sydney to place the box down on his desk.

She was like a fierce, protective kitten the way she glowered at Steve for him. A familiar yearning came over him. One he pushed away.

He wasn't that type of guy, no matter what the station used to whisper about him—he didn't go after taken women. *He wouldn't.* Everyone thought he was that kind of guy and he guessed he should have been. What with how everyone gossiped about him behind his back and how all the department wives looked at him. He could have easily slid into the sleaze ball category but he was better than that.

Except when dealing with a certain blonde.

He tried to distract himself but too late he was bombarded with images and sensations from last night when he'd had her pressed against the wall of Felix's house.

For some reason when he was in the heat of the moment his conscience always decided to take a vacation. He became nothing but a product of animalistic need and want, left later to rage at himself for his lack of moral judgment.

"Here's a pile of all the ones I was able to close." Steve dipped into the cardboard box and pulled out an impressive stack of folders, effectively drawing Merrick's attention away from thoughts of Sydney.

Merrick slid the cases across the desk to look through them.

Steve watched as he leaned against his desk. "Looking for anything in particular?"

"The MacGregor case." Merrick looked up. "It's not here. Where is it?"

Steve's face darkened. He pushed the box toward Merrick. "It must still be in here then."

Merrick didn't say a word. He got up and started to dig through the files.

"You've been gone a long time," Steve piped up. "I doubt you'll even need to finish those cases. I'd throw them all out if I were you."

"Well, it's a good thing you're not me," Merrick growled under his breath. He reached the bottom of the box. "It's not here. Is there another box anywhere?"

One look at Steve's face and Merrick knew he was going to make this difficult for him. He shouldn't have demanded the whereabouts of the folder. Steve didn't like being ordered around by someone who wasn't his superior.

Steve leaned back and shrugged. "Like I said, it was a long time ago. I'm pretty sure this was the only box."

Merrick bit down on his temper as he retook his seat. "Can you double check for me?" He swallowed his pride and gazed up at Steve. "Please?"

His strategically placed submissive seating and comment worked. Steve smiled and got to his feet. "I guess I can have another look since you asked so nicely. I'll be right back." He turned his smug grin on Sydney. She glared at him and his smile slipped.

Merrick held back a bark of laughter.

"I'm sorry I ever thought that man was anything but a jerk," Sydney said when the door clicked shut.

He waved her off as he leaned forward to continue poking through his old cases. "Don't beat yourself up about it. There's nothing wrong with you trying to see the good in everyone."

She made a thoughtful noise in her throat before scooting closer to him. "So why are you so determined to get your stuff back on that one case? Are you still going to solve it? What's it about?"

Merrick carefully put down the file he was holding. He glanced at Sydney through the corner of his eye. She was sitting patiently, hair falling around her face, eyes bright and eager to learn. He didn't mind her curiosity. In fact, her constant urge to learn was something he loved about her. She had an analytical mind, like him. It was that same reason why he hesitated in explaining the case to her. Would she put the pieces together after being in his house? Would she see the connection between his need to find this missing girl and the reason why he didn't have any more pictures of his sister?

He'd never really talked about his sister with anyone who wasn't family. She had her own special corner in his heart where he kept her locked safely away.

"Well?" Sydney prodded gently.

He opened his mouth, ready to tell her that it didn't really matter what the case was about. But instead he found himself telling her the truth. "The case is about a missing girl, Sandy MacGregor, age fourteen. She was taken from her home one day after school while she waited alone for her mom to get off work."

He could see the gears working in her head and he kept going before he lost his nerve. "I'm going to solve Sandy's case. Her mom deserves peace of mind. Even if it comes four months late." He only hoped she was still living in Anaheim, that she didn't get up and leave when Merrick failed to find her daughter.

"Because you never got peace of mind?" Sydney asked softly.

He flinched. She rested her hand on his arm, the connection felt all the way to his soul. They locked eyes. "It's because of your sister, isn't it?"

The question was like a punch to the gut.

"That's why you didn't say anything when I asked about her picture. At first I thought maybe you just had a falling out but that's not it, is it? She went missing?"

He couldn't stand the look in her eyes. "I wasn't there for her when I should have been. We were supposed to walk home from school together but I stayed after. I told her I'd catch up, only I never did."

His guilt ate at him. He'd done such a good job at burying it, and now he was ripping the wound wide open. He should have kept his mouth shut. He should have—

"My little brother died of cancer."

Merrick blinked.

Sydney was no longer looking at him. She was studying a stain on the floor. "I was his older sister, I was supposed to protect him from everything, but I wasn't able to shield him from disease. I had to witness him wasting away, unable to help him, unable to do anything but watch."

Merrick's chest swelled with emotion. Here they were, nearly two halves to the same whole.

His body acted on instinct. He wrenched her into his lap and fused their mouths together. Sydney clung to him desperately.

He kissed her hard and deep. Warmth burst from his chest, chasing away the lingering cold. She wiggled against his growing erection. Arousal spiked through him.

The back of his neck prickled once.

His hand hesitated, hovering between her shoulder blades. Not quite touching her sweater. But he wanted to. He wanted to know what she was thinking, what she was feeling.

He wanted to know if she thought they were Mirror Mates like he did.

Dammit, but he wanted to know.

His hand drew closer.

He froze less than an inch away from her.

But what if his plan backfired? What if all he saw was her thoughts about him not being good enough for her, not being what she wanted for the long run? Could he deal with seeing that?

He doubted there was a single mean thought in Sydney's head. But did he want to risk it?

You know better than most the evil that lurks within all human beings. Do you really want to see Sydney's?

He pulled away from her, frustration building.

For once in his fucking life he'd like to be able to touch a woman and not fear her thoughts about him.

"What is it?" Worried green eyes stared back at him, her entire face nothing but open.

It was on the tip of his tongue to ask her. *Are we Mirror Mates?* Was he really going to buy into the whole soul mate thing? Did he want her to be his?

Yes.

Soft footfalls came from outside Steve's office door.

"Steve's back." His voice came out gruff.

There was a brief flash of hurt in her expression as she extracted herself from his lap. He wanted to grab her wrist and erase any pain he'd caused her but the door handle turned.

Steve came back in holding another box. "This is the last of it." He dropped the container with a loud *thwack*.

Merrick found the MacGregor case and tucked it under his arm. "Thanks," he said to Steve. "I'll stop by another time to get the rest of it, if that's okay?"

Steve stared at the mess on his desk with disdain. "Yeah, fine." He waved Merrick out.

Merrick held the door open for Sydney as they made their way toward the front. He could hear the whispers as he passed the desks of his old co-workers. This was definitely something he didn't miss. He took Sydney's advice and didn't let the hushed voices get to him.

The front door came into sight and Merrick held the folder out to allow Sydney to precede him.

The file was snatched from his outstretched hand.

His eyes traveled from the hand holding his file to the arm it was attached to, then the body, and finally the head. Benjamin.

Cock sucking bastard.

Benjamin had been a co-worker, like Russell, who didn't mind opening his big mouth to piss Merrick off.

"Ben." Merrick forced the name through clenched teeth. Just looking at the man had his temper rising and the back of his neck tickling.

Ben flipped through the case with no regard to the notes he scattered along the floor.

"Hey," Sydney protested. "Watch what you're doing."

Ben cast Sydney a fleeting look. "I thought you'd flown the coop, Haskell." He returned his gaze to Merrick, smirking as he watched Merrick crouch down on the floor to pick up the papers Ben had dropped.

When he finished collecting the notes, Merrick rose to his full height and felt some satisfaction as he was able to stare down his nose at Ben. "I had a family emergency," he told him. "As you can see I'm back now."

Ben's lips twisted into some hideous rendition of a smile. "And we're so happy to hear that. Our number one crime solver is back in Anaheim. Who wouldn't be ecstatic?" Ben looked through the case one more time. "This isn't a new file. What are you playing at now, Haskell?"

Merrick held his hand out. "I'm not playing at anything. I'm not here to take your cases. That's one of my old ones. I need to tie off a few loose ends and would appreciate it if you'd give it back." *Before I pound your fucking face in.*

"You think you're so much better than us, don't you?" Ben held the folder out. "Nothing here is engaging enough so you fall back on your old cases, is that it? Why not just spit in our faces?"

The idea was more than tempting.

Merrick reached for the folder but Ben dropped it before he could close his fingers around it. The file fell to the floor, paperwork flying everywhere.

"Nice catch," Ben sneered.

Merrick saw red. He grabbed Ben by the collar of his shirt.

Sydney jumped in to intervene. Other officers froze in what they were doing.

Merrick barely noticed. He was no longer in his own head. He was in Ben's.

Ben was wearing the same shirt, the collar undone as he lay over Sally the receptionist, his pants down around his ankles. Sally's skirt was hiked up as Ben pounded into her, grunting with the effort.

Merrick stumbled back, gagging. He felt dirty from the inside out. Everyone stared at him like he was a freak.

Let them stare.

He kept his gaze level with Ben as he asked, "Does your wife know you're sleeping with Sally?"

If he'd thought the office was quiet before, it was nothing compared to the death silence that followed his question.

Ben's face turned purple. "You fucking bastard." His arm pulled back for a punch. "If you say one fucking word I'll kill you."

The stillness was broken and two nearby officers jumped in before Ben could do anything stupid like punch Merrick.

Merrick didn't wait around to see what became of Ben. He stormed out of there.

Sydney practically ran to keep up with him. "Are you all right?" she asked when he burst through the front doors out into the autumn breeze.

He inhaled deeply, the scent of car exhaust mingling with the smell of fast food. "Far from it, I'm afraid." He paced back and forth, hands clenched.

"You want me to take that before you ruin the papers inside?" she pointed to his tightened fist where he was crumpling the MacGregor case.

He swore and thrust it out to her.

She gently took it from him, her fingers brushing his experimentally. He pulled back. "Merrick…" she said.

He shook his head. "Just stop. This has nothing to do with that case or my sister. This is just me being pissed off at that fucking asshole, Benjamin." Who was nothing but a rat bastard that cheated on his wife.

He paced for a few more minutes, waiting for his head to clear. Sydney hefted herself up on the small hideous blocks that were used as decoration. She kicked her legs like a little kid as she waited for him to cool down.

He exhaled heavily, his anger leaving him. Sydney didn't want to spend her time with some anger crazed psycho. He needed to rein in his temper. What the hell had he expected when he came back to the station? Flowers and rainbows? He had been prepared for this kind of shit.

You simply underestimated how easily it was for them to get under your skin.

"I'm sorry." He leaned against the cement block next to her.

She continued to kick her feet. "No worries. It must be hard having to deal with everything that you…" she waved her hand, "…*see*. Did you see that man sleeping with another woman?"

Merrick barely repressed a repulsed shiver. "I was in his head while he was fuc—uh, sleeping with the receptionist."

She glanced back at the building. "You must have hated it here."

He snorted. That was an understatement.

A companionable silence fell over them.

Merrick kept replaying her words. How he hated it at the station. Somehow it sparked his memory of them in the hospital and how she'd hated it there. That's when it clicked.

"That's why you hate hospitals," he mumbled to himself.

At his side Sydney stopped kicking her feet.

He waited patiently until she raised her gaze to meet his. "It's because of your brother, isn't it?"

He thought he caught a glimpse of vulnerable fear within the emerald green of her eyes. "I've never told anyone about my brother before," she confessed. "Not Felix, or Cali, or even…" she drifted off.

"Joel," he finished for her.

She nodded miserably. "I don't know if Niella knows—with her you can never tell what she has Dreamed or not. Most of the time she doesn't share."

He felt humbled that she'd confided in him. More than that. He was honored, privileged—

His chest swelled with emotion.

He wanted to be the one she confided in. He wanted to know all about her fears and failures and successes. He wanted to be that steady rock in her life that she clung to in times of need.

"I won't tell anyone," he said softly. Then he did something he hadn't done since his sister had gone missing. He held his hand out, pinky extended. "I pinky promise."

The smile she gave him warmed a deep part of himself that he'd thought long dead. Her pinky curled around his. "I won't tell anyone about your sister," she promised back.

He held her pinky longer than customary.

Her face flushed.

"You ready to get out of here?" he asked, getting to his feet.

They started to make their way to her car when Merrick froze.

Sydney picked up on his posture immediately. "What is it?"

The hairs on the back of his neck stood up, and not in the regular powers manifesting kind of way. "I think someone's watching us."

Chapter 14

Sydney's mind instantly flew to Regina.

She'd found them!

The only problem was that Sydney didn't see anyone.

"Are you sure?" she asked Merrick. He was scanning the parking lot like a trained assassin. She could tell that he wanted to answer in the affirmative but there was no one out there.

The air in her lungs froze.

She knew better than anyone that just because you couldn't *see* someone didn't mean they weren't out there.

The back of her neck tingled and she threw her Shield up.

Across the street leaning against a beat-up building, the kid Sydney could only guess to be Jente appeared. She'd never actually seen Jente but Cali had described him to her a couple of times.

Tan skin? Young looking?

Check.

Black hair cut in a fantasy/anime sort of style?

Check.

She couldn't see from this distance but she was pretty sure that if she looked into his eyes she'd find one gray and one green. Cali said it was one of his most defining features.

Merrick zeroed in on him like a hawk.

It took Jente a couple of seconds before he noticed Merrick's stare. At first he simply stared back, then his posture stiffened. He pulled away from the wall he'd been lazing against as if realizing that he was no longer invisible.

She could all but hear the word his lips spoke. *Shit.*

He took off like a shot.

Merrick sprinted across the parking lot.

"Hey!" Sydney ran after him but with his longer legs he easily pulled ahead. Ten feet. Twenty. She was losing him. She had no idea how big of an area she could Shield. If Jente got out of range he'd be able to turn invisible again and they'd lose him for sure.

She pushed her legs as fast as they'd go. Her lungs were already burning.

Merrick disappeared down a residential street.

She wanted to call after him but she could barely get enough air as it was. She followed Merrick into the small neighborhood. He was already halfway down the block. Jente was nowhere in sight.

Merrick reached another corner. A large black van was parked near the curb. He raced past. An arm shot out knocking Merrick right in the side of the head. He stumbled.

Jente emerged from behind the cover of the van. He bounced on the balls of his feet like a boxer ready for action.

Merrick rubbed his jaw.

Sydney forced her stupid little legs to move faster. She grabbed her ribs as a side ache shot pain throughout her whole body.

Jente took another swing. Merrick stepped back dodging the blow.

Jente threw another, dropped into a crouch and aimed for Merrick's ankles.

Merrick barely caught himself.

Jente was fast. He also appeared to be a trained fighter. He carried himself with a certain kind of grace as he circled Merrick looking for any kind of weak spot. He feigned a punch. Merrick fell for it and got clipped in the jaw. Again.

Merrick threw a quick one-two at Jente. He danced out of the way and shot out with an uppercut.

Merrick caught his wrist and pulled him in close, locking his arms around his chest.

Jente struggled.

Merrick closed his eyes. They opened a few seconds later, locking with Sydney's. "Drop your powers. I need to get a reading off of him."

Jente's sunglasses had been discarded during his fight with Merrick so Sydney could see his green and gray eyes widen. "Oh, fuck no."

Sydney dropped her Shield.

Jente jammed his elbow into Merrick's ribs.

Merrick's hold broke.

Jente kicked back, forcing Merrick further from him.

Sydney ran to Merrick's side.

Jente went invisible.

"Let him go," Merrick said just before she pulled her Shield. He rubbed right beneath his sternum.

"Are you okay?"

Merrick wasn't paying her any attention. His gaze was off in the distance where she could barely make out the sound of running footsteps.

"Did you get anything from him?" she asked.

Merrick shook his head. "That kid has got a lot of issues. All the impressions I got from his shirt were mixed up in a jumbled mess. There might have been something there for us to use but I'll have to wait for all the sensation overload to settle down before I can take a look through it all, so to speak."

"You can do that?" she asked as they made their way back to the station.

He shrugged. "It's different with each person, but with that guy," he jerked his thumb in the direction Jente took off, "it's kind of like watching a movie in fast forward. I was bombarded with a whole bunch of images so I have no idea what I've seen but later I'll suddenly remember something that stood out. Make sense?"

"Kind of." She pulled her cell out.

"Who're you calling?"

"Cali. The guy that just attacked you is named Jente. We all thought he'd gone with Vander when he took off but I guess not." She held her phone up to her ear.

Cali answered on the fourth ring, out of breath. "What?"

Sydney frowned. "Is something wrong?"

"Huh? No. Was there something you needed, Sydney?"

"I wanted to let you know that we just ran into Jente."

There was a few seconds silence. "What did he want?"

"No idea. Merrick felt someone watching him and when I used my powers he appeared across the street."

"Which means Vander knows exactly where you guys are."

A chill went down Sydney's spine. Did that mean it was only a matter of time before Regina came to take Merrick back? They hadn't even started to look for Kevin's journal. She really hoped Merrick would find something pertaining to them in all those impressions he picked up from Jente. They needed to know what Vander was up to.

"Cali!" Felix's voice echoed through the phone.

"I see it," she shouted back. There was a crash followed by colorful cursing. "Look, I got to go, Sydney. I'll talk to you later."

"Wait." Sydney threw her hand out even though there was no way Cali would see it. "I need to talk to Felix about Kevin and Collette."

There was another crash and more cursing. "I'll have him call you." Cali hung up on her.

Sydney pulled the phone away and stared at the screen. What the heck was going on over there? She hoped it was nothing serious.

Felix liked to joke that their little vigilante super guild helped rescue animals but she didn't think he'd ever take on the task if it was presented to him. Maybe Niella had had a Dream about some animal and Felix decided to do something about it.

It wouldn't be the first time he played hero and she doubted it would be the last. She shrugged it off.

"What was going on?" Merrick gestured to her phone.

"No idea. It sounded like they were chasing some kind of animal, but I have no idea why unless Felix's pet rat got out again." She shuddered.

"Don't like rats?"

"No. In fact I'm terrified of them."

"Why?"

They'd reached the station and thus her car. Merrick waited with the passenger door open, gazing at her over the top of the car.

"Why don't I like rats?"

He gave a half shrug. "Why are you terrified of them? There has to be a reason, no one wakes up terrified of something without good reason."

She climbed into the driver's seat. Merrick followed suit and buckled his seat belt.

"When I was little I was locked in my aunt's attic while playing hide and go seek," she found herself saying as she made her way back toward Felix's. "She used to have a lot of rats up there but I never noticed before until I was trapped for an hour up there with them."

She shuddered, remembering how she'd spent the hour screaming for her parents to come get her.

"I'm afraid of sewers," Merrick offered out of the blue.

Sydney tapped the brake a little too quickly. "The sewer?" She snuck a look and found that he was totally serious. *No way*, she thought. Someone as tough as Merrick afraid of a sewer? It didn't even make sense.

"It was a dare my senior year of high school. The manhole was wide open, and my friends dared me to go inside. When I did the workers saw me and yelled at me to get the hell out of there. I freaked and fell into the water. It didn't help that I used to be afraid of mutated crocodiles in the water when I was little."

Sydney bit the inside of her cheek to keep from laughing. "What a pair we make, huh? You're afraid of sewers and I'm afraid of rats."

The dry look he gave her didn't help with keeping a straight face. "It wasn't funny."

"Oh please," she said while merging onto the freeway. "My story of asking Brandon Archer to the Backwards Dance was way more traumatizing."

"You want traumatizing?" he challenged. "The first girl I ever liked, Evelyn Clark in third grade, I nailed her in the face with a dodge ball."

Sydney burst out laughing. She couldn't help it. She pictured a miniature Merrick standing horrified in a schoolyard while the girl of his dreams lay on the ground with a bloody nose. "You're right, that is traumatizing. I'm surprised you ever got a girlfriend." That last part was a lie. She was sure he had no trouble in that department. Girls were probably throwing themselves at him as soon as he could smile at them.

"Once I stopped smashing their faces in with rubber balls they became a little more receptive," he said nonchalantly.

They shared a grin that set Sydney's heart pounding. Yup, she definitely would have been one of those girls to swoon over Merrick in high school.

She tore her eyes away from him and scanned the rearview mirror. She didn't see any motorcycles. According to Cali, Jente drove a motorcycle, and Sydney was going to be darn sure he didn't follow them. She'd Shield all day if she had to. The last thing she wanted was for Jente to report to Vander about any findings on Kevin's journal. Which reminded her…

"We need to start looking for that journal Vander is after," she said to Merrick.

He looked up from the case file. "Didn't you need to wait for Felix to call you back?"

She shook her head. "We don't have time to wait around if Vander is monitoring everything that we do. I'm going to stop by Felix's house and see what the heck is going down over there."

A half hour later she pulled into Felix's driveway.

As she stepped out of the Yaris she could hear shouts coming from inside. She exchanged a worried look with Merrick. "If it's Felix's rat that's on the loose I'm getting out of here as fast as possible."

He joined her in front of the door. "Don't worry," he said with a straight face. "I'll protect you." The corner of his mouth twitched.

Sydney glared at him. "That's not funny."

She rang the doorbell.

Cali opened it a few seconds later, took one look at them, and nearly slammed it closed right in her face. "Heeey…Syd." She winced.

Sydney cringed. "No offense, Cali, but don't ever call me Syd."

Cali nodded. "Right. Agreed. So what are you doing here?"

"I need to talk to Felix." She tried to get a look at the house around Cali but Cali was too tall.

"Oh. Yeah. That." She looked behind her then back at Sydney. "Give me a second." She disappeared. "Felix, get your pansy ass out here," Cali cried into the house.

Merrick's eyebrows rose.

"You get used to it," Sydney told him. "Trust me, the more insulting the name the more endearing."

Felix opened the door. His left arm was wrapped in white bandages that were spotted with red—

"Is that blood?" Sydney grabbed his arm. Felix hissed in pain. She released her grip. "What happened? What's going on with you guys?" Cali came up behind him. They exchanged looks.

Felix ran his hand through his hair. "We didn't want to say anything, but remember when I brought your car back from… wherever?"

She didn't like where this was leading. "Yeah?"

"Well, I might've brought something *else* back with it."

Sydney's gaze dropped back to the bandage on his arm. "What do you mean you *might've* brought something back with it?"

Felix stared at his feet. "See that's the thing, we don't really know what it is. We think it's a cat. But we're not sure. We can't tell if it was a cat at one point that just spent too long wherever it is things go when they are Erased, or if that goo your car was covered in mutated it. I didn't want to worry you about the goo without knowing anything first."

"Is it safe for her to be driving that thing?" Merrick asked Felix with a jerk of his thumb toward her Toyota.

She remembered the claw marks on the top of her back seats, as well as the dents and scratches that marred the side of her car.

Felix shot Merrick a dark look. "I wouldn't do anything to endanger Syd's life."

That seemed to satisfy Merrick.

"You say you think it's a cat," said Sydney. "Do you want me to take a look at it? I usually know a cat when I see one."

She could read Felix's reluctance. Felix had a very strong protective streak, one she would never hold against him.

"Sure," he said at last and opened the door for them.

Sydney swallowed thickly as she followed after him. Merrick placed a comforting hand on the small of her back. There one second, gone the next. She wished he kept it there, then flushed at her own thoughts. Her traitorous eyes sought the hallway they'd made out in. Her whole body grew warm and she pulled her eyes away as Felix led them into his living room.

The room was a disaster.

The sofas were shoved haphazardly away from the middle to clear an open space. Tables were shoved against the walls. Coasters littered the floor along with art supplies and papers.

In the center of the room sat one of Sydney's medium sized kennels. Atop that was Felix's extra-large water cooler that they'd brought to the beach numerous times. She could see miscellaneous objects sticking out from the cooler, no doubt to help weigh it down.

"Is that—?" She pointed to the kennel.

Felix gave her an apologetic look. "We stole one of your kennels when we dropped Luke off with Niella."

"You left Luke with Niella?"

Felix held his hands palms out. "He was the one who wanted to see the clinic. Niella was going to do some paperwork and offered to give him a tour."

Luke was interested in her clinic? The thought made her smile. She'd always wanted to hire more help, to expand her clinic, but never got around it.

A crash from inside the cage took the smile right off her face.

The sulfurous smell got stronger the closer she got to the kennel. A small animal paced within.

Felix had taken one of her nicer kennels, which meant little light could penetrate through the thick plastic walls. She hunched over to try to get a glimpse through the door.

Merrick peered into the large cooler and whistled. "What's with all the weight?"

Cali crossed her arms. Sydney noticed a white bandage on the back of her left hand. "Trust us, that *thing* is fucking strong."

Sydney swallowed another lump of fear as she crouched closer to the front of the kennel. "Why didn't you guys tranquilize it?"

Cali and Felix cast each other worried glances. Felix answered first. "We did."

Sydney waited. "And?"

Guilt blanketed his face. "And," Felix drew out, "we might have plowed through nearly your entire stock of sedatives last night to keep this thing knocked out. But today the last one we had wore off in eleven minutes."

"What?" She whipped her gaze up to Felix's face before dropping it back to the cage. The creature inside didn't look any bigger than a beagle. She squinted against the shadows inside the container. "Do you have a flashlight?"

Felix dug inside the cooler and pulled out a huge camping flashlight.

Sydney clutched it to her chest. Merrick crouched down next to her. "Do you want me to hold that for you?" he offered, pointing to the flashlight.

She shook her head. "I got it." She steadied her trembling hands, something she was always good at. You had to have steady hands to be a surgeon and she'd learned at a young age to repress her shakes even while nervous.

She inhaled once and flashed the light inside the kennel.

The creature shrieked. The metal door banged as the thing rushed it.

Sydney fell back. Merrick caught her in his arms, the warmth of his chest on her back a small comfort.

"T-that's not a cat." She stared unblinking at the container. A hiss came from the shadowed corner in the far back.

Felix squatted down in front of her. "You're sure?"

She leaned back against Merrick for comfort. His arms tightened around her.

Cali's eyes watched them studiously.

Sydney didn't care, her mind was awhirl with images of what she'd just seen. "I'm all but positive," she told Felix. "Cats have fur, unless it's a breed like the Sphynx, but that didn't look anything like a Sphynx. Its skin was…was discolored." She didn't even have a name for the color. Purple? Red? Some kind of maroon? Cali would be better at describing the color—she was the artist. Sydney was just the vet. "And don't get me started on the anatomy," she mumbled. The whole body had been misshapen. The arms and legs were too long, the joints in the wrong places and bent at unnatural angles. And the eyes…

Merrick's arms tightened around her as she shivered. "Could this have been a side effect of some kind of radiation exposure?" Merrick's breath tickled her ear. She suppressed another shiver and realized that the back of her body was pressed firmly to the front of his and that she could feel his reaction to her nearness pressing against her. On the heels of that thought came the horror that Felix and Cali were witnessing every minute of it.

She wanted to shoot from Merrick's arms but knew that would draw more unwanted attention than if she slowly extracted herself.

She held her hand out. "A little help here?" she said to Felix with a wiggle of her fingers.

Felix leaned over and grasped her hand, pulling her from Merrick's lap. "Could that be possible?" he asked.

"What?"

He motioned to Merrick, who was getting to his feet. "The radiation exposure. Could massive amounts of radiation do that to a…cat?"

She stared at the kennel. "I've never seen radiation do that outside of movies," she said truthfully. "Its body is all wrong, Felix. I don't know what to tell you."

His expression fell. Cali wrapped her arms around his waist. "Radiation might not be ruled out completely," she said to him. "You could be Erasing things to Fukushima. Right into the heart of the melted nuclear power plant."

Felix didn't look like he believed it, but he put on a brave smile anyway. "Yeah, maybe."

Sydney had known Felix for years and she knew how afraid he had been of his powers. He used to be terrified of where he might send something after Erasing it. They'd both hoped that once he became full-forced that he wouldn't have to fear Erasing anything ever again, but apparently life just wasn't that simple.

Chapter 15

After more cautious studying of the "cat," Felix Erased it back to wherever it came from. Sydney didn't mind seeing it go. She and Merrick stayed and helped rearrange Felix's living room back to its original form. By the time they finished Sydney had two missed calls from Joel.

She stepped out into the hall to get some privacy and called him back.

"Hey," Joel picked up cheerfully. "What were you up to that kept you so busy?"

She filled him in on Felix's cat from hell.

"Holy shit. Seriously?" Joel said when she finished.

"Seriously," she told him. "I don't know what could have done that to a cat, Joel."

"Don't worry about it. It's gone now," he said, picking up on her unease. "And if you're worried about your car I'm sure if you ask Felix real nice he'll Erase it for you again."

She smiled. "Maybe I'll have him Erase another Yaris from a car lot and then bring it back right away, that way I won't be out a car. I can't keep borrowing yours."

"You know I don't mind," he said absently. "But hot damn, are you considering thievery, Syd? I never thought I'd see the day. I'm so proud of you."

"I'm not seriously going to ask him."

Joel's voice dropped. "Aw, come on. A little bad will do you good."

"Except when I get caught with a stolen car."

"Where's that never ending optimism? Besides, I doubt you'd ever get pulled over. When was the last time you drove over seventy miles per hour on the freeway?" He made a few thinking noises. "Oh, I remember, when I accidentally broke my toe a year ago on that old, clunky metal frame you used to have on your bed."

"You screamed like a little girl." She laughed.

"I did not."

When she hung up with Joel she felt lighter inside. She'd missed their easy conversations. She missed the uncomplicated friendship between them.

"Everything all right with Joel?"

Sydney jumped.

Cali had snuck up behind her. Her shoulder propped against the wall, arms crossed over her dark purple thermal top.

Sydney tucked her phone away. "Yeah," she said with some relief.

Cali studied her carefully. "You still care for him, don't you?"

Sydney's relaxed muscles instantly stiffened. "What are you talking about? Of course I still care for Joel. He's one of my best friends."

Cali's gaze never wavered. "But that's all you see him as, isn't it? A friend."

Sydney's lips formed the protest but the words never came. She'd been with Joel for nearly three years, he was her first love…

And suddenly she realized that she already viewed him as her first love and not her only love. Because she had moved on. Somehow, somewhere deep inside, she'd lost the intimate connection with Joel. She still wanted him in her life but now when she pictured his arms coming around her, she only felt comfort. There was no heating of her blood, no tickling awareness of his body, she only thought of him like an older brother. Like Felix.

Cali took a step toward her with her arms out as if to catch her. "Are you okay? You just went white as my canvas."

"I'm over Joel," she mumbled numbly.

Cali tried to catch her eye. "Sydney?" She gave her shoulders a little shake. "Are you with me?"

Sydney blinked. Never in a million years would she have thought this would happen. She was going to have to break Joel's heart.

Her stomach twisted violently.

Cali backed up. "Okay, now you look green. What the fuck did you eat for lunch?"

You're going to break up the entire guild.

Tears burned the back of her throat. She blinked her eyes rapidly to keep them at bay and looked into Cali's eyes. She watched her carefully.

Everything Sydney wanted to tell her stuck in her throat. What if Cali thought her change of heart was a betrayal? Cali didn't have any qualms about speaking her mind. And Sydney didn't want to hear her worst fears voiced aloud.

She clamped her mouth shut.

"Sydney?" Cali searched her face.

"I'm fine," she lied. "I could use some water though."

Cali disappeared down the hall. Had Cali heard what she'd said? That she was over Joel?

What do you think?

She'd mumbled in front of a Silencer. Cali probably heard her loud and clear.

Not even ten seconds later Felix came down the hall. "Can I talk to you?"

She tampered down her sudden fear and nodded. Felix led her into his bedroom and closed the door behind them.

"What's up?" She tried to sound unconcerned.

Felix ran a hand through his hair. Never a good sign. "Merrick just finished asking me a whole bunch of questions about Mirror Mates. That's what's up."

Sydney wrapped her arms around her waist to stop the trembling. She'd completely screwed up. "What did he want to know?"

"Everything. What it felt like, how do you know if the woman you think is your Mirror Mate is the one? Sydney—" He ran another hand through his hair.

Terror froze her in place. Her whole world was crumbling. Chaos everywhere. No order. Now Felix suspected that she and Merrick were Mirror Mates and Cali knew she no longer had sexual feelings for Joel. If they put two and two together…

Her head throbbed and she rubbed at her temples. She'd been holding her Shield up for a long time now. Those few seconds respite when she'd dropped it to allow Felix to Erase the "cat" hadn't been long enough to reenergize.

That only brought into focus that she still had Jente to worry about. Not to mention they still had to find Kevin's journal. That took precedence over everything else.

Pushing her growing headache aside she slid past Felix before he could say anything more incriminating.

"Where are you going?" he asked before she could completely escape into the hallway.

She forced her thundering heart to slow. "We have to find Kevin's journal."

He cupped her elbow to keep her in place, his brilliant blue-green eyes staring down into hers. "Sydney, this isn't something to brush off. I think Merrick thinks you're his Mirror Mate."

She was suddenly very glad Felix wasn't touching her hands because her palms instantly started to sweat.

He searched her eyes with his. His expression was nothing if not sympathetic and understanding. She could tell Felix anything. But he was Joel's best friend. Just because she knew him longer didn't automatically make him her friend more than Joel's.

If Joel left the guild would Felix be forced to choose between them?

What if he chose Joel?

Her stomach started to cramp again.

Felix's fingers tightened around her elbow. "It's okay," he said softly.

She looked away. "It's close to dinner time. I'll go pick up a pizza from Tom's."

It took her nearly ten minutes to convince Merrick that she could go alone to pick up a pizza. It wasn't until she was on her way out that Cali pointed out she could pick up Niella and Luke from the clinic.

She'd wanted to be alone but she guessed some time to herself was better than none.

She slipped into Tom's Pizzeria and inhaled the smell of garlic bread and pizza sauce. She must've been a little early because the dinner crowd hadn't arrived yet.

"Hey, Sydney." Tom came out from the back with his visor crooked as usual. She didn't think she'd ever seen it on straight. "I thought you were on vacation." There was no suspicious glint to his eye, just genuine curiosity. Sydney relaxed fractionally.

She forced a smile. "Not even a vacation can keep me away from your delicious pizza."

He leaned against the other side of the counter. "That's just sad," he said while giving her one of his grins that used to make her heart flutter when she was a teen.

Thomas Larkin had owned the pizzeria a few doors down from her parent's clinic for years. She'd met him when she was eighteen and worked part time with her parents at the clinic while attending college. She'd instantly developed a crush on the twenty-three-year-old pizza maker. It hadn't been hard. Tom had clear green eyes, unkempt dirty blond hair, and a smile that had melted her eighteen-year-old heart. She'd tried numerous times to flirt with him but nothing had ever come out of it. It was one of her biggest regrets not pursuing Tom to see if anything could have developed between them. Yet at the same time she was grateful nothing had ever happened, it would have ruined their friendship and right now she needed someone like Tom—a close friend with no ties or biases whatsoever to the guild.

"Can I talk to you about something?"

The easy smile faded from his handsome face. His forehead wrinkled in worry. "What's wrong?" He came around the counter.

She scuffed her shoe against the floor. "Nothing's wrong, I just…need some advice."

Tom went over to the front door and flipped the sign to "Closed." "Come on into the back so we can get some privacy."

This was why she loved Tom. She smiled gratefully at him.

In the back of the pizzeria she watched as he put together her order. "So," he said after he loaded their pizza into the oven. "What's on your mind?"

She snagged a green pepper out of a topping container and popped it in her mouth to buy herself some time to think. "What do you do when your feelings for someone you really care about change?"

Tom took a moment to dust his hands off. "I'm going to take a guess and say this is about Joel?"

She nodded.

Tom exhaled and joined her leaning up against the counter. "First of all, I think that changing feelings is natural. It's a part of growing up."

She gave him a flat stare. "I'm not sixteen."

"Hey, you'll always be that little eighteen-year-old to me." He wrapped his arm around her and rubbed the knuckles on his other hand gently on top of her head.

She pushed him away. "I don't want anyone to get hurt," she confessed. "And you know how close-knit my guil—uh, my group of friends are. I don't want to ruin the whole dynamic."

"I hate to say this, Sydney, but you can't stay with Joel out of some twisted obligation you feel for your friends. That's not fair to you—or Joel. It's perfectly normal to want to move on. That's why we date, to figure out what we're looking for in a life partner and what we're not. You'll find that one guy for you."

"What if I already have?" she mumbled.

Tom stopped nibbling on his piece of Canadian bacon. "You already have? Meaning—? Ohhh."

She waited for the disappointment, the condemnation. It never came. "You're not a bad person because of this, Sydney. You got me?"

"Easier said than felt," she said.

"I'm serious." His expression hardened. "You're not a bad person. You can't help what you feel. It's as simple as that."

"Okay," she said because she didn't know what else to say. She'd never seen Tom so fierce before.

He relaxed back into his easygoing demeanor. "Good. Don't lose sleep over this either. You look exhausted."

She was. She'd dropped her Shield on the way over. Cali could listen for Jente if he was hanging around Felix's and she didn't need to Shield herself while going to get pizza. Her body needed the rest.

Tom wrapped his arm around her shoulders again and she felt a comforting tingle throughout her whole body.

When Tom released her she felt loads better. Rejuvenated.

She gazed up at him. "What did you do to me?"

Tom tilted his head. "What do you mean?"

"When you hugged me…I felt…tingly." Realizing her words could be taken in a totally different meaning, she flushed. "I didn't mean—"

Tom laughed. "Don't worry about it. I'm sure you were just exhausted and when you relaxed it helped ease some of that weight you've been carrying on your shoulders." He pushed off the counter to tend to her pizza.

Her eyes followed him, her brow furrowed in thought. "I guess," she muttered.

While Tom was busy she slipped back to the front of the pizzeria. Bad idea. The dinner crowd had arrived and they spotted Sydney.

"Uh, Tom?" she called to the back. "It looks like there's an angry mob outside your place. You want me to flip the sign and let them in?"

"Give me a second," he answered. She heard movement as he bustled around in the back before he came out holding her pizza all boxed up and ready to go. "Here." He handed it to her. "Let me know how everything works out, okay?"

She didn't want to lie to Tom, but she didn't know if she'd be able to go through with breaking up with Joel. Their three-year anniversary was only a few days away. It would devastate him.

But which would hurt him more: breaking up with him before, or right after?

She could barely meet Tom's eyes. "Okay," she told him.

His green eyes warmed. "You can do it, you're stronger than you think."

At that moment she didn't think so. She'd never been particularly strong or adventurous. If she was she'd have thought her powers would have reflected it. But what did she do? She Shielded. It was a fancy word for hiding. For cowardice.

A warm hand gripped her shoulder. Tom was still watching her. "I'm just a phone call away if you need anything."

She smiled at him. "Thanks."

*

"Finally." Niella rolled out from behind the reception desk when Sydney came in. "Come on, Skywalker, our ride is here," she yelled to the back.

Sydney hid her smirk. Niella liked to think she kept her distance from the guild, but what she didn't realize was that when she used Joel's nicknames and helped create titles, she was a part of the guild as much as anyone else.

Luke emerged from the back, his brown/blond hair falling into his eyes. He needed a haircut, Sydney thought absently.

He smiled when he saw her. "Your clinic is amazing," he gushed. "I can't believe you run this whole thing."

Pride swelled in Sydney's chest. "My clinic isn't that amazing," she said on instinct, even though she thought it was. It wasn't very big but it was hers and she loved it. The first time Cali had seen it she'd commented on how small the place was. Sydney liked Luke's reaction much better.

"Well, I think it's amazing," Luke said as she locked up. "Do you ever need, like, help or anything?"

Sydney pulled back from the door to look Luke up and down. He was no longer dressed in his scrubs. He had on worn jeans and a black jacket that wasn't quite zipped up all the way revealing a… *Star Wars* shirt?

Joel…

She shook her head at the idea of Joel happily giving Luke a shirt to wear.

With his outfit Luke looked like any regular kid. But what was he before he was kidnapped by Vander? Had he been homeless? She knew Juliet had a family to return to. Hazel admitted to having no one but she hadn't elaborated beyond that.

"Luke," Sydney said, "did you have a home you needed to return to? Parents that you needed to contact?"

"Uh." Luke studied the floor, shifting nervously.

Sydney waited patiently. She knew that he was twenty years old, so he didn't have to go anywhere he didn't want to go.

"I'm not going to force you to do anything. You know that, right?"

He lifted his blue eyes from the ground. "I-I know." He twisted his hands a few times before continuing. "I was in the foster care system for a while. The home I was taken from…the people were really nice."

He shrugged. "I just don't see what good talking to them will do. I mean they were great and all and I'm really glad I was placed with them but I don't want to cause them any more problems. I'd rather stay away. They probably thought I ran away anyway." He continued to fiddle with his hands, his eyes darting around.

She decided not to press him anymore. "Why don't you help Niella get situated in the Hummer?"

He looked grateful to have something to do and disappeared to the back of the car to help Niella.

When they reached Felix's, Sydney's heart flipped at the sight of Joel's truck parked out front.

She felt Niella's eyes on her and tried to keep her outward appearance calm and collected.

Tom's words floated through her head as she brought the pizza in. Felix, Cali, Merrick, and Joel were all seated on the couches. Joel and Merrick were on the same couch. Sitting side by side the two looked so different, yet so similar.

Everyone turned when she entered the room and Sydney found her eyes locked with Merrick's. Her heart pounded in her chest.

"Where are the others?" Cali asked.

She pulled her gaze from Merrick and pointed behind her. "Luke's helping Niella."

"Nice." Felix came over and took the pizza box. "Who's hungry?"

Merrick and Joel got to their feet. Sydney was stuck rooted to the ground. Joel gave her a smile though it didn't quite reach his eyes. He pulled her in tight for a hug. She closed her eyes instantly so she wouldn't see Merrick's expression over Joel's shoulder.

"Sorry I had to work," Joel said as he released her.

"It's fine." She forced her own smile while her heart raced. It was so hard to stare into his face when she knew she had to break it off with him. She'd spent the entire car ride back to Felix's bolstering her confidence. She had to do what was right. Right?

Indecision warred within her.

Chapter 16

Merrick climbed into the back of the Hummer where Luke was practically jumping up and down.

"This is so cool," said Luke. "We're going to break into a hospital so you can use your powers."

"Technically," Felix said from the driver's seat, "we're not breaking in. We're visiting during visiting hours but the rest of that statement is true. You think you're going to be able to get anything?" Felix directed that last question at Merrick.

"I won't know until I get there," he said honestly.

Joel sat silently in the passenger seat. Merrick tried not to watch him but he couldn't help it. Once Sydney had returned with the pizza Joel had never left her side. As if he wanted to keep Sydney away from Merrick on purpose.

Stop being such a fucking asshole. That's his girlfriend and he has every right to want to spend time with her.

Sydney might be Joel's girlfriend but after Merrick's conversation with Felix about Mirror Mates, Merrick was almost positive that Sydney was his.

Everything Felix had described had happened between them. A jolt through his system when they touched, an ache in his chest when they were apart, and an overwhelming need to be with Sydney—to taste her and touch her.

He bit back a groan of frustration as his cock hardened.

All these sensations couldn't have been one sided. Sydney had to have felt them too, which begged the question: why didn't she do anything about it? Did she not want Merrick as a Mirror Mate?

I thought you weren't buying into this soul mate shit?

He sighed. He didn't know what to think anymore. Was it too much to hope for a woman he could get close to and not have to fear her inner thoughts?

"You think Juliet and Hazel are all right?" Luke's voice snapped Merrick out of his inner musings.

He glanced over at the kid and saw real concern on his face. "I'm sure they're fine. I told Hazel to call if she needed anything. If she's in trouble, we'll know."

Or at least he hoped so. Regina hadn't shown her pretty little mug since they came to Southern California. He would have thought Vander would send her after him, or that she'd at least volunteer, but he hoped that not seeing her meant she was ordered to stay in San Francisco.

Luke nodded. "I miss them," he mumbled.

Merrick blinked in surprise. He hadn't thought their friendships had grown that strong, but then he remembered that all his time was spent with Sydney.

And look how attached you got to her.

"I'm sure they miss you too," he said earnestly.

Some of the sadness left Luke's face. "I bet they would have had fun going on this mission."

Merrick felt like telling him that it wasn't really a mission. They were walking into a hospital room, end of story. But he didn't want to ruin Luke's illusion.

They arrived at the hospital with a little less than an hour to "visit."

Felix led them to a private wing. A few nurses eyed them skeptically but no one stopped them. Merrick kept a close eye out for anything suspicious. He had that tickle at the back of his neck again, like someone was watching him. Could it be that Jente guy again?

They shouldn't have left Sydney at the house.

They had no way of knowing if they were being followed but she had looked beyond exhausted and Merrick had agreed with Joel and Felix that she needed to stay behind and rest.

"Here we are," Felix announced as they stepped into a sterile smelling room. The temperature was on the cool side. Merrick instinctively scanned the room. There wasn't much to look at. There was nothing there. No flowers, nothing to indicate that anyone came to visit.

Merrick stepped closer to the bed. It was surreal to look down into the faces of Collette and Kevin and feel like he already knew them. He'd seen them awake, walking and talking. He'd been inside Kevin's head, feeling what he felt.

They both looked washed out now. White faces, drab hair, and sunken cheekbones.

Felix stared at both of them with a strange expression on his face. Some kind of mix between sympathy and loathing.

Joel remained off to the side, arms crossed over his chest. Luke stood nearby looking as if he wanted to come closer but wasn't sure if it was appropriate.

Merrick stood between the two beds acutely aware of all the tubes that were attached to both Collette and Kevin. Maybe it was a good thing Sydney had stayed away. She hated hospitals; he couldn't imagine what seeing someone like this would do to her.

"Have you ever gotten information off of an actual person before?" asked Felix.

"No, just things they've touched. I'm not sure this'll even work. I've never tried to read something off of someone in a coma before. They might not give off impressions like a normally active person would."

"Just give it your best. We might as well start at the main source." Felix moved away to give him more room.

Merrick ran his fingers along the sheets as he focused. He'd never tried to get inside a person's head before. Not to mention one that was in a coma. Was it possible for him to become trapped inside another person's mind?

He fucking hoped not.

He inhaled. The back of his neck prickled. He reached out and brushed the limp brown hair off of Kevin's forehead. His skin was lukewarm. Merrick repressed a shiver.

You won't get trapped.

He pressed his fingers more firmly against Kevin's skin and shut his eyes.

Nothing happened.

He gave it a few more seconds but no visions came.

"Anything?" asked Felix.

Merrick shook his head in awe. "Nothing." He couldn't read people. A tightness in his chest released. "I'll try his clothes and the sheets, just to make sure." He touched Kevin's hospital gown and instantly got sucked into a strange black void. He was aware of being moved and that was it. He jerked his hand back.

Holy shit, had that been Kevin's thoughts?

He touched the clothing again. This time he didn't get any black voids. He picked up on the nurses: their boredom, their sympathy. He pulled away when a few nurses got curious about how hung Kevin was.

He moved onto the sheets. More nurses. He was ready to pull away when he stopped. He closed his eyes and concentrated. He skimmed the sheets like someone would skim the pages of a book until he found what he was looking for. There.

"Where is she?"

It was Vander.

"You hid her from me, didn't you? Why?" Vander grunted. *"It doesn't matter. It was a fool's mistake. You forget I hold Collette's life in my hands. One phone call to the hospital and every machine that's keeping her alive will be unplugged. This might not matter to you now but it will. I've found a way to bring you back to me. It might take time but we've both got plenty of that."*

Shouts erupted.

It took Merrick a moment to realize that they weren't coming from his visions. He wrenched his hand away from Kevin's bed in time to see Luke get shot in the chest by a taser. His body convulsed, then dropped.

"Shit." Joel caught him on the way down.

Felix waved his hand and the taser disappeared from existence. He launched himself at the men in the doorway. Joel placed his hand flat on Luke's chest. He held on for a second before jumping into the fray with Felix.

Merrick rushed to help. A fist shot out and took him in the solar plexus. He staggered back. The man who'd hit him crouched next to Luke and gripped him under the arms. He heaved but Luke's body didn't move an inch. It was like he was glued to the floor.

Not glued, Merrick realized, but Locked. He laughed aloud at Joel's genius and flew into the fight with renewed vigor. His fist smashed into the face of the man trying to abduct Luke. The man flew, knocking into the back of Felix's knees. Felix stumbled and took a hit in the gut.

Merrick winced. Cali was going to beat his ass if she ever found out about that.

Felix's eyes locked with his.

My bad, Merrick mouthed.

Felix grinned before slammed his elbow into his closest attacker's ribcage. The man doubled over. Merrick kneed him in the face.

They systematically worked their way through their assailants. Joel Locked them in place and Felix and Merrick took them out. By the time they were through Merrick could taste his own blood in his mouth. They'd moved into the hallway but there were no nurses or doctors to be found.

"Convenient," said Merrick.

"Come on." Joel went back into the Bauers' room to unlock Luke from the floor. "More could be on their way. We better head back." He was sporting a cut on his forehead and a swollen lip.

"I'll keep watch—you guys try to wake his ass up," said Felix.

Joel shook Luke by the shoulders. "Come on, Skywalker, a little electricity never hurt anyone. I mean, look how fast Luke bounced back after being jolted by the emperor in the movies. This is nothing."

Merrick gripped Luke's other arm and together he and Joel lifted him to his feet.

Luke blinked.

"I think he's coming around," said Merrick.

Luke gave a pained groan.

Joel and Merrick walked him out of the hospital room. By the time they reached the elevators he could stand on his own. Merrick reached out and steadied him when he started to sway again.

"You're fine," Joel kept repeating. "You're invincible, remember?"

"I don't want to be invincible if it means I have to take all the hard hits," Luke said as he rubbed the back of his head.

Felix patted him on the shoulder. "I'll bet after a few more big hits like that you won't even feel pain anymore."

Luke stared at him incredulously.

"Welcome to the Guild of Truth," Felix said with a grin.

"The Guild of Aletheia," Joel said, exacerbated. He dabbed at his swollen lip with the hem of his shirt. "You know that fight would have gone a lot smoother if you would have brought back the taser for us to use," he said to Felix.

Felix punched the button for the lobby. "Sorry, it's force of habit to not bring something back."

Joel grunted. "I'm going to have to think of a better excuse at work for all my bruises besides 'I like to box.' Everyone's going to think I'm into S&M or something."

"S and M?" asked Luke.

Felix and Joel exchanged a look. Felix raised his eyebrows as if to tell Joel that Luke was his trainee.

"Sadomasochism," Merrick spoke up. "It means getting off on pain."

Luke shuddered. "Who'd ever want that?"

"There are some…unique people out there," Felix said carefully. It was very politically correct of him.

Merrick remembered the man in San Francisco whose power caused pain on contact. He studied Luke, took note of the way he held his arms around himself as if to ward off the world. He was pretty sure Luke would never want to experience pain ever again if he could avoid it.

The lobby was bustling with people and it took everything Merrick had to keep his head high as he walked out as if nothing had happened, as if he wasn't sporting the beginnings of a black eye or a split lip.

A few workers stared openly. Some pointed. Merrick kept an eye out if any one of them pulled out a cell phone. Someone had to have alerted Vander that they were here.

"Well, that was pointless," Felix said once in the safety of his vehicle.

"Not completely," said Merrick as he buckled up. He told the rest of them what Vander had said to Kevin's unconscious body.

"Well, shit," said Felix when he was done. "What the hell did he mean he can bring him back?"

"No idea." But he wished he did know. If Kevin woke up would Vander leave him alone? Vander had said it would take time, which meant that for now he would keep pursuing Merrick.

*

"Would you two knock it off?" said Niella. "What the hell is wrong with you guys?"

Sydney and Cali both stopped their pacing.

Cali rubbed at her chest. "Felix is away from me, that's what's wrong."

Niella waved her off. "Yeah, fine. You I understand. You…" She pointed to Sydney. "What's your problem? Why are you so antsy?"

Sydney dropped her hands before she felt tempted to rub at the hollow ache in her chest. She was nervous, anxious. As soon as Merrick drove away she wanted to race after him.

Both women watched her carefully.

She forced herself to sit. "I'm worried about them. All of them," she stressed in case they got any ideas.

"Well, quit it, you're making me nervous." Niella rolled her shoulders.

Could it be that Niella was worried too?

"Are you worried about Luke?" Sydney asked.

The glare shot her way was answer enough.

"You are. That's so cute," Sydney teased, glad to divert the attention away from herself.

"Look, the kid has had a tough life. He doesn't need any more complications."

Cali continued to pace. Sydney wanted to join her but concentrated back on Niella. "I know he was in the foster care system, that had to be rough."

"You want to know why he was in the foster care system?" Niella asked. "It's because he had an abusive father. Luke and his sister were separated and he went from home to home until this last one kept him for a few years."

"He told you all this?"

"He mentioned it and then while he was touring the clinic again on his own I had a Dream about him. His past."

"Did you tell him that?"

"Nah, I'm sure he doesn't want anyone to know, so you better keep your mouth shut." Her hazel eyes hardened.

Sydney leaned back. "I promise."

Cali let out a relieved sigh.

Sydney looked up. The tightness in her chest had lessened, which meant—

She shot to her feet as the front door opened.

The men shuffled into the living room all bruised and bloodied except for Luke. Luke looked shaken, his hair frizzing out like he'd stuck his finger in an electrical socket.

Sydney's attention flew to Merrick. He had a black eye and a split lip. "Are you all right?" She ran to him and only realized her mistake when she clutched Merrick's face in her hands.

A deathly quiet settled over the room.

Sydney dropped her arms and spun to find the rest of the guild gaping at her. Her eyes instantly sought Joel.

He stood off to the side sporting a cut on his forehead and a swollen lip. He stared at her dazed, as if someone had bashed him over the head from behind.

He blinked and the dazed look was gone. In its place was hurt and betrayal.

Sydney took a step toward him.

His midnight blue eyes narrowed. His anger couldn't quite mask the pain she saw in his face.

"Joel," she croaked. "I—"

"What the hell, Syd?" His gazed flickered around the room to where the rest of the guild was watching them. His face flushed with humiliation. He stepped forward and took her arm. "Can we talk somewhere private?" he whispered between clenched teeth.

He didn't wait for an answer. He started to pull her toward the hallway that led to the bedrooms.

"Joel, wait," she protested meekly. She didn't want to have this conversation while he was pissed. She didn't want to have this conversation somewhere the entire guild could overhear them. She didn't want to have this conversation period.

His fingers tightened around her arm. "Joel, stop. Please let go."

He made it three steps with her stumbling after him before he stopped. She peeked around his body to see Merrick blocking their way. His eyes were shining like blue fire.

Joel's body stiffened. The tension in the room rose another notch. "Get out of our way," Joel seethed.

Merrick crossed his arms and widened his stance. "She doesn't want to go with you."

Sydney could barely hear over the roaring in her ears.

Joel's fingers twitched against her arm. "And you think she'd want to go with you?"

Merrick's eyes briefly met hers. For one second she could have sworn she saw a flicker of vulnerability. It was gone in the next instant, replaced with hard ice. "She asked you to let her go." He avoided Joel's question.

"This doesn't concern you," said Joel. "She's my girlfriend and I want to talk to her alone."

"If Sydney doesn't want to do something then it concerns me," Merrick said flatly.

"And since when did it become your responsibility to protect Syd?"

Merrick took a menacing step toward Joel. "Since you failed to do so."

Sydney gasped. "Merrick—"

Joel dropped her arm.

A split second later his fist slammed into Merrick's face. Blood gushed from his nose. He stepped back to regain his balance and threw his fist.

Sydney heard the crack of bone and cried out as Joel flew off his feet.

"Shit." Cali jumped out of the way.

Felix rushed to Joel's side. His blue-green eyes caught with Sydney's and he gave her a look like "what the hell are you doing?" She wasn't rushing to Joel's side. She was anchored to the floor, her gaze darting between Joel and Merrick.

Merrick held his clenched fist close to his body, his chest heaving.

Their eyes locked. Something like fear and anticipation coursed through her body. Her breasts ached and her sex pulsed.

She tore her gaze away and ran to Joel.

"Joel." She knelt next to him. Cali handed her a roll of paper towels. She brought them to his face where his hand was cupped to catch the blood from his nose. "Here." She tried to shoo his hand away. "Let me."

"Get away from me." He pushed her away. She fell back onto her butt. Numb.

Cali took the towels from her hand and shot her an apologetic half-smile. She took her place at Joel's side and handed him the paper towels.

Sydney mechanically got to her feet. She stared from the outside as Felix, Cali, and Luke helped Joel.

A delicate hand grasped hers.

She jumped.

Niella squeezed her hand once and let it drop. She rolled over to the rest of the group and handed them more tissues.

Tears welled in Sydney's eyes. It was all her fault. She'd done this. Her greatest fear of breaking up the guild was happening right before her eyes.

She felt Merrick come up behind her. She quickly stepped away, not looking at him. "Just stay away," she pleaded, though the words broke something fragile inside of her. She wanted nothing more than to curl into his strong, warm arms and forget the sight before her.

Out of the corner of her eye she could see Merrick's white knuckles. He backed off into the adjoining kitchen.

Felix helped Joel to his feet. His face was swollen and Sydney could already make out the beginnings of two black eyes. "Joel, I'm so sorry—"

He walked right past her.

Felix gave her an apologetic look and followed Joel out, talking to him in a hushed voice.

Numb didn't even begin to describe what she was feeling. She was dead inside. Joel wouldn't even look at her.

A car started in the front yard.

A few seconds later Felix came back in, looking uncharacteristically somber. He studied the blood stains on his carpet and Sydney felt even more terrible. "I'll help you clean up," she offered.

Felix held up a hand. "I think we all need to just calm down, go home and recuperate. We didn't find anything out tonight so there's no rush to do anything."

"Is there a phone I can use to call a cab?" Merrick asked.

Felix pitched him his cell.

The offer to drive him home was sitting on the tip of her tongue but Sydney swallowed it down. Right now she was feeling crushed and vulnerable. She didn't know what she'd do if left alone in Merrick's presence. And she wasn't willing to find out.

After Merrick left Sydney helped Felix with his carpet despite his protests. Once that was finished she searched for anything else she could do to occupy her mind and time. When there was nothing left she conceded defeat and collected her purse and keys.

Niella blocked Sydney's path to the door.

"What?"

Niella's face betrayed nothing. "Take me home." It wasn't a question.

Sydney's fingers tightened around her keys but all the anger drained from her when she realized the extra time would keep her mind away from thoughts of Merrick and Joel. Her shoulders slumped. "Fine."

Niella's wheelchair would barely fit in the back of her Yaris but they'd gotten it in once before.

Felix offered the guest room to Luke. He turned in as soon as possible. Sydney felt bad for ruining everyone's night but Felix said Luke was probably exhausted from being tasered.

"What?" Niella and Sydney both cried.

Cali, who was sitting on the sofa, leaned back in a relaxed pose. "Ah, tasers, that brings me back."

Felix shot her a mischievous grin.

The joke wasn't lost on Sydney. She'd been there after Cali had knocked Collette out cold with a taser.

"Don't worry," Felix said to Niella and Sydney. "A little rest and he'll be fine. He regenerates, remember?"

Niella grumbled about poor treatment of new recruits.

The car ride to Niella's started out in relative silence. Niella played with the radio until she settled for some upbeat dance song. When they were about halfway to her place she turned the volume down.

"So are you going to tell me what happened back there?" she asked.

Sydney kept her attention front and center. After a few minutes of following the car in front of her, she finally answered. "I didn't want anyone to get hurt," she confessed. There was no point lying to a Dreamer. Niella would find out about it eventually. The more she concentrated on a subject or object the more likely she was to Dream about it.

"Well, you failed on that front," Niella said bluntly.

Sydney winced. "I know. It's just—"

"Merrick is your Mirror Mate?" she supplied helpfully.

The air left Sydney's lungs in a rush. "How long have you known?"

"How long have you?" Niella countered.

Sydney adjusted her hands on the steering wheel restlessly. "I suspected as much when I saw him in June locked up beneath the Kratos building." She stopped at a red light and turned to Niella.

Her eyebrows were raised in surprise. "That's a long time, Syd."

"I know, but I couldn't say anything to Joel. He cares for me so much and this is so…unfair to him." The light turned green and she concentrated on the road.

"You're always so worried about everyone else. You're trying to please too many people. What do *you* want?"

"Merrick." His name burst from her lips without conscious thought.

She whirled her head around to gauge Niella's reaction but she was only smiling at her. "Then you have your answer."

"But what about Joel?"

Niella leaned her head back against the seat rest. "Joel will be fine in time. Trust me."

Sydney frowned.

Chapter 17

Merrick tipped the cab driver and made his way to his apartment. The door handle was loose and on further inspection there were scratch marks on the doorframe. Merrick jiggled the handle before sticking his key in.

Still locked.

He shook his head. Some punk kids were testing out their skills on breaking and entering and failed. Much to his relief. Maybe it was a sign that his luck was changing.

He pushed open his door and flipped the lights before relocking the front and engaging the flimsy chain. It was the first time he'd been back in his apartment by himself. His gaze drifted to the dog dishes by the fridge.

The apartment was eerily silent and he wondered if perhaps he should get another dog to quell the loneliness he was currently trying to hold off. He threw his keys onto the counter and opened his fridge out of habit. There was nothing inside of it. Nothing edible anyway.

He pulled a glass from the cupboards and filled it with some tap water. He held it without taking a drink as he surveyed his empty living space. He stared down into his water and dumped the glass in the sink, rubbing his chest as he entered the living room.

Maybe a book would help—

He froze in mid-reach and spun on his heel.

In the far corner near his window Vander and Jente appeared out of thin air.

Merrick recalled the scratches on his front lock. And here he'd thought luck was on his side.

He snorted mentally.

Idiot.

Vander had aged even more since the last time he saw him. His entire head of hair was silver now, emphasizing his dark eyes and brows. Merrick also got his first good look at Jente. He couldn't have been that much older than Luke. He had tan skin and black hair. Merrick would put him roughly around the six feet area in height but his most defining feature would be the mismatched coloring of his eyes. The coloring of his skin already made the gray in his eyes stand out, but the splash of green in his right eye stood out even more. When paired with the flat stare he was currently giving Merrick, Jente's gaze could be quite disconcerting.

This is a man that can go invisible at any moment, he warned himself. *Be on guard.*

"Not even going to reach for a gun?" asked Vander.

"Believe me, I would have if there was one close by."

Vander made a thoughtful noise in the back of his throat before straightening his suit jacket. "Very well. That'll make this whole conversation much easier then." He stepped deeper into Merrick's living room, comfortable as could be. Jente remained in the corner where it would be easy for Merrick to forget he was there.

"If it was a conversation you were looking for a phone call would have sufficed." Merrick trailed Vander with his eyes.

Vander settled onto his couch and propped his feet on the coffee table. "We both know you wouldn't have answered."

"And what makes you think I'm going to talk to you now?" He moved slowly toward the kitchen where there were many knifes waiting for him in his drawers.

Vander sighed and pulled a Glock 19 from under his jacket. He pointed it levelly at Merrick's chest.

Merrick froze, hands instantly splaying. "No tasers?" he asked.

Vander flashed his teeth. "I'm afraid not. And with my powers being on temporary shutdown I'm sure you understand why I have to resort to such…barbaric methods of persuasion."

At the mention of powers Merrick's eyes instantly shot to the corner of his living room.

Jente was gone.

Shit.

He could be anywhere.

"And he could be aiming god only knows what at you as well," Vander said as if reading his mind. He easily tucked his gun back into his jacket.

Merrick ground his teeth. The hair on the back of his neck stood on end. "What do you want?" he growled.

Vander held his hand out to the chair on his left. "Sit."

Merrick remained standing until he heard the distinct click of a gun somewhere off to his side. Keeping his hands near chest level he sank into his armchair. Once seated he carefully placed his hands palms down on his knees where they were in plain sight. "Now, what the fuck do you want?"

Vander folded his hands together. "I'm afraid it's the same thing I've wanted since the beginning. Your compliance."

"Bullshit. You never wanted my compliance, you wanted that journal. And just in case your invisible spy hasn't noticed—I don't have it."

Vander's eyes glittered darkly. "On the contrary, Mr. Haskell, I believe we can help each other tremendously. My resources are infinite. You can ask Mr. Mitchell if you'd like." He held his hand out to gesture to his invisible companion.

Merrick filed the last name away.

"My resources could be a valuable asset for someone like yourself."

"For someone like me?" He scoffed. "You forget that I've been doing fine with my cases on my own."

"I'm not talking about your PI cases," Vander said calmly. "I'm talking about your missing sister."

Merrick's heart ceased beating.

A slow, satisfied smile spread across Vander's face. "You do want to find her, don't you? Imagine having a multi-million dollar company at your fingertips. A company, I might add, that, what's the phrase? Has their fingers in many different pies?"

Merrick breathed slowly.

Don't let him know how much he's getting to you.

An image of his sister rose unbidden to the forefront of his mind.

Alyssa…

"Still not enticing enough?" said Vander.

Merrick found his voice. "There's no guarantee that I'll find her with your resources. I've collected quite a bit on my own."

"And how has that worked out for you?"

He clenched his jaw.

"That's what I thought. If my resources aren't enough then I promise a guarantee that you'll find her, but it may take time."

"How?"

"Not how. Whom." His dark eyes bore into Merrick's. "I believe you visited him tonight."

Merrick heard Vander's voice through his head, telling Kevin that he was going to bring him back. "Kevin," he breathed.

Vander leaned forward, elbows on knees. A crazed look came over his face. "You don't understand the power associated with having a…Dreamer in your pocket. Anything you could ever want would be yours in a manner of seconds."

Merrick thought of Niella sitting all alone in her wheelchair. What would Vander do if he learned that she was a Dreamer? Images of Dennis and Regina converging on her flooded his mind. He'd never submit someone to that kind of fate.

"How are you going to wake Kevin up?" he asked.

That shark's smile was back. "I can't tell you all my secrets, now can I? The only thing I will tell you is that it involves another person with an ability."

It didn't take a genius to figure out that person needed the ability to heal. He instantly thought of Luke. Was that why Vander had tried to kidnap him again?

No. Luke could only heal himself rapidly. He didn't possess the power to heal others. Maybe he'd gain that power when he became full-forced?

"Why did you try to take Luke tonight?" Merrick asked. If Luke was Vander's target then he needed to warn the others.

Vander depthless eyes stared straight through him. "Money is power, Mr. Haskell, and Mr. Teagan has his uses, none of which are any of your concern."

"If I worked for you it'd be my concern," he said evenly.

"That's where you're mistaken. If you worked for me it still wouldn't be any of your concern. Now, what is your answer?"

Merrick pretended to think about it. "I'm afraid I'm going to have to say, go fuck yourself."

Vander's face still held its pleasant expression but Merrick could make out the tick in his jaw. Vander got to his feet in one fluid motion. He reached into his jacket and Merrick braced himself for the pain of being shot.

Vander didn't retrieve his gun. He pulled a business card. "I'll get that journal, Mr. Haskell. I'll be watching you. I'll keep in touch but just in case you wish to contact me." He held the card up before placing it face up on the coffee table. Vander unlocked the front door and walked out without a backwards glance, the door left ajar.

Merrick stared.

Had Jente followed him or was he still watching him right at this moment?

His eyes traveled over every piece of furniture in his home but he couldn't find anything to give away Jente's presence if he was indeed still with him.

"If you're in here," Merrick growled. "You better get the fuck out, now."

He held the door open but heard no footsteps. After a few more moments of feeling like an idiot he slammed the door shut and locked it.

He stormed into his bedroom and booted up his computer. A few minutes later he was staring at the digital scans on his sister's case. *Unsolved,* he read in one of the corners. The word haunted him. Somewhere out there Alyssa could still be suffering. Alone.

Merrick cradled his head in his hands.

He was no closer to finding Alyssa than he'd been years ago when he'd picked up her case.

Vander's promise slid against his mind like a lover's caress, taunting him, tempting him. He fisted his hair.

All it would take to find her was one Dream. One Dream and all his years of searching would come to an end.

What if he found the journal and then bartered with it? Then he wouldn't have to work for Vander. They'd both get what they wanted.

But Merrick would still be stuck with having to wait.

If he worked with Vander he would be given unlimited resources. If he didn't work for Vander but bartered the journal for Alyssa's whereabouts he'd have to wait until Kevin woke up. He'd have to trust Vander's word that he'd keep his end of the bargain.

You could always keep the journal until Kevin woke up.

But by that time the journal would be obsolete.

Maybe Niella could find Alyssa for you.

He lifted his head and stared at the search bar on his computer screen. Something about Niella pulled at his memory. The name wasn't common and something about her face stood out to him.

He typed her first name into the internet search bar. A few different hits came up but one caught his eye. *Niella Souveray: Olympic Athlete Mangled in Freak Car Accident.*

Merrick clicked the link.

Now he remembered why she seemed so familiar. He'd watched her in the Olympic trials. He scanned the article. Niella had been a sprinter. She'd qualified for the Olympic Games when one night after practice reporters claimed she'd been so tired after a night of celebrating that she'd fallen asleep at the wheel of her car and crashed.

As Merrick continued to surf the web he found different takes on the accident. Some claimed it was self-inflicted, that the pressure of the games were too much for Niella and she'd purposely injured herself. Either way, Niella had been on her way to victory when in a matter of seconds her whole athletic career had been taken from her.

No wonder she seems so bitter.

There wasn't much more on Niella after the accident. She'd moved from San Diego further up the coast. What she was doing with her life now, reporters didn't know.

Merrick stared at an image of the car wreck. No one else had been injured. "Falling asleep at the wheel…," he muttered aloud.

He sat up straighter as something clicked. Dreamers. Dreaming. Niella had been suffering from a Dream while she'd been driving.

Merrick's heart went out to her.

He shut down his computer. He didn't need anything else to depress him. He'd reached his quota for the day.

He lay down in bed staring at the ceiling wondering how he'd ask a woman who'd lost all her dreams because of her powers to use those powers for him.

*

A knock on the door woke Merrick from a dead sleep.

He shot up, eyes gritty from trying to stay awake all night in an attempt to sniff Jente out. He'd obviously failed.

He rubbed the sleep from his eyes and shuffled to the door to see who was on the other side.

His heart kicked against his ribs.

Sydney.

His fingers tightened on the knob. He inhaled and loosened his grip. He pulled open the door. "Hey."

"Hey." She stood before him immaculate as ever. Her hair hung in perfect loose waves down past her shoulders. She wore a three-quarter sleeved top against the late September chill that brought out the green in her eyes. She hardly wore any makeup but Merrick loved that about her.

She stared at him, mouth slightly parted. Merrick glanced down at his chest. He'd forgotten to don a shirt in his haste to answer the door.

The hungry glint in Sydney's eyes had his blood quickening. His hand gripped the door. "What do you want?"

She dropped her gaze to the floor but she couldn't hide the flash of hurt fast enough. Merrick ground his teeth. He flung the door the rest of the way open and stepped back. "Come in," he said gruffly.

Sydney hesitated before she entered.

Merrick scanned his apartment for any sudden appearances. "Are you Shielding right now?"

"What?"

"Are you using your powers?" He quickly went back to his bedroom.

Curiosity must've got the better of Sydney because her hesitancy melted away and she trailed after him. "Yes, why?"

Merrick ripped open his closet, the bathroom, anywhere Jente could hide.

Nothing.

Merrick exhaled in relief. So he had left with Vander last night.

"Is everything all right? No offense, but you look horrible."

Merrick caught sight of himself in the bathroom mirror. Sydney wasn't wrong. He looked like shit. The bags under his eyes were accentuated by his paler skin and dark hair. His lips had dried blood on them, his nose was swollen, and bruises were forming all over his face. His black eye was coming in nicely as well. He was also sporting a couple bruises along his chest. He snagged a shirt from his closet and slipped it over his head.

"I didn't sleep very well last night," he said on his way to the kitchen. He searched for some instant coffee and found nothing. "Can I get you something to drink? Water or…water?"

Sydney perched herself on the arm of the couch. "Water is fine."

He filled a glass for both of them and handed her one. "So what are you doing here?"

She stared into her glass. "I was going to call but then I realized I didn't have your number. I hope you don't mind me stopping by like this. Anyway, I wanted to talk to you about Kevin's journal and our next steps."

Merrick very carefully put down his glass. "I don't think we should look for it anymore."

Sydney nearly spilled her drink. "What?"

He'd been thinking about Kevin's journal a lot last night and either way Vander was going to get it. He explained as much to Sydney. "If we leave it hidden wherever it's hidden then the chances of him finding it lessen."

"But he's never going to stop. At least if we found it we could keep it safe."

"Keep it safe how?" he challenged. "He's a billionaire who could break into anywhere. There's nowhere safe to hide it."

"The Guild can protect it," she said stubbornly.

Merrick crossed his arms. "The Guild? Do you know how much work that would be? The manpower that would take? You'd be a constant target. Vander would never stop, especially once he found out the location. You can't Shield forever, Sydney. I saw you yesterday, you were exhausted and that was a single day. One day. Can you imagine doing that for weeks on end?"

"It might get easier the more I practice," she shot back.

Merrick wanted to roll his eyes. "Say that did happen, would you want to spend the rest of your life staying close to the journal? Because you seemed to have forgotten that all our powers seem to be based off of proximity."

"At least I'm willing to give it a shot here. You seem to have given up. If Vander ever found his Mirror Mate and bonded with her there's no telling what would happen with his powers. You've seen what he does in his spare time. You've experienced it and you don't want to stop that from happening? Vander uses people like us, Merrick, to gain money and power, and I can't believe you're willing to sit back and forget everything that ever happened."

Her fingers where white around his glass as she caught her breath.

"Look, I know things…" She stopped and tried again. "Last night…" She inhaled. "If you don't want to be a part of our guild then that's fine," she said quietly. "I don't blame you. But we could really use you in this one thing. Please. Then you never have to see any of us ever again."

Merrick took the glass of water from her hands and set it down on a nearby table. He gripped her hands and pulled Sydney to her feet. She was trembling. He wrapped an arm around her waist and pulled her closer. Her free hand rested against his chest. He wondered if she could feel his pounding heart.

"What if I don't want to never see you again?" he said.

Her breath hitched. He could smell the vanilla coming from her skin. He inhaled greedily, the scent ratcheting his blood higher.

She licked her lips nervously. "Merrick…"

"I'll help you," he said.

"You will?"

"I only want one thing in return."

"Sure. Of course. Anything."

He leaned down and brushed his lips against her ear. "I want you."

Sydney jumped from his arms like a startled rabbit. She smashed into the side of the couch.

"Why do you fight it?" Merrick sighed.

"Fight what?"

He gripped her in his arms again. A jolt went through his system. Sydney's eyes widened. "This," he said, refusing to break eye contact. "I know you feel it too, so don't lie to me. We're Mirror Mates." The color drained from her face and Merrick briefly wondered where this sudden recklessness was coming from. "You keep hiding behind Joel like you're afraid of what could happen between us."

At the mention of Joel some of her regular fire returned to her eyes. She shoved him back. "I'm not afraid. I've loved Joel for three years, all right? I-I can't..."

Silence fell.

Merrick's hands ached from how hard he was clenching them. He spun on his heel.

"Wait," Sydney called out.

He froze. His control was slipping. There was too much crushing down on him and his desire for Sydney wasn't helping. If she didn't want him then she needed to say it so that he could move on.

But we're Mirror Mates.

He'd never be able to move on.

He whirled back around and grasped her by the shoulders. "I don't care if you love Joel. You're mine."

His lips crushed against hers, his tongue forcing her lips apart to gain access to her mouth.

Chapter 18

Sydney could do nothing but cling to Merrick as his tongue slid deep into her mouth. A moan rose from her, her fingers digging into the flesh of his arms. His muscles were coiled tight beneath her hands and she shivered in anticipation at all the raw strength Merrick was holding back.

He wants you. He knows you're Mirror Mates and he wants you.

Desire rode her hard and she tore her lips away to suck in a lungful of air. Her whole body was on pins and needles, hyperaware of every brush of Merrick against her body. She craved his touch, wanted to feel him deep inside her.

She slid her hands up his chest and let her fingers tangle in his black locks. She wrenched his mouth back to hers for a hard kiss.

His answering groan set her blood on fire. Her sex pulsed in need and she shamelessly ground her hips against his growing erection.

His arms tightened around her almost painfully.

When his fingers skimmed the bare flesh beneath her shirt, she jumped. His fingers trailed up her stomach to her chest where they slipped beneath her bra to cup one of her tiny breasts.

"I know they're not much," she mumbled in apology.

Merrick pulled away to stare down at her. "What are you talking about?"

She avoided his gaze. "My boobs. I have the body of a prepubescent boy."

He grasped her chin and forced her eyes up to his. "As someone with experience in that field, you don't, Sydney. You're perfect. Everything about you is perfect."

He kissed her then. Slow and gentle. Warmth bloomed in her chest.

She reached for the hem of his shirt and pulled it over his head with some difficulty. She stared at his broad chest, her stomach flipping. "I've wanted to touch you like this since the first time I saw you shirtless," she confessed.

He smirked down at her. "Then what are you waiting for?" He drew her hand to his chest and slid it over his heart. "Touch me."

Sydney's mouth went dry.

Merrick laughed at her expression and scooped her up into his arms before depositing her on his bed. Sydney didn't even remember the journey from the living room to the bedroom.

Merrick crawled over her like a predator, his fingers skimming the waistband of her pants. His mouth settled over hers. Sydney opened for him eagerly, her tongue twining with his.

His hands worked her pants loose. Her heart jumped. He slipped the material down her legs.

"Are you wet for me?" he asked against her tingling lips.

He kissed her again before she could respond. Her mind reeled. She wrapped her arms around his neck and hung on as he painstakingly removed her panties. His fingers brushed against her and she shivered.

Merrick groaned when he found her ready for him. He slipped a finger deep inside her.

Sydney gasped. Her mind went blank. She rocked against his hand, eager for the pressure, the pleasure he could give her.

"Fuck," Merrick broke away from her mouth and tore her top from her body. He stared down at her with raw passion.

Her heart quivered. She tried to cover herself but he held her open and exposed. She could feel his gaze like an intimate caress.

"God, you're beautiful," he whispered. He stole a kiss before his mouth trailed down the side of her neck. His hands cupped and squeezed her breasts. When his mouth reached her chest he replaced one hand with his mouth, sucking an aching nipple between his lips.

Sydney moaned and then cried out when the fingers of his free hand found her between the legs once more. He slid two fingers inside and gently thrust, his thumb rubbing against her throbbing clit.

She was panting in seconds, her climax building. "Merrick." She arched against him.

"Not yet." He withdrew his fingers.

She protested but he silenced her with a fierce kiss.

"I want to feel you coming around me." He squeezed her breast to punctuate his sentence. Her hands instantly dropped to the waist of his pants.

He chuckled as she worked the button and zipper frantically. Her body was poised right on the edge and she couldn't take a minute more of it. She was an aching ball of need. She shoved his pants down to his thighs, freeing his erection. Her eyes widened. Her inner muscles clenched in anticipation.

He gently pushed her onto her back, covering her body with his. Her legs wound around his waist as if they'd done this countless times before.

His lips drank from hers lazily.

She could feel him poised at the center of her. He brushed a loose strand of hair away from her face, his eyes locked on hers.

The emotion she saw touched her down to her soul.

He slid into her.

She hissed in pleasure, unable to break eye contact as he filled her completely.

His Adam's apple bobbed, the tendons in his neck standing out as he held himself back.

He slowly rotated his hips, a low rumble coming from deep within his throat. "You feel like heaven," he growled.

Sydney laughed. She couldn't help herself. "You're only saying that because you haven't had sex in such a long time."

He pulled out and slowly thrust back in. He smirked down at her. "Maybe."

She gasped in outrage but it quickly turned to a moan as he started to move faster. His hips rocked hard against hers. Her eyes drifted shut and Merrick dropped his head to seal their lips together. She wound her hand tight in his hair and trailed the other down his back, marveling at the feel of his muscles contracting under her palm.

She arched her back to meet him thrust for thrust, pleasure streaking through every fiber of her being.

Her pleasure built. Merrick's grunt sounded in her ear. Her legs tightened around his waist.

She was so close.

So—

She cried out as her climax claimed her.

Merrick gripped her bottom and pulled her up to thrust deeper inside her. She yelled out at the pleasure of it. His body jerked, his cock jumping within her before he came. His lips latched onto her chest, just above her heart.

She clutched him to her as the aftershocks skittered along her skin.

Merrick rolled off of her a few seconds later.

They were both covered with a thin sheen of sweat. Without Merrick's warm body to cover her the chill air caused goose bumps to rise all along her skin. She shivered.

Merrick pulled the bed covers over her body as he settled in against her side.

Despite the early hour in which she'd gone to bed the night before, Sydney hadn't been able to sleep. Now, nestled in Merrick's arms, she drifted into a warm, content sleep, her chest lighter than it had been in months.

*

Sydney awoke to a firm pressure on her bladder. She blinked and searched for a clock. It was still early in the day. She'd only been asleep for three hours. Steady, warm breathing along the back of her neck signaled that Merrick was still sleeping behind her. His hand rested solid and heavy on her hip and she slowly eased out from under it to get to the bathroom.

After she finished relieving her bladder she stood for a long second in front of the mirror staring at the hickey just above her left breast. Right over her heart. She rubbed the mark absently as mixed emotions coursed through her.

She went back to the bed and stared down at Merrick's sleeping face. It was covered in black and blue bruises, but even with all his injuries he was the sexiest man she'd ever seen.

She'd never felt so connected to another human being. She never wanted to leave his side; she wanted to wake next to him every morning.

You have to break it off with Joel.

The idea might have frightened her before but all she felt now was a calm acceptance. Joel wasn't meant for her. She'd always love him, and she'd been lucky to have him for as long as she did, but now it was time to move on.

I can do this.

She picked up her discarded clothes and went into the living room to try Joel's cell phone again. Still no answer. She tucked her phone away and decided to search the kitchen for something to eat. While she was warming some soup her phone went off.

She answered it instantly, not bothering to check the caller. "Hello?"

"Hey, Syd." Felix's cheerful voice came through the other end. "I'm off work and wanted to know how you were doing and if you wanted to come over. Cali mentioned something about finding Collette's address."

"She found Collette's address? Where?"

"Not sure, she kept boasting about how she was the next computer genius. I hung up on her when she wouldn't shut up."

Sydney laughed at Felix's glee. No doubt Cali would be pissed about being cut off on the phone and he was sure to get hell when he got home, but Felix loved nothing more than to push Cali's buttons.

Sydney's eyes strayed to Merrick's bedroom.

"So are you going to meet us here?" Felix asked.

Sydney turned down the stove before the soup boiled over. "Sure. I'll be over within the hour."

"See you then."

She hung up and divided the soup into two separate bowls. She fished out some stale crackers from the back of the cupboard.

"Is that for us?"

Sydney screamed. She spun around and found Merrick leaning against the wall. Naked. Her eyes instantly dropped to his stirring erection.

She forced her eyes back to his face, moisture flooding her sex as an ache pulsed through her.

His erection continued to grow. The heat in Merrick's eyes seared her. She grabbed the bowl of soup and held it in front of her like a shield. "I made us soup," she said lamely. "I found crackers in the back of the pantry but they're a little stale." She turned to grab the box. When she turned around Merrick was right before her.

She stared at his chest, heart pounding, before she tilted her head back to look him in the face. The hunger in his eyes had nothing to do with food.

"F-Felix called and said Cali found where Collette lived."

Merrick took the soup from her hands and put it back on the counter. "Why are you dressed?" He started to undo her pants. She stood frozen as his hand slipped inside. His fingers brushed aside her panties before pushing into her aching sex.

Her world spun and she grabbed him to steady herself. His fingers found a rhythm that had her moaning helplessly. Her legs opened wider in surrender.

Merrick's cock strained against her, pulsing.

He worked another finger into her and her knees buckled.

"Merrick." Her voice was breathless. "Take me back to the bed."

His mouth teased hers. "What's wrong with the kitchen?"

She sucked his tongue, long and hard. "It's not appropriate," she said once her mouth was her own.

"Appropriate?" Merrick chuckled and ground the heel of his hand against her clit.

She cried out.

He hummed in the back of his throat. "I'm going to enjoy taking you out of your comfort zone," he promised darkly.

She shivered before her orgasm washed over her in heavy waves.

When the last of her aftershocks wore off Merrick withdrew his hand. "Dump the soup," he told her. "We'll go out for lunch."

She reached out before he could escape and grasped where he was obviously aching. Every muscle in his body went rigid. She could hardly breathe after that last climax but she managed a quiet, "Where you do you think you're going?"

She walked him up against the fridge, her hand pumping him. Merrick's eyes nearly rolled into the back of his head.

Power flooded her veins. It was downright intoxicating.

She grinned as she cupped his balls with the other and worked him. His muscles stood out against the skin of his body as he tensed. He came with a shout and his forehead dropped into the crook of her neck, his breath hot and hard against her chest.

She licked his ear. "Better?" she asked.

He raised his head, eyes glittering.

She jumped out of his reach before he could snatch her. "Felix is waiting for us," she yelled over her shoulder as she raced from Merrick. There wasn't much room to run, especially when she tried to keep clear of the bedroom. He caught her near the bookcase, his mouth hot and demanding. She kissed him back with equal force.

She didn't realize he'd picked her up off her feet until he put her back down. The floor helped ground her.

Merrick grinned when she stumbled. "Let's get some lunch and then we'll go find where Collette lives."

Chapter 19

"Ha!" Cali crooned triumphantly. "Who says we need Joel for all the computer hacking?" She turned her laptop around to show Sydney the address.

Sydney studied the map on the internet. "Are you sure?" She stared at the rundown area of Santa Ana.

Cali glared at her.

Sydney backed off. "I'm just making sure."

"Well, I'm almost positive this is where she used to live." Her chest puffed up proudly. Felix came up behind her and gently bopped her on the head with the newspaper. Cali whirled in her chair, obsidian eyes sparking. Felix met her challenging eyes with a confident smirk.

Sydney could feel the sexual tension between them and carefully looked away. Is that what everyone else felt when she and Merrick locked eyes?

No wonder everyone could see through your lies.

Both Cali and Felix had eyed them peculiarly when they'd walked in. Sydney still worried that they'd been able to tell that she'd had sex with Merrick.

"You sure you don't want us to come with you?" Felix broke his staring contest with Cali.

"We'll be fine." Merrick pushed off the counter where he was leaning in the kitchen, keeping his distance.

Felix looked to her. "Syd?"

Felix might have forgiven Merrick for last night but that didn't mean he'd forgotten. He wouldn't show open hostility but he didn't mind openly questioning Merrick's authority. He wanted to make sure she was okay with being alone with Merrick. After what had happened a few hours ago, she was more than comfortable being alone with Merrick, but she couldn't tell them that. Felix didn't trust Merrick because he didn't know him, but he trusted her.

"We'll be fine," she assured him.

That was all it took. Felix nodded. He handed her the address. "Let me know if you guys find anything."

She tucked the piece of paper into her pocket. "Of course."

By the time they reached Santa Ana it was well into the afternoon. The cloudy sky made it seem later than usual and Sydney hugged her jacket closer to her body as the wind kicked up. Merrick wound an arm around her shoulders. A jolt of pleasure raced through her.

They walked in silence for a few steps before she spoke. "Thank you."

"For what?"

"For not doing anything in front of Cali or Felix."

His body stiffened. He dropped his arm from around her. "Sure," he said curtly.

He started to walk faster. "Wait, Merrick." She pushed her legs to move faster. It didn't help. She broke out into a light jog. "I didn't mean anything by that." She'd upset him and she didn't know why.

"I know exactly what you meant, Sydney," he ground out. "I shouldn't have expected anything more, really. You wanted my help, I told you my terms, you met them, and here we are."

His words were like a slap to the face. "Excuse me?"

They had reached Collette's house. It was a rundown home with broken windows and dead grass. Sydney didn't even give it a spare glance. She raced after Merrick.

He was already inside when she caught up to him. "How dare you think I'm someone who exchanges sex for favors. Is that really all you see me as? A prostitute of some sort?"

Tears were creeping up her throat and she wanted to scream because of it. How could her life have turned so dramatically so quickly? They'd been fine five minutes ago.

*

Merrick saw the glistening of tears starting in Sydney's eyes and looked away. His hands curled into fists. He wanted to punch someone out, preferably himself. He'd been the one to make her cry.

He strategically avoided answering her question. He'd been an idiot to think that Sydney would want him over Joel. To think that she was different from all the other women he'd dated. She was ashamed to be with him, didn't want the others to know that she'd sullied herself by sleeping with him.

He ground his teeth and stormed deeper into the house. "Split up," he barked and left her in the entryway.

He'd been a fucking moron. And here he hadn't even needed to read her clothing to learn about her regret with being with him—her embarrassment. She'd outright told him.

At least she was honest.

Merrick grunted. It was his own fault, really. He was the one who'd wanted to fuck her so badly. Did he really think that she'd choose him for good?

But then why did she run to him first last night when he'd returned with the others from the hospital?

Women.

Now he remembered why he'd avoided them. They caused nothing but pain.

Fool.

He slammed his fist into the closest wall. Plaster cracked and a low groan went through the house. He shook out his hand to ease the stinging and continued into some large living area. Piles of old clothes and random belongings were in each corner. A worn duffel rested in front of the fireplace.

Merrick frowned and stepped deeper into the room. The scent of unwashed bodies lingered in the air and he knelt down next to a pile of clothing and picked up the top piece. He rubbed the fabric between his thumb and forefinger but got no impressions off of it.

"Sydney," he mumbled. She was using her powers.

He dropped the shirt and got to his feet. It didn't matter. He didn't need his powers to know that there were squatters in this house. The only thing he had to worry about was when they'd come back.

He listened carefully for Sydney and heard distant shuffling from another room. Satisfied that she was safe he moved upstairs.

He searched for any kind of master bedroom that might still hold something of Collette's. Or if he was lucky, something useful of Kevin's. When he found the master bedroom it was completely ransacked, so he moved on. He lucked out on the second guest bedroom.

An old dresser was propped up against the far wall. He strode toward it and pulled open drawer after drawer. Old rags littered the floor. It looked like whoever got this room didn't want to bother folding their clothes up to use the dresser. That was fine with Merrick—the fewer people to touch the dresser the more likely he was to find the impression he was looking for.

The last drawer held an old-fashioned brush, with soft bristles and a decorative backing. He snatched it up. A personal object was even better than the dresser.

"Drop your powers," he yelled down to Sydney.

There was an answering gasp. His shout must have startled her. A few seconds later his neck started to tingle. He gripped the handle on the brush, picking up on numerous hands. He closed his eyes and concentrated on Collette's face, searching for her through a sea of people.

He opened his eyes.

Nothing.

He eyed the brush. Maybe he'd been wrong and this was one of the squatters' personal objects. He put it back and ran his hands along the dresser. He flipped through all the people searching for money and found a faint imprint of two young men moving the dresser from the master bedroom. Grandsons. This was ttheir grandmother's dresser.

Merrick stepped back. This was not Collette's house.

A stifled cry from downstairs caught his attention.

"Sydney?" He raced for the room he thought she'd be in and came to an abrupt halt when he reached it.

Two homeless men were attacking her. One held her against him, his hand over her mouth as she kicked out at the other one who was trying to tie her feet together.

Merrick's vision turned red.

The men spotted Merrick and froze.

"I-I told you there was another one searching for our stash," the man holding Sydney said to his companion. "We should just kill them both and move on. They know where we live now, we're not safe."

"Shut the fuck up," the man at Sydney's feet said. While he was distracted she kicked out and nailed him in the jaw, snapping his mouth shut.

Merrick pounced. He grabbed the side of the man's skull and shoved it straight into the wall. His eyes rolled back and his body dropped.

Merrick turned around to the man holding Sydney. His face was sunken with malnutrition, emphasizing the dark circles under his eyes. He moved his hand down to her throat and squeezed. "Not another step." He started to retreat and slipped. He dragged Sydney down with him and Merrick lunged for her. The druggie screamed and tried to pull Sydney by her hair.

She cried out and clawed his hand. He dropped her and ran.

Merrick let him go. "Are you all right?" He dropped to Sydney's side and helped her up. She was covered with dirt and dust.

She was shaking but sat up on her own. "Fine."

Merrick helped her to her feet. "Let's go. This isn't Collette's house anyway."

She stared up at him, incredulous. "It's not?"

He shook his head. "I found an original piece of furniture in one of the upstairs rooms that belonged to an old woman who used to live here."

Sydney massaged the top of her head. "Looks like Cali wasn't as computer savvy as she thought."

Her hand moved to her neck and rubbed gently. It was an angry red and Merrick's rage returned full force as he yearned to go after the one he let get away. The back of his neck prickled.

But instead of going on the hunt he found his hands reaching out to carefully touch her neck. "Are you sure you're okay?" he asked softy. "No scratch marks? No broken skin anywhere?" The men had been filthy and there was no telling what they could have passed on. Probably a zombie virus.

Sydney gazed up at him with those guileless green eyes of hers. "I thought you were mad at me?"

He dropped his hands to her shoulders, not realizing his mistake until the fabric touched his skin.

He was instantly flooded with Sydney's thoughts and emotions. He saw himself through her eyes—glorious, sexy, her fierce Mirror Mate. Her heart had torn inside her chest as he'd walked away from her earlier. She wanted him by her side. She wanted his hands on her body. He made her feel whole. His smile set her blood racing. His touch set her heart pounding. His eyes touched her to her very soul—

Merrick stumbled back, chest heaving.

Too many emotions flooded him and he couldn't differentiate between what were his and what were Sydney's.

"Merrick?" Concern was etched into her face. She reached for him and he hastily stepped away.

Tenderness…anger…desire…it all rode him. He was on a rollercoaster and couldn't hit the brakes.

"Just give me a second," he told her, not wanting to upset her anymore.

"What happen—?" Understanding dawned and she retreated, her arms pulling in close to her chest. "You read me?"

Now it was his turn to reach out to her but he stopped halfway. "I didn't mean to."

"What did you see?"

Their eyes met.

He didn't answer.

She visibly shivered.

"Let's get you out of here," he said at last. He couldn't look at her for fear of what he'd see.

Had he been wrong about Sydney this entire time?

He didn't dare hope. He pushed aside everything except their need to leave before more homeless came back and mistook them for stash stealers. He'd been lucky that the last two who attacked Sydney hadn't been carrying.

He scanned the front yard before ushering Sydney ahead of him. She kept her distance. When they made it to her car he held out his hand to her. "Keys."

"I'm perfectly capable of driving," she protested.

"You were attacked, your nerves are shot. Let me drive."

She handed him her keys. "What good are powers when you're still helpless with them?" she asked fifteen minutes into their drive.

He watched her cross her arms over her chest and stare out the window through the corner of his eye. "You're not helpless," he told her. "I saw you struggle. You were outnumbered and you were still giving those guys a tough time."

Sydney harrumphed. "They were druggies who weighed less than me and I still couldn't throw them off."

"True," Merrick conceded and received a dark glare. "But you've also been using your powers for two days straight. Am I right?"

She fell into contemplative silence and Merrick continued to drive back to his place. "Why are we here?" Sydney asked when he let her into his apartment.

"Cali's information was useless," he said. "I'm going to put in some calls and e-mails to some of my contacts at the station and see if I can pull any strings to get the information we need."

"Good idea." She pulled out her phone and stepped into a secluded corner of his living room in an attempt at privacy. He tracked her every step, wishing he didn't care so much who she was going to call. "I have a few phone calls to make," she called over her shoulder.

He disappeared into his room so he wouldn't have to hear them.

*

Joel stared down at his phone as it went off for perhaps the sixth time that day. Sydney's picture and number popped up. His chest ached and he reached for his phone instinctively before he stopped himself.

He let the voicemail pick it up.

He'd acted like a royal pain in the ass last night and he was determined to make it up to her. Felix had always told him his over-protectiveness was going to bite him in the ass and now it finally had. But he couldn't help it. He usually wasn't so damn clingy, but with Syd's distant behavior over the last few months he was terrified that he was losing her.

Punching out one of the men he'd helped save from Vander probably hadn't helped either.

Technically he punched you out.

Joel tentatively touched his swollen nose. His two black eyes had attracted a lot of attention at work—so much so that his boss had called him over to make sure everything was okay. He'd even given Joel the rest of the day off.

Joel had been so tempted to find Sydney and spend his day off with her. But he still needed to cool off. He needed to think about his actions and compile an apology worth her forgiveness.

He pulled open his desk drawer and pulled out the black velvet box he'd picked up from the jewelry store after work. It was Sydney's three-year anniversary gift. He'd had it specially made for her. He imagined her bright green eyes sparkling when he showed it to her. It'd been so long since he'd seen her eyes light up like that.

No...

He remembered the look on her face when she'd brought the pizza from Tom's and how her face had lit up at the sight of Merrick—how her eyes had instantly sought him out over Joel.

He shoved her gift back into the drawer and slammed it shut, his heart pounding.

It wasn't possible—Merrick couldn't be...

Joel cut off his train of thought swiftly, denying everything he'd seen over the past week. No, the only reason Syd was pulling away from him was because he'd allowed the excitement to fade from their relationship. He wasn't interesting enough. She was showing attention to Merrick because he was someone new and interesting.

He swallowed his humiliation when he thought again of being knocked out by Merrick. His manhood had been wounded and Sydney had witnessed it.

His fingers flew over his keyboard. If he could get it back then he'd get Syd back. He had to show her that he was still that same capable, fun loving guy she'd fallen in love with three years ago.

He searched through the Kratos database looking for anything that could be useful in his mission. "Come on," he muttered. "Give me something good." He needed something that could dismantle the Kratos Corporation. Something big that would really win Syd over.

A file caught his eye and he double clicked on it. It was a companywide e-mail. A posting for a new job opening. In IT work.

Joel clasped his hands together and stared skyward. "Thank you."

This was just what he needed. He could apply for the job, hack into the computer so only the worst candidates that applied got through. That way he'd look like the golden goose. He could go undercover, gain all the ins and outs. He could have unlimited access to Kratos's computer work.

He rubbed his hands together in anticipation. If he got into their computer system then he'd be able to bypass any and all security. He could destroy them from the inside out. A complete systems meltdown could seriously hinder them.

Joel smiled gleefully as he got to work.

"Sydney is going to love me for this."

Chapter 20

Sydney finished her call to Felix and rubbed her aching temples. Her brain was throbbing inside her skull.

She could still hear Merrick on his home phone and moved into the kitchen in search of some kind of pain reliever. She found some aspirin in the cupboard and popped two pills. She washed them down with a glass of water. She set the glass in the sink before joining Merrick to see if he'd learned anything new.

She found him sitting in front of his computer, typing furiously. She wanted nothing more than to wrap her arms around his shoulders and lean into him. "Find anything?" she asked, stopping a good two feet away from him.

"Not yet. That was Steven on the phone, he told me to try e-mailing someone new in the department. Of course he was an asshole about the whole thing. Wouldn't give me the contact information until I told him what I was up to."

"What'd you tell him?"

"That I was on a new case. That just pissed him off more because I'd only been back a day and I was already getting new work."

His voice was laced with bitterness and her heart went out to him. Without meaning to she stepped closer and ran her hand through his hair in a comforting gesture. Merrick froze in his chair as her fingers trailed through his silky black hair. It was so soft. She'd never tire of the feel of it slipping through her fingers. "Steven is just jealous," she said at last. "They all are. You're ten times better than they are and they know it."

He turned slowly in his chair to stare up at her. She smiled, then winced as a deep throb went through her head.

"What is it?" He cupped her cheek.

"I wouldn't touch me if I were you," she said and realized her mistake as he pulled away, hurt. "No, that's not what I meant. I meant because I'm dirty." She stared down at herself. "I mean, look at me. And I'm fine, it's just a headache."

He eyed her for a few heartbeats before getting to his feet. "You're using your powers too much," he chided.

Another shot of pain went through her and she decided that maybe she was pushing herself a little too hard. She dropped her Shield. "Maybe I'll lie down for a little bit." She took a step and stumbled.

Merrick's warm, strong arms wrapped around her, pulling her back flush against his chest. Her stomach hiccupped. His breath brushed against her ear. "You're not going to lie down on my bed covered in God knows what. Come on, Syd, let's get you cleaned up."

She smiled as he maneuvered her into his bathroom.

He deposited her on the toilet where she watched him turn on the shower, still smiling.

"What?" he asked.

"You called me Syd," she said brightly.

"Yeah, so?"

"So," she used the wall to help her get to her feet, "only my friends call me Syd." Which meant that he didn't hate her.

He arched one ebony brow. "Cali doesn't call you Syd."

"Cali doesn't count; it sounds weird when she tries to call me Syd. But you…" She stepped closer. "You called me Syd, which means you think of me as a friend." She grinned.

The bathroom was starting to fill with fog from the heat of the shower.

Something glittered in Merrick's eyes and Sydney felt an answering clench between her legs. He stepped closer to her and leaned down. "Believe me," he whispered against her damp lips. "I think of you as more than just a friend."

She swallowed thickly.

But then he straightened, without even kissing her. What the heck?

"Now come on," he said. "Let's get you washed up." He reached for the hem of her shirt and started to pull it up.

She stepped back and knocked his hand away. "I'm perfectly capable of undressing myself, thank you."

"Oh, perfectly," he agreed. "But I'm not going anywhere. If you pass out and bash your head on something in *my* bathroom than that's a liability to me. You're not dying on my watch."

She fisted her hands on her hips. "So you're only in here to protect your assets? Not because you want to see me naked?"

"Exactly," he said easily and pulled her top over her head before she could protest.

She gasped.

Merrick's eyes roved over her greedily.

She wrapped her arms around herself self-consciously.

"It's nothing I haven't seen, or touched, or licked, or sucked—" he growled the last word, "—before, Syd."

Heat scalded her cheeks. "I don't care. I'm not going to stand here naked while you're fully dressed, happy as could be."

The ice blue of his eyes sparked. "I'm far from happy as can be," he rumbled.

She avoided her eyes from the bulge in his pants.

"And as for being dressed while you're naked…fine." He pulled his shirt over his head. "I wouldn't want you to feel uncomfortable."

Sydney stared, heart pounding. If she thought she was uncomfortable before, that was nothing compared to now. "P-put your shirt back on," she squeaked.

The steam in the bathroom was becoming oppressive. It added to her discomfort, made her skin damp and sticky.

"Why?" Merrick's hands dropped to the front of his pants.

She stared avidly as he popped the top button. Her heart skipped a beat and she shook herself mentally. "I don't need a chaperone to shower. Besides," she tried her best to cast a disgusted look at his groin, "the shower is not the place for sex."

Both Merrick's brows rose before a slow, feral smile broke out over his face. "Are you telling me Miss Prim and Proper hasn't gotten down and dirty in the shower before?"

"What did you call me?" she asked, affronted.

Suddenly Merrick was right in front of her. She stared at all that hard muscle like a possum caught in the headlights of a car.

Merrick chuckled and she felt his fingers under her chin, lifting her gaze up. "I'm up here. And I called you Miss Prim and Proper. Care to prove me wrong?"

Desire slithered through her whole body. She lifted her chin further—stubbornly. "I don't care what you call me," she lied. "I don't need an escort to shower. Now get out."

He stepped back and she shivered as he took all that heat with him. Even in a room full of steam he radiated more warmth than was in the air.

"I'll leave."

She sighed in relief.

"*If…*"

Her body stiffened.

"…you can take your pants off without losing your balance or using anything for support."

"That's like a trick question," she protested instantly. "There's no way to do it without losing my balance."

"Are you saying it can't be done?"

"That's exactly what I'm saying."

He pulled the zipper down on his jeans and smoothly pulled them down his legs, first lifting one leg out, then the other. All without losing his balance.

Sydney couldn't breathe.

He wore no underwear under those pants. He stood gloriously naked before her and she couldn't help but ogle his muscled frame—his long, wide cock. It seemed to pulse before her eyes and moisture flooded her sex. She wanted him buried deep inside her.

A faint rumble went through the air and it took her a second to realize that it came from Merrick. "If you keep staring at me like that I'm not going to be responsible for my actions." His voice was gruff with arousal.

She dropped her eyes to his pants on the floor, remembering his challenge. "You cheated," she blurted. With all that naked flesh before her she couldn't recall if he'd lost his balance or not.

He crossed his arms over his chest. "You know I didn't. Now drop your pants without falling over or I'm staying right here."

Sydney wrinkled her nose in distaste. "Fine."

The aspirin must have started kicking in because the throbbing in her head had been reduced to a dull ache. She hoped it was enough.

She unfastened her pants and slid them down her legs. When they got around her ankles she inhaled and lifted her leg, determined not to reach out for something to steady her.

One leg through…

She lifted the other and her world tilted. The tile floor rose up to meet her, then suddenly she was encased in warm heat. Flesh.

Merrick.

She blinked.

She was in his arms, bridal style.

His ice blue eyes were sparkling with amusement but underneath she could see the worry. "Looks like I'm staying right here," he said to her.

He placed her back on her feet but kept an arm around her waist. He removed her bra but when his fingers tugged at her panties she pushed him away. "I can do it." Her voice came out shaky. Her whole body was on fire and she tried not to notice the weight of Merrick's gaze as he stared at her naked body. Her breasts plumped and ached. A deep throb started between her legs.

She hastily stepped toward the shower.

Merrick's hand tightened around her waist, sending her heart racing. "Easy," he said. "It's going to be slippery in there and you're not very steady on your feet."

To her horror he stepped into the shower with her. It was a combination bath and shower and he'd had to help her step over the lip of the tub. Once they were inside he pulled the curtain shut to keep the water in.

His erection pressed against her hip—hot and hard. "This is totally unnecessary," she told him.

The steam was clogging her lungs, making it difficult to breathe.

It's not the steam that's making it hard to breathe, her inner voice said, *it's the masculine body pressed against yours.*

She cleared her throat. "Look, why don't you shower at your end and I'll shower over here in my end."

"Fine."

She didn't bother turning around to see his face. She didn't want to see his hair wet and glistening. She didn't want to see all that water sluicing down his body—caressing his skin like she wanted to.

"But I'm keeping my hand right here." His hot palm rested against her hip. She wanted to protest but decided not to push her luck. He was giving her as much space as possible in this dinky shower.

"Fine," she muttered back and reached for the shampoo.

She'd never been so aware of a man before in her life. As she washed her hair she could feel him behind her. The hand on her hip burned like a brand and every once in a while she caught a glimpse of naked flesh out of the corner of her eye.

When she was done scrubbing her scalp she paused. She needed to get under the shower head to rinse her hair.

She made the mistake of turning around to face Merrick and found him rinsing out his own hair—his head thrown back under the spray of water, eyes closed. The water rushed down his sculpted body. He might've been held in captivity for four months but he still looked great. She couldn't imagine how incredibly hot he'd be once he gained all his muscle back. He'd look like a Greek god.

Her eyes stared transfixed as a stream of water ran down his chest, down his abdomen, continuing south. She wanted to follow the trail with her tongue.

The fingers on her hip tightened and she jerked her gaze up to see Merrick watching her.

She had to swallow twice before she could speak. "I need to rinse." She pointed lamely to her soapy head.

Without a word he stepped out from under the water. They circled each other until she was under the spray and she closed her eyes and ducked her head under, pretending not to feel his heated gaze on every sensitive part of her body. Her nipples hardened and her legs shook beneath her.

Sydney went as fast as humanly possible. Merrick was still staring at her when she was finished, his eyes blue fire. She started to tremble and moved out from under the water, trying to get back to the conditioner—when her foot slid along the bottom of the tub.

Merrick caught her easily and she found herself pressed against all that wet muscle. The scent of his body teased her and she tried to pull away. "I'm fine." She looked anywhere but at his body.

He refused to release her. His hand brushed back a strand of her wet hair. "You look flustered," he commented calmly.

Irate, she glared up at him. "Well, I wouldn't be so dang flustered if you'd let me shower on my own."

He smiled as if she hadn't spoken a word. He ran his fingers through her hair again. "You're cute when you're flustered."

She blanched. "What?"

He lowered his head and pressed his damp lips against hers, softly at first, then slowly with more intensity.

Everything she'd been holding back came flooding out. She gripped his hair and ground her mouth against his fiercely. Electricity flashed through her whole body and she pressed herself closer to Merrick, wanting to feel all that wet skin against her own.

Merrick growled low in his throat and wrapped his arms firmly around her. His tongue slid between her lips and she met him halfway. Her head spun from the taste of him. He tasted just like he smelled—masculine. It made her heart pound and her sex throb.

She kissed him harder, stroking her tongue against his.

Hot water pounded against her back as Merrick walked her to the shower wall. His wet hands dropped from around her waist. He cupped her bottom, squeezed, and continued to let his hands explore.

She was shivery and achy from need. His hands caressed her sides before cupping her breasts. She sighed against his mouth, her own hands slipping and sliding along his back. She traced every ridge and muscle and squeezed his butt before dragging her hands to his chest. She tried to mirror his moves as best she could so that he could feel what it was like to be driven insane. The only problem was that he didn't have breasts. But she still grazed her fingernails around his nipples.

They hardened under her fingers.

She grinned. Merrick nipped at her lip playfully. She nipped back. He nipped harder. So did she.

Merrick growled, the sound resonating through her. It empowered her and she dropped her hands, trailing them over his abs, then lower still until she took him into her hands.

His body jerked.

Sydney fell back, the cold tile against her heated flesh making her yelp.

He tore his mouth from hers and breathed raggedly into her ear. "Spread your legs."

She tightened her hold on his throbbing shaft to let him know who was in charge.

He groaned and dropped his head to start licking the water from her collarbone. His fingers danced along her hip, her thigh, before settling at her very center. Lost to desire, she parted her legs for him.

He took one of her nipples into his mouth as he pushed a finger deep inside her. Her arm shot out to grip the shower wall. It was cold on her palm.

As Merrick suckled her breast she was hit with a wicked idea.

The hand around his cock pumped him once before dropping away. She replaced it with the one she'd had against the cold tile.

"Fuck!" Merrick bucked as her freezing hand wrapped around him.

She laughed. "Does that feel good?" she asked impishly.

His fingers slipped out of her. "I don't know," he said. "Why don't you tell me?"

Two cold fingers thrust between her legs and Sydney cried out at the shock of that cold going deep inside her. She hadn't realized that Merrick had been holding himself against the shower wall with one hand. His skin was well and truly frigid and she moaned from the sharp contrasting temperatures.

"You like that?" Merrick's gaze was wild, feral, as he watched her ground down on his hand.

Sydney bit down on her lip as she felt her orgasm building. She nodded.

His thumb pressed against her clit. Her breath hitched, her inner muscles clenching. She lost her hold on his cock and gripped his shoulder to keep herself from falling. "Merrick..."

His fingers thrust faster, his thumb rubbing her clit insistently. "Come on, Sydney," he goaded her.

She came apart with a scream.

Hands gripped her roughly under her bottom. Her feet left

the floor. Water pounded on top of her from overhead before her back met another cold tile wall. She gasped, her legs locking around Merrick's waist. He sheathed himself inside her with one easy stroke.

They both groaned.

Sydney dug her fingers into his shoulders as her body was bombarded with sensation. The cold tile against her back, Merrick's hot, throbbing cock within her.

He started to thrust and she felt him all the way to her soul. He was so hard. She whimpered as the aftershocks of her climax faded in place of another orgasm building.

Wet hair dripped into her face and she blew at it uselessly.

Merrick raised his head from where it rested in the crook of her neck. Their gazes tangled and her soul quivered. Raw emotion stared back at her.

She had no idea what he saw in her eyes but suddenly he started to thrust faster, harder, his grunts punctuated by her moans. He held her gaze as he pounded into her. It was the most intimate feeling she'd ever experienced. Pleasure skittered along the edges of her consciousness. Her climax was so close. She arched her back, drawing Merrick deeper into her body.

His black hair was plastered around his face and she wiped it away, exposing his defined jaw and cheekbones.

She loved his face. She loved his body. She loved what he did to her and what he made her feel.

She loved *him*.

The realization tipped her over the edge and she came hard around him.

He kissed her, hard and demanding, as he continued to thrust into her, seeking his own release.

She clutched her legs tight around his waist. He groaned into her mouth as his body jerked against hers, coming.

Chapter 21

"Sir."

Vander turned from the monitors in front of him.

David was typing furiously on his keyboard.

"What is it?" Vander asked.

David double clicked on a window. "There was a security detection but all that's popping up is a work resume applying for the recent IT position."

Vander frowned.

David brought up the screen on his own monitors.

Vander scanned the resume. "Were there any other applicants with this one?"

"No, sir. In fact, everything else that's been coming in has been less than qualified."

Vander's eyes narrowed. "Can you trace this back to the one who submitted it?"

David cracked his fingers. "Of course, sir."

Vander smirked. David had been a resent investment that was turning out to be worth the cost. Ever since Cali's little group had broken into his database he'd been increasing his security both physically and electronically. The only problem was that there weren't enough Davids to go around.

A few minutes later David uttered another sound of frustration. The noise grated on Vander's nerves. "What?" he barked at the young initiate.

David jumped in his seat. "Nothing, sir, only…whoever this person is, their own personal security rivals my own work."

Vander's interest spiked. "Is that so?"

He shut the monitors off in front of him. He was learning nothing new by watching his recent captives. There were no displays of powers and he was getting agitated.

He was no closer to finding a new Dreamer than he was to finding the one to heal Kevin. And that bastard, Haskell, wasn't making any new discoveries on the whereabouts of Kevin's journal.

He had one more lead concerning Kevin's recovery but that would take some time yet. The time to act wasn't upon him.

"Well?" he asked when David remained silent, his fingers flying over his keys.

David chewed his lip in concentration. The screens froze momentarily. David continued to type.

"What's happening?" Vander demanded.

A new file popped up before the screens flashed blue then shut down.

"Aha!" David leaned back, his hands in the air.

Vander grabbed him around the collar and wrenched him halfway out of his chair. "What happened? If you compromised my security in any way…I will kill you."

David's brown eyes widened. "No, sir. I'd never compromise the system. You see, I allowed a temporary shut down so that whoever was on the other side would think I didn't get what I was looking for."

Vander tightened his hold. "And what did you get?"

David swallowed. He pointed to the screen that was rebooting. "That document. It's the resume, a real one. The one sent in I traced back and found that there was an original copy on the person's server, which meant that this was a decoy of sorts. I was able to copy the original resume onto our hard drive." David fell back into his chair with an *oomph* as Vander released him.

"Bring it up on the screen," Vander snarled. Now he was going to see who was trying to screw with him.

It took David a few seconds before he brought up what Vander desired. It looked like the exact same document—only the name was different, as were the names of the schools he'd attended.

Vander leaned in closer to the monitor.

Joel Kegler.

The name tickled something in the back of his mind.

"Run that name through our database. I want to know why it sounds familiar."

David's fingers were already moving. "Right here, sir." He brought up a window with everything on Joel Kegler they had.

"Well, well," Vander drawled. "Look who doesn't know how to stay away." Cali's guild was getting most annoying. Joel had also been the one to break into his facility in San Francisco. He was an impressive hacker and a valued member of Cali's group. Surely he'd be missed…

"Send him a request to meet for the position," he ordered David.

"Sir?" David stared at him, incredulous. "You're not thinking of giving him a job, are you?"

"Do as I say," Vander repeated.

David got to work. Vander left him to make a phone call.

"Jente," he said when the young man picked up the phone. "I need you to pick someone up for me."

*

Sydney's phone went off in the bathroom, the sound echoing through the small room and out into the bedroom. She stirred.

The ringing stopped then started again.

She groaned. There was only one person who'd call over and over again. And if Sydney didn't answer she'd only keep on calling. She moved to get out of Merrick's bed.

His arm slid around her and pulled her flush against his body. He was already hard.

"Let it ring," he mumbled sleepily.

She turned over and faced him. His hair was unkempt and he looked so adorable. She cupped his cheek, loving this feeling of waking up next to him. "Trust me, if I don't answer it now it'll never stop."

As if on cue the phone briefly paused in its ringing before starting up again.

Merrick sighed and flung himself onto his back.

Sydney kissed him gently on the cheek and rolled out of bed. "Yes, Cali?" she answered.

"Finally! What the hell? Felix has been wanting to talk to you all morning. He left a voicemail like two hours ago so I decided to call for him."

"How thoughtful," she said dryly as she rubbed the sleep from her eyes. "I was sleeping." She briefly glanced down on her phone to find that it was well into the day. She remembered last night and how Merrick had ordered in for them. They'd spent the rest of the night in bed, sating their newfound lust over and over again until they knew each other's bodies like the backs of their hands.

She grew warm just thinking about it.

"Syd?" Felix's voice came on over the line.

She instantly shoved those thoughts out of her head. "Hey, Felix. What's up?"

"What happened last night? You called and told me that you found nothing because Cali gave you the wrong information." There was a protest from Cali in the background. "You said Merrick was going to check his PI contacts. Have you heard anything?"

She stepped out of the bathroom and found Merrick on his computer, still naked.

He sure does like to walk around in the nude.

Not that she minded. After all, she was nude too.

She walked up to him and rested her hand on his shoulder. "Have you heard back from anyone?" she asked Merrick.

He was checking his e-mail. "Nothing yet."

She relayed her find to Felix who was uncharacteristically quiet on the other line. "Felix?"

"Are you at Merrick's?" he asked neutrally.

"Yeah, why?"

Again silence. "Cali said that you'd just woken up."

"I did—" Sydney clamped her mouth shut. Horror flooded her. "I-I mean I had just woken up when Cali called but I was already on my way to Merrick's." She winced at her own lame excuse.

"Uh-huh," Felix said, unconvinced.

"No, really—" she tried again.

"Sydney," Felix broke in easily. The use of her full name from him had her shutting up instantly. "You don't have to lie to me," he said gently. "You're one of my best friends. You can tell me anything."

The words took her back, years ago, to Felix's parents' backyard, where he'd first shown her his powers. He'd been so scared to lose her, but she'd stuck by him. She'd told him that he could tell her anything.

She exhaled and walked out of Merrick's bedroom. "I know, and I will tell you everything, Felix. I promise. Just not yet."

"Okay," he said. "I trust you. But Syd?"

"Yeah?"

"Be careful."

"I will."

"I mean be careful with what you're doing now as well as being careful about Kevin's journal."

"I know and I will. The last thing I want to do is hurt anyone, Felix."

He sighed. "I know, and whatever happens I'm always here for you, okay?"

She smiled. "Okay."

"All right, I've kept you on the phone long enough. Get back to whatever you were doing but keep me updated."

"I'll let you know as soon as we find anything," she promised.

"Everything okay?" Merrick asked when she walked back into his bedroom.

She brushed her hair from her face and dropped her phone on his dresser. "Everything's fine."

He turned off his monitor and got to his feet. "So I take it Felix knows about us?"

She frowned at his tone of voice. "Yeah," she said slowly.

"And you're okay with that now when you didn't want him to know yesterday? You're not ashamed of me anymore?"

Understanding dawned and she stepped closer to him. "Merrick, I was never ashamed of you."

He was starting to close her out; she could see it in his demeanor.

"The reason I didn't want anyone to know yesterday was… well, because I was scared. My guild is my family and I don't want to lose them. I was so afraid of what they might think…"

"So you're not afraid anymore?"

"No, I'm still terrified, but I have to make my own decisions— including about who I want to be with."

"And who's that?"

She fisted her hands on her hips. "It's you."

His eyes sparked but he remained aloof. "What about Joel? He's all you know, you've loved him for the past three years."

He'd thrown some of her own words back at her, but she refused to back down. "He *was* all I knew. But I know you now. And did love him for the past three years—I still love him, but it's not the same type of love. It's time for me to move on. I've been trying to get a hold of him since two nights ago to break things off. He hasn't been answering my calls."

Again there was something in his eyes, as if he wanted to believe what she was saying but couldn't quite do it. "You're going to break up with him?" he asked carefully.

She stepped closer to him until they were nearly touching. She rested her hand over his heart. It pounded beneath her palm.

"I am breaking up with him. I'm choosing you, Merrick. I want you."

I love you. It was on the tip of her tongue but she couldn't say it.

Merrick's grin lit up his whole face. He scooped her into his arms and together they fell onto his bed. He slid into her like he was coming home and Sydney moaned as he thrust, slow and steady, as if they had all the time in the world.

And she guessed they did. They had the rest of their lives together.

*

Joel pulled out his phone, half expecting to see Sydney's picture and number. But it wasn't her. She hadn't called all day. He swallowed his disappointment and tried to place the area code.

With a jolt he realized that it was the Kratos Corporation.

"Holy shit," he muttered and hurried into a deserted part of his work building. "Hello?"

"Mr. Johnson? Samuel Johnson?" A male voice answered.

"Yes?" Joel kept his eye on a nearby clock. He wouldn't stay on the phone longer than necessary in case they were tracking it. Just yesterday someone in Kratos had tried to hack into his own computer. He needed to be wary.

"This is the Kratos Corporation calling because of your impressive resume. We'd like to set up an interview if you are still available?"

Could it be a set-up? Or had the attack on his computer system been because he'd been snooping around too much yesterday?

He took the gamble.

"I'm still available."

"Excellent. Unfortunately, we no longer have a building in the Southern California area and apologize for our lack of professionalism. Would a meeting over coffee work for you?"

A few minutes later Joel hung up with the time and place for his meeting. It was at a local café—somewhere public, which meant that this had to be a real interview.

Are you sure? Don't forget that Cali was lured in with a false interview months ago when Vander wanted her.

True.

He eyed his contact list, his finger hovering over Felix's number. He could call in backup.

An image of himself flying off his feet as Merrick punched him stole through his mind.

He tucked his phone away. He could do this. He didn't need backup. He'd prove that he could take on Kratos by himself.

He gingerly touched his nose and eyes. His face was still multicolored, he'd need to pick up some cosmetics to cover the worst of his bruising.

He talked to his boss and requested another half-day. Reluctantly his boss agreed. It probably had something to do with the fact that Joel was supposed to be on vacation but had come in when they'd been understaffed. The wonders of guilt.

His meeting wasn't for a few hours, so he spent that time getting ready. He applied face makeup to cover his injuries. He bought colored contacts and slipped them into his eyes. As far as disguises went it wasn't amazing. He decided to go with little changes—like Clark Kent. All he needed was a pair of glasses.

Joel slicked his hair back and added some white spray dye to his temples to give the illusion of aging.

He eyed himself in the mirror.

"Not bad." He pulled at his suit jacket. His eyes were itching like a motherfucker but he pushed through the pain. Grabbing his keys he headed out to start phase one of his win-Syd-back plan.

*

"I got something," Merrick called to Sydney. She was busy brushing her teeth. In his bathroom.

The image of her in his apartment—using his things like she belonged there, like they lived together—was enough to make him hard all over again.

She was his.

The urge to take her again rose up from deep within but he fought it back. No matter how bad he wanted to feel her inner muscles clenching around him, he'd promised to find Kevin's journal.

They'd agreed to find it and then burn it. There was no point in keeping it if there was any chance of it falling into Vander's hands.

Merrick had told Sydney about Vander's offer to help find his sister. She'd sympathized and promised that after they got rid of Kevin's journal that she'd talk to Niella. There were no guarantees with Niella, but it was better than nothing. No matter how tempting Vander's offer, he was not to be trusted. Merrick had to continually tell himself that Vander would never help him find Alyssa, even if he did work for him. Vander would never overlook the fact that Merrick had once been playing for the "good" team. He'd had his chance to accept Vander back when he was a captive in that room in San Francisco. He made his choice long ago and he was going to have to live with it.

Arms wrapped around his shoulders from behind. The scent of vanilla teased him. He groaned low in his throat as Sydney pressed a kiss to his cheek. He turned his head to capture her mouth with his, stroking his tongue deep into her mouth. She tasted like mint.

Her eyes were heated and glazed when he finished kissing her. His cock throbbed, demanding he take relief inside her sweet body. Demanding he make her moan and writhe beneath him.

Merrick clenched his jaw.

"What'd you find?" she asked.

He focused all his attention back on his computer and pulled up the e-mail from the station. "They looked up Collette Lizeroux's information for me and forwarded all the files. It looks like she lived in Garden Grove. The house hasn't been foreclosed or resold yet."

"How much you want to bet that's Vander's doing?" Sydney leaned closer to read the address, and Merrick noticed she was wearing one of his old t-shirts. The sight of her in his clothes made his body burn. Her clothes were still dirty from being dragged across the floor of that abandoned house yesterday.

He ran his hand lazily up the back of her thigh, lifting the hem of his shirt to find her bare beneath it.

Sydney jumped at the touch and straightened. The shirt fell back down to her mid-thigh but that still didn't erase the image of her naked flesh from his mind. His groin tightened painfully.

"Hey, none of that." She waggled her finger in front of him. "We've got work to do." She made her way back to the bathroom. No doubt to dress.

He caught her before she made it five steps.

"Merrick." Her voice was shaky—excited. She'd tried for exacerbation and failed miserably.

"Tell me you don't want it." He reached down and felt how wet she was.

Her body trembled.

He walked her to the wall and pressed her chest against it. He dropped his jeans, freeing his aching shaft. He gripped her hips and lifted her until she was on her tiptoes. She was panting and when he pushed into her she dropped her head in surrender.

Her body squeezed around him and he bit back his roar of pleasure. She was so tight—so hot. He pulled out to the tip and thrust back in. Sydney whimpered.

Merrick rode her hard and fast, demanding a climax out of her until she was shaking and exhausted.

He'd never tire of her. Every time he took her it only made him want her again, made him want her more. He'd never been so addicted to a woman—her touch, her scent, her flavor.

He felt himself hardening again.

Sydney gasped as she no doubt felt him growing inside her. "You can't seriously—"

He took her against the wall again, until the scent of vanilla could be smelled on his skin.

After they had finished he watched her dress on shaky legs, her whole body flushed a becoming pink. He loved taking her out of her comfort zone. He doubted she'd ever had sex anywhere other than on a bed. It made him grin to know that he was the first to take her in a shower and up against a wall. The first to make her peak in a kitchen.

"Do you need to call Felix to let him know what's going on?"

She had her shirt held up to her face, nose wrinkled. "I figure I'll call him when we actually find something. Do you have a washing machine here?"

They decided to stop by Sydney's house to get her fresh clothes.

Merrick took the opportunity to snoop. Sydney's home, like its owner, was as immaculate as ever. It looked like one big IKEA advertisement. Sydney's room was painted bright yellow. He felt like he was standing in the center of the sun.

"How can you see in here?" He pretended to shield his eyes.

"Ha ha." Sydney dug around in her closet. "You'd better get used to it because when we live together I'm not giving up my home for an apartment. No offense. You're too far from the clinic too."

Merrick froze where he was looking at the pictures on her dresser. "Did you say live together?"

She turned from the closet, a bundle of clothes in her arms. Color dotted her cheeks. "I mean—"

Merrick strode toward her and kissed her hard on the lips. "I'd endure a million yellow rooms if it meant being with you."

The grin she gave him made her look like a teenager.

Merrick's heart seized in his chest. How had she wheedled her way into his life so completely?

She disappeared into the bathroom to wash off and change. A box on the top shelf of her closet caught his attention and he pulled it down.

The lid popped open easily. Inside there was a worn baseball cap, a signed baseball, an old blue T-shirt, and pictures. On top of the shirt a photo smiled up at him. Merrick picked it up carefully. Sydney was easily recognizable by the bright smile on her face. It was at a baseball game. She looked to be around nine years old, her arm slung protectively around the boy next to her. He wore a bright blue shirt and a baseball cap to hide the fact that he had no hair. Even though he was smiling, Merrick could make out the fatigued lines in his young face.

It was Sydney's brother.

He thought of the shrine of things he had of Alyssa's hidden away in his own closet. Then he felt like a real asshole because he'd gone looking through Sydney's personal belongings. If she'd found Alyssa's box without his consent he didn't know how he'd feel about that. Definitely not warm and fuzzy.

He returned the box to the shelf just as it was. Maybe in time they'd both be able to bring out their boxes and share with each other the horror of losing the siblings they were supposed to protect.

"You ready?" Sydney poked her head through the door. Her blonde hair was damp and fell around her face in soft waves.

"Let's go."

Chapter 22

"Now this is more like it," Sydney said as she gazed out the window.

Merrick pulled in front of a large mansion of a house. It was in a posh part of town, complete with expensive SUVs and stay at home wives that walked their little dogs.

Merrick threw Sydney's car into park and stared at the house through the windshield. He scanned the neighborhood. There weren't too many people out and about, but there were enough. The cloudy weather from yesterday was gone, leaving them with nothing but bright sunshine. It made them easy targets to spot.

"We'll need to go around back to sneak in." He searched the streets for any kind of pool service van. If they could borrow a few things from the company to disguise themselves as they slipped into Collette's backyard it would make this a whole lot easier. The last thing Merrick needed was the cops to find him breaking and entering into a house whose address he'd gotten from them.

There were no pool service vehicles. Only a dark blue SUV and a motorcycle were parked on the curb. Everything else was safely tucked away into the driveways or five car garages.

"Maybe Collette hid a key somewhere by the front door." Sydney pointed to the various potted plants that led up to the front of the house.

"I can't check all of them, that'll look suspicious."

"I don't think so. I mean, look how we're dressed and look what we're driving. We're not exactly thug material here."

Merrick thought it over.

"Besides, we're going to have a better chance of finding a key in the front then we are the back."

"Fine." He got out of the car. "We need to do this fast."

"Start with the welcome mat," Sydney called when she couldn't keep up with his longer stride. "We'll pretend to be relatives if anyone comes up and asks."

He stopped and turned, giving her a chance to catch up. "You look nothing like Collette."

"No," she conceded, "but you do. You both have dark hair and Collette had blue/gray eyes. You have blue so it's close enough. We'll tell them you're a cousin or something."

Merrick shook his head and kept walking, checking his speed so as not to leave her behind.

Her fingers laced through his, startling him. "Thank you." She eyed his legs pointedly.

He squeezed her hand. "You're welcome."

They made it to the front door hand in hand and pretended to ring the doorbell like visiting relatives.

"Now what?" Sydney whispered as they stood there.

He held his hand up to the door. "Now you drop your Shield."

His neck prickled as soon as she did and he touched the hard wood. He pulled back a few seconds later. "We'll get nothing there," he said aloud for Sydney's sake. "Too many impressions of door-to-door salesmen."

She stepped off the welcome mat. He did the same and crouched down to pick it up. As soon as his fingers touched it he saw Regina.

She knelt down and tucked a spare key under the mat. "Lead us to the treasure, baby." She blew a kiss, Merrick's naked body as she bathed him fresh in her mind.

"—ell?"

Merrick shot up.

Sydney eyed him funnily. "Well? Nothing down there?"

Merrick toed the mat aside for Sydney to get a good look at the key.

Her face lit up and she went to pick it up. He pulled her back against one of the walls by the door. "What are you doing?" she hissed.

"We're being watched," he hissed back.

Her body froze.

"Regina put that key there for me to find, which means they're waiting for me."

"What should we do?"

"Fuck if I know. Vander must've realized that I wasn't going to give him the journal. We should just leave."

"Wait." She stopped him from moving. "The journal might not be here. If we find a clue as to where it is then we can lose Regina and whoever else is watching us. If they left the key then that must mean Vander already searched the place and came up empty handed. He needed you to search because he found nothing out in the open."

"If he didn't find anything here then he has no idea where it is. Wouldn't it just be safer to leave the journal wherever it is? We don't need it for anything."

"That's not necessarily true. We have no idea what Kevin wrote down. There could be a whole list of people with powers in it. We could help them. There might be more things about Vander in it—things that could help us stop him."

"You really think Vander's own worker would write how to stop Vander in his journal?"

"Anything is possible. Felix has this theory that Kevin led Vander astray to Cali—one, because he wanted some kind of revenge on Felix and two, because whatever he saw in the future when Vander became full-forced—it wasn't pretty."

Merrick let out a weary breath. He picked up the key and quickly opened the front door. Sydney slid in first. Merrick kept an eye on the neighborhood before following after her. He shut the door and locked it.

"Wow."

He turned around and stopped. "Holy fuck." Hanging from the ceiling was the biggest crystal chandelier Merrick had ever seen. It probably cost more than Sydney's car.

"I think I might reconsider working for Vander." He crept deeper into the house, eyes still on the chandelier.

"That's not funny," Sydney called from another room. "Now start searching."

He found her in a room with a grand piano and a china cabinet full of more crystal. "How about a quickie on the piano first?"

Sydney looked up from where she was searching an old fashioned desk. "I'm serious."

"So am I," he said. "Don't tell me the offer doesn't appeal to you."

Her eyes flickered to the piano then back to him. "Fine, it does appeal to me—a lot."

His blood quickened at her admission.

"But we don't have time. We're being watched, remember? Regina could be standing right outside."

The use of Regina's name was like a bucket of cold water. She was right. What the hell was wrong with him?

It had to be the celibacy. Now that he'd had a taste of what he'd been missing he was like a sex fiend.

Or maybe it was just the woman in question. His eyes followed Sydney as she searched in the top of the grand piano. She had to bend over to look inside. His gaze fastened on her ass. He remembered the feel of her in his hands, how she felt pushed up against him as he slid inside her.

His jaw clenched. It had to be Sydney. He'd never been this consumed by a woman before. Every move she made was somehow erotic to him. He wanted to drag her beneath him and take her and screw whoever was watching. He wanted her with a longing that traveled all the way down to his soul.

He'd do anything for her, which included finding this damn journal so that Vander would leave them the hell alone. Once it was gone Vander would have no use for Merrick. And if Vander tried to kill him then he'd hide Sydney away and deal with Vander himself. He'd love nothing more than to beat the shit out of the man who'd held him in captivity for four months.

Resolved to get the job done, he strode to Sydney. "Find anything suspicious?" he asked.

She pulled her head out of the piano and shook her head. "I don't even know what the inside of a piano is supposed to look like, so I have no idea if something is out of place."

He took a look inside, searching for any kind of cuts in the wood. "I don't see anything."

He moved over to the piano bench and lifted the seat. He only found worn music sheets.

"Try pressing the keys," Sydney suggested.

Merrick arched his brow, a smirk playing at his lips. Her time around Joel was showing. "You think there's some kind of hidden bat cave in here?"

She looked down sheepishly. "You never know."

"Let's keep looking and if we don't find anything I'll try the piano." Merrick methodologically started his way around the house, fingers skimming any and all surfaces for some kind of clue. Sydney trailed behind him with nothing to do but wait. She volunteered to search other rooms but with no idea where Regina was or when she'd strike he wanted Sydney close by.

Forty-five minutes later, Merrick's brain was overloaded with pointless thoughts and visions of everyday life from when Collette used to live in her home. Her thoughts continuously circled her work, Kevin, and Felix. Sometimes he caught brief flashes of Cali in her thoughts and feelings but he never strayed long enough to get the full vision. It wasn't until his hand was tracing the edges of her jewelry box in the master bedroom that he found something.

Sydney slammed into his back when he came to an abrupt halt. "You found something?"

He closed his eyes and watched in his mind as Collette gathered valuable necklaces to put in the safe buried beneath the carpet of her closet.

"Fuck, yes." Merrick flew to the large walk-in. Shit, it was as big as his kitchen.

"Wow." Sydney stood mesmerized by the shelf upon shelf of shoes.

He snapped his fingers in front of her face. "Not now. I need your help." He dropped to the floor and crawled his hands along the carpet until he found a faint impression of Collette pulling the carpet up.

"Is that a safe?" Sydney knelt beside him and took the peeled back carpet without needing to be asked. She held it out of his way as he pressed his fingers against the keypad.

A few seconds later he typed in the code.

"I can't believe you found it." Sydney bounced excitedly.

"We're not out of the woods yet," he said, but still his adrenaline was pumping. Could this be it? Had they found Kevin's journal? Was this whole ordeal finally at an end?

As soon as he lifted back the lid he knew that wasn't the case. There was no beat up spiral notebook to be found.

"So?" Sydney tried to look over the opened door but couldn't quite make it. "What's in there?"

Merrick dug his hand in and came out with envelopes and jewelry.

Sydney's nose wrinkled. "That's it?"

An object slid out of his hand and landed back in the safe with a *clank*. He and Sydney looked at each other before he dived back in to retrieve the object.

"What is it?"

"It's a key." He closed his fingers around it. Collette's thoughts briefly flickered through his mind. It was obvious she never really touched the key. It was something of Kevin's. "It's a key to a lock at a storage lot."

"Do you know which one?" Sydney got to her feet with him.

He tucked the key into his pocket. "I think so."

They made their way downstairs. Sydney paused by the front door. "What is it?"

She stepped away so he could see the handle. It wasn't locked. Son of a bitch.

"Are you using your powers?"

"Yes." Her eyes darted around, on the alert. There wasn't a soul in sight.

"It must've been Jente," said Sydney.

Merrick swore under his breath. "How much do you think he heard?"

"Enough. He's gone now but just in case he tries to follow us I'll keep my Shield up."

He nodded. It was all they could do.

He fisted the key in his pocket. "Let's go see where this leads us."

*

The storage facility was deserted.

Merrick leaned out the driver's window and typed in the code for the gate. It opened with an ominous rattle.

"Are you sure this is the right place?" Sydney asked as they drove through.

Merrick circled around the back, scanning the storage numbers until he found what he was looking for. "I'm positive," he told her as he shut off the car.

The storage unit that Kevin possessed wasn't exposed to the outside. They had to go through another door that opened into a dim lit hallway. Storage units lined both sides.

Sydney wrapped both arms around herself as if to ward off the chill. She eyed one of the broken light bulbs and swallowed. "I don't like it in here."

He counted down the cells until they reached Kevin's. "We'll be out soon enough," he promised her and took the lock in his hand. The key slid in easy enough. He exchanged a look with Sydney and then gave a twist.

The lock popped open. Merrick flashed a grin over his shoulder. Sydney smiled right back.

He threw up the metal shutters that kept the storage unit enclosed. Boxes upon boxes were stacked everywhere. Christmas decorations were abandoned in a far corner along with a beach cruiser bike.

Merrick stepped into the dark storage cubby. He caught sight of a flashlight and clicked it on. "I think you're going to have to drop your Shields, Syd. None of these boxes are labeled."

She stepped in with him. "They're down and I'll help you move some boxes."

He leaned over and kissed her. Her lips met his eagerly, soft and pliant. "We're probably going to get dusty and dirty so prepare for a shower when we get back," he said.

Her eyes darkened with desire. "I'm looking forward to it."

Merrick's groin tightened. "Then what the hell are we waiting for? Let's find this damn journal and get out of here."

*

Merrick dropped a box by Sydney's feet out in the hallway. He wiped his forehead with the sleeve of his shirt. The storage unit was now divided with boxes they'd opened and checked and boxes they hadn't. "What are we on?" he asked. "Lucky number twenty-three?"

Sydney started in on the box lid. "No idea."

She'd just pulled a flap free when the door at the end of the hall opened.

Merrick froze as a man he'd never seen before poked his head in. He spotted Merrick and Sydney before opening the door wider to let in more light.

"Is that your unit?" the man hollered down the hall.

Merrick squinted against the bright sun. He snatched up the lock and key from the floor and held it up.

The man nodded. "Just checking. We've had a couple break-ins the past few weeks." He held the door open for a few seconds longer than necessary before letting it close behind him.

Sydney shot him a worried glance. "That was a little weird."

He returned to the box and ripped it the rest of the way open. "We should hurry. I don't trust him. I couldn't tell if he was wearing a uniform or not. He could have been putting on an act for all we know."

"Merrick…" Sydney's voice drew his attention back to the box and he blinked as notebook upon notebook stared him in the face. "We found it."

"No shit." He picked up a worn red spiral and closed his eyes. Kevin's thoughts and emotions bombarded him. He dropped the journal and held onto the box. He frowned.

Someone else knew about this box. Had been—

The door at the end of the hall flew open. Merrick shot to his feet.

A faint click came from his left. Jente appeared a second later, gun raised. "Don't move."

"How the hell—?" Merrick started to ask but he stopped. He remembered the man holding the door open as if for no reason. Now it looked like he did have a reason—he'd been holding it open to allow Jente in. And with Sydney not using her Shields so he could get readings off the boxes it was the perfect plan.

He cursed under his breath.

Regina and gang strode down the hall toward them. Regina smiled seductively at him. Merrick's stomach turned. He eyed the box of notebooks then glanced at Sydney. Her green eyes were wide. Her gaze darted down to the box as if to ask, "What do we do? The box is right there."

He held his hand out and gestured for them to stay put. If they wanted any kind of chance to get away without being shot they needed to wait until everyone was within grabbing distance. Human shields were a wondrous thing. He'd grab Regina the first chance he got. She could use a few more holes in her.

Sydney carefully got to her feet.

Jente pointed the gun at her. "Don't even think about using your powers."

She nodded shakily.

Merrick growled protectively. If Jente so much as harmed one hair on Sydney's head he'd kill him.

"Well, well," Regina cooed. "I didn't think you went for the ones built like children." She raked her gaze over Sydney's petite frame, sneering.

Sydney glared at her.

"Cut the bullshit, Regina, and get the damn box," Jente said, bored. "I've got more important things to do than take care of your assignments."

Regina's face darkened. She motioned with her hand and a few unknowns from the back of the group came forward to get the box. Regina stared down at all the notebooks. "What kind of grown man keeps this many journals?"

"One on the brink of insanity," Sydney snapped at her.

Regina shrugged. "You'd think if he could look into the future he'd write down winning lottery numbers or something."

"Hurry the fuck up," Jente said, exacerbated.

Merrick watched his gun hand. The men bent down to lift the box. His gaze locked with Sydney's. He looked from her to the metal bat they'd unearthed in the storage unit then back to her. She gave the smallest nod.

With the box in their hands the two men couldn't do anything.

Merrick lunged for Regina. He grasped her around the shoulders and swung her into Jente. The two collided. A shot went off. A light bulb exploded. Sydney yelped and grabbed the bat. She swung for the nearest man and hit him in the knee.

He fell, and the box of notebooks tipped. Journals went everywhere.

Regina screamed. "Pick them up."

Light burst into the hallway once more as the door was wrenched open. More hired muscle funneled in. They were going to run out of space fast. Merrick scrambled for where Jente was getting to his feet. He tried to surprise him from the back but the kid was fast on his feet. As if he sensed Merrick behind him, he spun and smacked him across the face with the butt of the gun.

Pain exploded along his jaw but he ignored it as he grabbed Jente's wrist and twisted.

Jente hissed in pain.

Merrick twisted harder.

Jente grit his teeth but eventually he dropped the gun.

Merrick dropped to get it and received a knee to the stomach. He did his best to push the pain away. With one hand clutching his abdomen he grabbed the gun and pitched it into the far corner of Kevin's storage unit where it fell behind a mountain of boxes.

Hands grabbed him from behind and nearly pulled him off his feet. He relaxed his body and dropped like dead weight. The men staggered. Merrick kicked back and heard a grunt.

"Merrick!" Sydney shouted.

He looked up and saw her holding the bat like she was ready to hit a home run. Jente and Regina were fleeing with the box, the man Sydney had nailed in the knee hobbling after them.

As if noticing the others making a run for it, the men holding Merrick threw him into Sydney. He caught her in his arms and together they crashed into the box towers.

"Are you hurt?" he asked her immediately.

She pushed herself up. "I'm okay. Merrick, we have to get that box back." She started to run after them.

He grabbed her around the waist and pulled her back. "Easy. No we don't."

She frowned at his calm expression. "What do you mean 'no we don't'? They have Kevin's journals."

"True, but they don't have *the* journal." He smiled. "Now come on, we should leave. We got what we needed."

"We did?"

He ushered her out and locked up. There was no sign of Regina and their thugs. Good riddance.

"Merrick, I'm confused," Sydney said as they made their way back to her car.

"I'll explain everything, I promise, but first call Felix and see if he's home. We need to plan and we don't have that much time. I don't know how long it'll take for Vander to realize the journal he's looking for isn't in the box."

"What do you mean it's not in the box? There were tons of journals in that box."

He pulled out of the storage facility. "I know, but the one Vander's looking for isn't among them. I saw someone else get to the box before we did. I think Felix was right. Whatever Kevin saw he didn't want Vander to get his hands on his Mirror Mate. A trusted friend of Kevin's took the journal. He's the one who has it. His name is Greg Kelley."

*

Sydney sat back and watched as Merrick told Felix and Luke what had transpired at the storage facility and Collette's home. They were still waiting for Niella and Cali, but Merrick didn't want to wait. Time was limited. The longer Vander believed he had the right journal the more time they had to find the real one without having to look over their shoulders.

Sydney had to admit it was nice to not have to worry about Shielding because Jente was hiding out in the bushes. She doubted any Kratos Guild member was within a ten mile radius of them.

She pulled out her phone and checked it. She'd texted Joel to meet at Felix's as soon as possible but she hadn't heard back.

Cali and Niella burst through the front door as if someone was hot on their tail. They both instantly sought her out. "Where's your idiot boyfriend?" Niella demanded.

Sydney's eyes went to Merrick before she realized it.

"Not your Mirror Mate, I mean Joel. Where is he? Have you heard from him?"

"What's a Mirror Mate?" she heard Luke whisper to Felix.

Felix shushed him.

"I haven't heard from Joel." Her stomach started to sink. "Why? Did you Dream about him?"

Cali swore.

It was all the answer she needed.

Niella expression looked pained. "Vander has him," she said gently.

Felix exploded. "What? When the fuck did this happen?"

Niella looked lost; it was a rare show of vulnerability on her part. "I don't know. All I know is that he's about to be in pain. At first I thought it was emotional pain—that you finally grew a pair and broke it off with him, but you haven't heard from him." She looked ill. "Which means the pain I saw was physical."

Chapter 23

Joel awoke groggily to the swaying sensation of being in the back of a car. "Fucking hell." He grabbed his head as it throbbed. What the hell had happened?

He remembered the café, the interview, being given the job, and shaking his employer's hand. They'd walked out together when he'd started stumbling.

His coffee.

They'd drugged his coffee.

Motherfuckers.

How long had he been out?

He couldn't see anything in the back of the van. There were no windows and his phone was missing.

His eyes felt dried out and he went to rub them before remembering the contacts. He pulled them out, his eyes tearing up. He rubbed his eyes. His hands weren't tied together. Neither were his feet.

He didn't know whether that was a good thing or a bad thing. On the one hand it could be a good thing because he could fight his way out of there. On the other hand he might not be tied up because whoever was holding him had powers and could easily take him out—thus he wasn't a threat and there was no need to tie him up.

Knowing Vander he went with the second option.

He was so screwed.

He didn't know how long he remained in the back of that van before it came to a stop. It felt like an hour but he had no way of knowing.

The car shut off. He edged his way closer to the back doors. If he could Lock his kidnapper's hands to the back doors he could make a run for it.

The front doors slammed. Footsteps sounded around the side. He heard voices.

Shit. There was more than one of them.

He shifted his weight from one foot to the other anxiously. He could do this. He pressed his hands against the two back doors of the van. He heard the key and waited until they opened the door. He needed to make sure the guy's hands were touching the metal.

The van groaned as the back doors were pulled open. Joel Locked the metal and kicked out with his foot. The man who opened the door took the hit in the shoulder and flew back. His arm was stuck to the van and pulled him back like a bungee cord. He cried out.

"Nice trick, want to see mine?"

Joel turned to find the man from San Francisco. He grabbed Joel and hung on. Pain exploded beneath his skin. He screamed as the burning sensation increased under his skin, like he was being boiled alive on the inside. He wrenched away and dropped to his knee.

"Not so fast," the pain master said. He held his hands up menacingly. "Drop whatever you did to my colleague and I won't hurt you more than I have to."

Joel weighed his options. His muscles screamed and spasmed, his legs were shaking. He'd never experienced a pain like that before. It was as if every nerve ending had been on fire. He wasn't ready to feel it again. He eyed his surroundings.

A crappy motel, how fitting. He glanced back at the man flailing against the van door in an attempt to unlatch his arm. *Good luck with that, buddy.*

He was tempted to watch the poor sucker to see how long he'd go at it before he realized there was no way he was coming away from that door unless Joel willed it. However, he didn't want to feel like his insides were melting either. Keeping a careful eye on the pain master he put his hand against the van door and dropped his Lock.

The man fell back on his ass and Joel grinned.

Once he was back on his feet the man stormed Joel, his arm held back as if to throw a punch.

Joel stared him right in the eye. "Touch me and I'll freeze your lungs right in your chest."

The man hesitated. He looked to his colleague as if to ask him if that was possible.

Joel had no idea if his powers allowed him to do that but this fucker didn't need to know that.

The pain master shrugged at his idiot companion. Idiot companion dropped his arm and instead glared balefully at Joel.

Joel returned his glare with a pleasant smile.

"Move it." He motioned for Joel to start walking.

He was taken to a motel room on the far side of the building, as far away from the front office as possible. *The better to hide your screams, my dear.* He thought of Little Red Riding Hood as he was led to the big bad wolf. Vander Donahughe stood inside the room waiting for them. He looked as if he'd aged forty years in the three months since Joel had last seen him. The sight was startling. *Grandma, what gray hair you have.*

Sitting huddled on the bed behind him was a young woman. Looked like he wasn't the only captive.

"You're right on time," Vander greeted him. "I just got off the phone. It appears that your bargaining chip purposes have been made void."

Joel frowned.

"The journal is in my possession, which means your usefulness has all but run out."

Joel didn't take the bait. He wouldn't ask what he'd be used for if Vander wasn't going to barter him off to Sydney for Kevin's journal.

How the hell had Vander gotten to it before her?

Fear slid through him. He hoped Syd was okay. If she was hurt in any way he didn't care what happened to him, he'd take Vander down right where he stood. The man looked ready to break a hip at any moment. If Joel got to him before he used his powers then he might have a chance.

"Not going to ask what I'm going to use you for?" said Vander.

Joel crossed his arms and feigned nonchalance. "Considering what I've seen from you I have a pretty good idea."

Vander bowed his head in concession. "Then there's no point in wasting time talking about it."

Joel was grabbed from behind and propelled toward the bed. He landed on the edge of it.

The woman clutched her knees closer to her chest. She was dressed in RN scrubs. What the hell was Vander playing at?

"Everything's going to be fine," Joel promised her.

Her doe-like eyes latched onto him. He didn't think she heard a word he said. Poor thing.

The next thing he knew he was being held from behind, his arm gripped in idiot companion's hands. "What the fuck?" Joel struggled but pain flared bright hot through his body in warning.

Pain master held him immobile as idiot companion waited for some kind of signal from Vander.

Vander drew closer and touched the woman on the shoulder. "You're an incredible nurse," he told her calmly. "I've seen your records. The recovery rates are off the charts."

The woman shivered beneath his hand. "I'm just a nurse," she all but sobbed. "I don't know why I'm here. Please let me go."

Vander continued to speak as if he hadn't heard her. "You don't like to see people in pain, do you?"

She shook her head, tears leaking from her eyes. Joel's stomach churned painfully. "Please don't hurt me," she whispered.

"You're a natural born healer," said Vander.

"I'm just a nurse," the woman repeated. "You keep calling me a healer but I don't do anything special, I just do my job. Please…"

"Show me how good of a healer you are." Vander nodded at idiot companion.

Joel felt a snap in his forearm and screamed.

*

"We have to get the real journal and trade Joel for it." Sydney paced Felix's living room. Worry had her stomach cramping. This was all her fault. She should have gone over to his place when he didn't answer his phone.

"For that to work we need to get the real journal." Felix stood a few feet away, participating in his own pacing. "Where does this Greg Kelley live?" he asked Merrick.

"I only caught glimpses. I put in a call to the city station and should hear back shortly. We're going to have to tread carefully. We can't go barging into this man's house."

"Why the hell not?" Cali asked from the couch.

"Because he has powers," Merrick said flatly.

"What kind of powers?" said Felix.

"I didn't see that much," said Merrick. "And with no idea what he can do, we need to plan this out. Kevin must've realized how valuable his information was, so he trusted it to someone he knew could protect it. That's saying something about this man's power."

Felix swore.

Sydney was right along with him. This was such bull. She couldn't sit by and wait while she knew Joel was being hurt.

"Look," Niella said. "You guys go after this Greg guy and I'll stay behind and see if I can Dream up anything about Joel. Specifically his whereabouts."

"Do you want me to stay behind with you?" Luke spoke up for the first time.

Niella looked startled that anyone would even offer but she quickly got control over her expression. She shook her head. "It's fine. I know how much you want to go along with them."

"I don't know if bringing him is such a good idea," Sydney

said. Luke was only twenty years old. If anything happened to him she'd feel even worse. She didn't even think he knew how to fight.

"Are you kidding?" said Cali. "He's perfect. If we have no idea what we're going up against, we'll just shove Luke in first."

Luke's face paled.

Cali leaned over and chucked him under the chin. "I'm kidding."

Luke relaxed.

"But only partly."

Felix grinned at Cali's antics.

Before they could say anything else and give Luke a heart attack, Sydney intervened. "We need to come up with a plan. We don't have any time to waste."

"Agreed," said Merrick.

The Newport police station got back to Merrick within the hour. Sydney sent up a silent thank you that this Greg character didn't live in Anaheim. She never wanted to deal with Merrick's old co-workers ever again.

The address was some private estate that was very secluded.

"Shit," Cali commented as they looked up the address on the internet. "I don't think he has a neighbor within a mile of his house. Is that good for us or bad?"

Felix cracked his knuckles. "It's good. Everyone ready?"

"All set," said Merrick.

They piled into Felix's Hummer. Sydney went over the plan again and again. She hoped she could do this.

A warm hand covered her knee. "You okay?"

She looked over to Merrick. "I just hope I don't screw this up," she told him in a hushed tone.

His fingers tightened on her leg. "You'll do fine. No pressure."

She gave a quiet laugh. No pressure, sure. It was only her responsibility to Shield everyone periodically so they could take Greg by surprise. She'd have to be on high alert to watch for any signs of his powers so that she could temporarily shut them down before dropping her Shield so the others could use their powers in offense. It was like one big choreographed dance, only she didn't know if she remembered all the steps. Attack, Shield. Shield, attack.

It'd be a lot easier if she could see Greg during this whole operation so she could read his body language and facial expressions, but they probably weren't going to come across him until the halfway point.

"Someone want to tell me how Kevin befriended someone this wealthy?" Cali stared out the front windshield at the large double door gates that blocked off the estate.

"Maybe he gave him some good financial advice or some stock market tips," Merrick said dryly.

Cali turned around in her seat and grinned cheekily.

Felix continued down the street and parked a half a block away. "Everyone know what they're doing?"

They all nodded, Luke a little less confidently then the rest of them.

Felix's eyes latched onto him. "Cali and I are going to clear the way for Merrick to get any reading on where the journal might be kept. Sydney is going to be on the watch for any super powers and if we're in danger she's going to Shield us. Luke, you'll bring up the rear. You're our backup."

He nodded shakily. "You're not going to Shield if I'm hit are you?" he asked Sydney.

"Don't worry," she told him. "You're not going to have to take a bullet for anyone else. And if on the off chance that you do, I promise not to Shield, that way you'll heal just like you always do."

That seemed to put him at ease.

"You can always stay behind in the car if you don't want to come with us," Merrick said.

"No." Luke shook his head. "Joel helped break me out in San Francisco and I want to help him if I can."

When they were all out of the Hummer, Felix came around and clapped Luke on the shoulder. Luke flinched mildly. "Welcome to the Guild of Truth," said Felix. "You're official now."

Luke beamed.

Felix and Cali led the way back to the estate. As they came upon the gate Felix motioned them to the wall. "Cameras," he whispered. He waved his hand and the two little black cameras mounted on the top of the gate vanished.

Merrick blinked.

Sydney smiled and touched his arm. "You'll get used to it," she told him.

He nodded.

Felix turned to Merrick. "Give me a boost?" He motioned to the large wall.

"Why don't you Erase the gate?" Sydney asked.

"Because that's going to look suspicious. If I can get on top of the gate I'll be able to see the lock and Erase it, letting you guys in."

Sydney eyed the large wooden doors. The lock was probably a giant latch on the other side.

Merrick and Luke both helped boost Felix up enough so that he could grab the edge of the wall and haul himself up. He sat on the wall for a moment, his hand waving. No doubt he was taking out any threats that he could see. He jumped down from the wall and a few seconds later the two large gates swung open soundlessly.

"Nice landscaping," Luke said in awe as they all got their first good look at the front yard.

It was huge. Bright plants were everywhere. The driveway was lined with professionally designed hedges that were shaped into long spirals. A koi pond was off to one side of the place while a fountain was off on the other. All in all, the one word Sydney could think to describe the place was *exotic*. "At least we know he doesn't have kids," Merrick said as they made their way down toward the mansion type house.

"How can you tell?" asked Cali.

Merrick gestured to the grass. "There are no toys lying around anywhere. In my experience that means no kids."

"One less obstacle," said Felix.

They moved slow and steady until they climbed the stoop leading to the front door.

"Anyone else think this has been too easy?" Felix asked.

Sydney hadn't wanted to say anything but they hadn't come into contact with any resistance. Not even a guard dog. "Maybe he left?"

Felix looked doubtful but didn't say anything. "Get ready for anything," he warned her.

She stepped back.

Felix waved his hand and the lock and handle on the door disappeared. The door slid open, again soundlessly. Sydney wondered if they were just lucky that this man oiled his hinges or if Cali was at work. She cast a quick look in Cali's direction but the Silencer only smiled back.

Once all inside, Luke pushed the door closed as best he could but it continued to slide open.

If Sydney thought Collette's house was nice, then this place was amazing. Two curving staircases, one on each side, joined up in the middle to lead to the second floor. There was a hallway straight ahead and two rooms on either side.

A dark object moved too fast for Sydney to catch on the second floor. "Did you guys see that?" Her voice came out warped, as if she were speaking underwater.

"No, what?" She heard Felix's voice perfectly but there was something off about it. As if she heard it in her mind and not around her.

She turned to Cali. She smiled again and tapped her ear. She was using her powers. Somehow she was manipulating their voices when they spoke so that they'd be able to hear each other but no one else would.

"Something moved upstairs," she said.

Merrick's warm body came up behind her and for a moment she wanted to lean back against him and absorb all that heat. "Do you think it's Greg?" he asked.

She shrugged, some part of herself doubting that she even saw anything. "I know this is going to sound crazy," she said. "But what if we were to ask him for the journal? We're both on the same side. He might be sick of having to protect the journal from Vander—if we tell him we're going to take it maybe he'll be happy to be rid of it."

"The only problem with your plan is that we're not going to keep the journal from Vander. We're going to barter it for Joel's life," said Felix.

"Technically we don't have to tell him that," Cali commented.

Felix stared at Cali before turning around to look at the rest of them. "Is that what we want to do then? Try the diplomatic angle first?"

"There might be less pain that way," said Sydney.

Felix shrugged. "I guess—" A large object flew from one of the side rooms and smashed into his shoulder.

He staggered back. Cali raced to his side as another object came flying.

"Cali, watch out," Sydney cried.

Cali took the hit in the side of the ribs. Her face contorted in pain but she continued to Felix's side.

The dark shape reappeared on the second floor and Sydney stared into Greg Kelley's eyes.

A flurry of miscellaneous objects came hurdling toward them.

"Sydney!" Merrick shouted from behind her.

She tore her gaze away from Greg and threw up her Shield. The objects fell to the floor useless. Greg disappeared out of sight.

"Holy shit." Felix rubbed his shoulder absently as he bent to inspect Cali's side. "Out of all the fucking powers we had to get landed with Mr. Telekinesis?"

Sydney barely heard him. She rushed for the stairs. She couldn't let Greg get away.

"Syd!"

She kept running. On the second floor landing she went left where she saw Greg disappear. She followed her instinct and picked the furthest hallway to travel. She passed room after room, some connecting with others. There were tons of places Greg could have backtracked. She shook her head and pressed on.

"Syd!" Merrick's voice barely reached her.

Movement caught her attention and she veered left into a large room that was filled with boards and planks and other wooden items.

Greg stood alone in the center.

"You can't hit me with anything," she told him.

Greg slid a hand carved bat from one of the shelves. "I can't hit you with my mind," he corrected her.

She swallowed in fear but kept her footing. "Look, we're on the same side. We both want to keep that journal from Vander. If you help us—"

"I was warned about you." Greg stepped back and raised his bat. "You're the one's Kevin warned me about. Under no circumstances were you to get his journal. You'd ruin everything with it."

Sydney drew back. "What? No—we'd never... our friend is in danger."

"I don't care who's in danger. You're not getting that journal."

"You can't stop us. You're outnumbered and it's only a matter of time. Help us. Please."

Greg swung.

Sydney cried out as she dropped to the floor. The wood of his bat crashed into another shelf. Wooden objects flew everywhere, raining down on her.

She threw her hands up to protect her head.

"Sydney!" Merrick roared through the whole house. Footsteps thundered down a nearby hallway.

"Fuck diplomacy," she heard Felix say as she scrambled for the door. Her hand closed around a large figurine and she threw it at Greg with all her might.

He batted it away and brought his weapon up for another swing. "You can't stop my powers if you're knocked unconscious."

She screamed.

The bat swung for her head.

Merrick flew through the doorway. He tackled Greg to the floor. Greg's swing went wide but it still sent Sydney into another shelf.

Pain exploded behind her eyes and her vision went black—

She blinked up from the floor.

Luke was crouched next to her. "You're all right." He smiled. "How's your head?"

For the first time she noticed the blood on his hands. She tentatively touched the side of her head that throbbed with her heartbeat and felt the matted blood. Felix and Cali stood around them like a protective shield. Wooden objects were flying everywhere as if they were in the middle of a tornado. Felix was Erasing left and right while Cali used her sound waves to push away any object that came too close. She was covered in bruises, as was Felix.

Sydney pushed to a sitting position. "What happened?"

Luke helped her upright. "Merrick's attempting to kick Greg's ass—er, butt," Luke hastily corrected at her flat stare. "The only problem is that Greg's not going down without a fight." He motioned to the spinning cyclone of wood they were presently encased in.

Merrick.

"Where's Merrick? Is he hurt?" She tried to get to her feet and nearly fell over as she became lightheaded. She tried to use her powers and nearly cried out as pain tore through her skull.

"Easy." Luke kept her steady. "No sudden movements. Trust me, I've had my share of head wounds."

She didn't want to think of just how he'd received those head wounds. Niella's words about his father drifted through her mind unbidden but she pushed them away. "I have to fix this. I have to help Merrick, this is all my fault." If she wouldn't have been so darn stupid and waited for everyone before going after Greg they might have been able to avoid this. But no, she had to try to be the hero. For once in her life she wanted to be able to help the guild without anyone else's assistance.

All you did was make things worse.

Well, now she was going to make things right. Bracing herself for the pain she threw her Shield up. Luke had to hold her up as pain erupted in her head.

Wooden objects fell to the floor with a clatter.

Greg cried out as Merrick advanced on him. "No!" Greg shouted, his gaze locking with Sydney's. "You don't know what you're doing."

Merrick caught him in a head lock and put him to sleep. It was over within seconds. Sydney dropped her Shield, exhausted.

"I got you." Luke wrapped her arm around his shoulders and held her up.

"Thanks, Luke, I'm so glad we found you."

He blushed and dropped his dreamy blue eyes.

Merrick was at her side instantly. His hands hovered near her head. "Shit." He brushed aside her hair. "I should have killed that bastard for hurting you."

"You did the right thing," she told him. "He was only doing his job."

"Well, he did a pretty fucking good job of it," said Cali. Her exposed forearms were covered in angry red marks, some already bruising. She had a cut along her forehead and dried blood in her side bangs.

Felix wrapped his arm around Cali's shoulders and drew her into his chest. He wasn't nearly as battered as Cali, though he did have a nasty gash on his ear that was still bleeding. "We should start searching the place. There are a lot of rooms to cover."

"What about him?" Luke nodded to Greg.

Merrick eyed him balefully. "We'll tie him up." He stepped over to Greg and grabbed his clothes in his hands before closing his eyes. A few seconds later he released Greg. "This might not take as long as you think, Felix," he said.

"You know where Greg hid it?" Sydney asked hopefully.

"I know what room, but he was very careful in keeping his thoughts to himself. I've never seen anything like it before. It was as if he knew what to expect."

Sydney frowned as she remembered Greg's warning.

Chapter 24

Felix dragged Greg around by the duct tape and rope they had tied around his ankles.

Merrick kept glancing back every few seconds to make sure the bastard stayed unconscious. He would have been happy to make it permanent but Sydney would never have accepted that. She was too good of a person. She'd tried to help them by talking to Greg one on one but that man had been holed up in his house for years. Whatever Kevin had told him, he'd taken it straight to heart.

Merrick had never seen such paranoia in a person before. This was why they needed to destroy the journal. If they kept it around Sydney, Felix, and anyone else in their guild, they would be charged with guarding it and their fate would ultimately turn into Greg's. They'd never be able to leave for fear of someone getting their hands on the notebook.

He'd been right all along. It needed to stay hidden or be destroyed. He looked over his shoulder at Greg.

Felix caught him staring. "Don't worry, if he wakes up I'll put him back to sleep." The feral smile he shot Merrick told him how much he'd enjoy putting him to sleep.

Merrick's gaze slid over to Cali who was rubbing stubbornly at her bruises, as if that would make them heal faster.

He'd asked Felix a few days ago how someone identified their Mirror Mate, how they bonded. It'd taken Felix a couple seconds to answer.

Your souls…they connect, but it's more than that. Cali once told me that when your soul cries out for the other and that call is returned— that's when you're bonded. I can't put it into better words. All I know is that Cali and I were in a situation and we were trying to reach each other. Suddenly I heard her voice in my head, my heart, everywhere. I called out to her and then the world turned blazing white. After that it's like you have a little mini sun burning deep inside your chest, a constant heat to know that you're not alone. Ever.

Merrick's eyes latched onto Sydney's swinging blonde ponytail. His gut tightened. To know that he'd never have to be alone…

He couldn't even imagine.

To have someone that would never shun him, someone he'd never have to fear betraying him or fearing him. The thought was amazing.

Sydney paused and turned around to face him, as if she could feel his eyes on her. "Am I still going in the right direction?" she asked him.

"The door is right up ahead."

She smiled that beautiful smile at him and his breath caught. She grasped the handles on the double doors and pulled. The smile on her face dropped.

"Holy fuckballs." Cali went through the threshold and paused at the end of the balcony where Sydney had walked.

Merrick's spirit plummeted as he entered the vast two story library.

"Did anyone else get a sudden image of the beast's library from Disney's *Beauty and the Beast* just now?" asked Felix as he dragged in Greg.

Luke raised his hand. "I did."

"And the journal is somewhere in this room?" Sydney stared down at the wooden tables on the bottom floor. Some were covered with stacks of books, others papers and magazines. Every nook and cranny was stuffed with books—and not just leather bound old tome looking things either. Merrick saw books of every shape and size and to his horror there were spiral notebooks stuffed into shelves throughout the entire room.

"Please tell me you got more off of Greg then just what room the journal was in," said Felix.

Merrick didn't bother answering him. It would just depress them all. "We should split up," he said instead.

A collective groan went through the group.

"I'll take downstairs," Felix said cheerfully and pulled Greg toward the staircase at the north end of the room.

"Felix, don't you dare," said Sydney. "You'll drag him around upstairs, we don't need you throwing him down stairs and giving him a permanent concussion. Besides, we might need him later."

Felix sighed. "Fine, I won't drag him down the stairs. Why don't you, Merrick, and Luke take downstairs? Cali and I will cover up here. What are we looking for again?"

Merrick turned around and plucked a spiral notebook out of the shelf. "The journal is like this, only a worn out blue. If you find more than one just start making a pile and I'll go through them."

Cali gave a mock salute and kicked Greg as she made her way past Felix to start searching.

Merrick grinned. Cali was really starting to grow on him. In fact, the entire guild was.

The realization was startling. He'd never had a large group of friends, not since his days at the academy. Ever since his powers came into play he'd been on his own. He'd forgotten how much fun it could be to be a part of a unit.

He met Sydney at the large staircase and held his arm out to her. "Shall we, my lady?"

She tucked her hand into the crook of his arm. "Why, thank you, good sir."

Greg only woke up once in the four hours it took to sweep the entire library.

There was a commotion upstairs that came swiftly to an end before Merrick or Sydney could make it up the stairs.

"What happened?" Sydney asked.

Felix had still had his arm around Greg's throat. He gave an innocent shrug. "Greg was being uncooperative so I gave him a time out."

Sydney hadn't looked amused but she'd gone back downstairs to continue their search.

By the end of the four hours they had over three hundred and fifty blue notebooks.

They all converged on the bottom floor and spread out their finds over four tables. There was nothing the others could do after that. Felix and Cali took a seat and waited at another table and Luke went off to a table that held a large atlas while Sydney sat down by Merrick's side. Merrick exchanged looks with Sydney. He exhaled and picked up the first notebook. He closed his eyes to cut out any distractions and let his mind drift into the notebook, searching for any impressions of Kevin.

He put the notebook on the floor by his feet. "Nothing."

And so began the process.

By the three hundredth notebook, he could see the hope draining from Sydney's face. The library was eerily silent, the only sound coming from Luke turning the worn pages of the atlas.

"This can't be right," Merrick said when he discarded another journal about mathematics from high school algebra. "There had to be more that we just overlooked."

Sydney placed her hand on his forearm in a comforting gesture that only spiked Merrick's anger. He shook her off. "No, you don't understand, it has to be in here." He continued to grab the journals and started throwing them over his shoulder when they didn't bare the impressions he was looking for. He grew more frantic.

Sydney watched him with sad eyes. "Merrick, it's not here. Greg must've been messing with us. What better way to slow us down than by leading us to the library to search through millions of books? It was a wild goose chase."

He refused to believe it. He tore through the remaining notebooks before turning on Greg. Felix had draped him over the hard leather sofa by one of the large windows.

Everyone shot to their feet as he stormed across the floor.

"Take it easy," said Felix. "Shaking him isn't going to wake him up. We'll wait and then ask him where he put the journal. You don't want to do anything rash."

Merrick was about to blow through Felix when Luke's quiet voice stopped him short. "Guys, come look at this."

Merrick whirled.

Luke stood in front of the atlas, which apparently wasn't an atlas at all. At least, not a full one.

"Luke," Sydney breathed. "You found it."

Cut into the back pages of the large book was a square hole big enough to hold a blue spiral notebook.

Felix wrapped his arm around Luke's shoulders. Cali beamed.

Sydney threw her arms around Merrick's neck and kissed him. Her lips on his broke through any shock he may have been experiencing and he kissed her back. It was hot and demanding. His groin tightened and he plunged his tongue deep into her mouth where she met him stroke for stroke.

Someone cleared their throat and Merrick remembered that they had an audience. Sydney jumped back, her face red. The others stared at them as if not quite sure what to do. Luke's face was as red as Sydney's. Felix looked a little shocked and mortified as if he'd just caught his baby sister making out for the first time, and Cali was trying to suppress a smile and failing at it.

Merrick cleared his own throat and picked up the notebook. He instantly felt Kevin's thoughts and emotions. He pulled himself away from them. "Shall we go?" he said to the group at large as if nothing were amiss.

Sydney's pants pocket started vibrating. She hastily pulled her phone out and checked the ID. "It's Niella." She put the phone up to her ear. "Hello?"

Merrick watched the expressions that played over Sydney's face.

She hung up. "Niella knows where Joel is."

*

"So what's our plan of action again?" Cali asked as they all stared out the side windows of Felix's Hummer.

They were parked outside a crappy motel with chipping paint and rusted railing. The pool area was closed off because the water was green and Merrick was pretty sure their continental breakfast would make you sick for a week.

He pulled back from the window to go over their rough mission plan. "We scope out how many people are inside, especially if Vander is one of them. We offer to trade Joel for the journal. We don't give him the journal until Joel is safely in our hands and we are near enough to the car to make an escape. Felix will Erase it as we drive away. Luke, you're staying in the car because for whatever reason Vander still wants you. Plus, we need a getaway driver. You do know how to drive, right?"

"I'm twenty, not fifteen," said Luke.

"Right. Everyone got it?"

They all nodded.

Felix turned to Cali. "You have an estimate of how many people we're dealing with here?"

Cali's head was cocked as if listening for something. She kept closing and opening her eyes. "There are a good number of heartbeats coming from the furthest room. I'm guessing that's where they're holding Joel. I hear at least two females and maybe three or four males? I'm not sure."

"How can you tell there are females in there?" asked Luke.

"One spoke and another one is sobbing." Her head perked up like a dog.

"What is it?" asked Sydney.

The hate on Cali's face said it all. "Vander."

Felix popped his knuckles.

"We all want a piece of Vander," said Sydney, "but remember

we're here for Joel. Our first priority is getting him out. Okay?"

Felix gave a tight nod before starting the car back up and driving around toward the far end where Joel was being kept. They parked around back and left Luke to guard the Hummer.

Felix handed Luke the keys. "If anything happens, get the hell out of here."

"And if you happen to see an old man running from the room, it'll most likely be Vander. Feel free to run him over," Cali piped up helpfully.

Luke looked sick at the idea of running over a person.

Felix playfully shoved Cali away. "Don't run over anyone. I don't want to have to wash blood off my car."

Luke's face paled even more.

"Would you two stop it? This is serious," Sydney hissed at them.

Felix held his hands up in innocence.

Cali's smile instantly dropped. Her head jerked to the side.

"What is it?" Felix asked.

Cali shoved Felix out of the way and sprinted across the parking lot toward the motel rooms. "We don't have time for a sneak attack. We need to go now, I just heard the words 'want them dead.'"

Merrick swore and set off at a dead run. Half of him wanted to keep pace with Sydney but the other half told him to go ahead—Felix would need him.

Cali got to the room first and blew the door open with a sonic blast that had Merrick's ears ringing.

Shouts erupted from within. A woman screamed.

Merrick's grip tightened on the journal. He could feel Kevin's impressions tingling against the skin of his hand, as if eager for him to read them, as if they wanted him to learn the secrets he was holding.

He hesitated at the threshold and let himself get sucked into Kevin's world.

Chapter 25

Having short legs sucked.

Sydney pumped her arms as she trailed behind Cali, Felix, and Merrick. Cali and Felix rushed into the motel room while Merrick hung back near the door.

Was he waiting for her?

The thought warmed her and she didn't feel so bad about her height. She reached his side and briefly threaded her fingers through his. "Come on," she urged him. She was anxious to get to Joel. She hadn't seen him in days. Niella had said she'd seen him in pain. Her stomach cramped at the thought of Joel hurting. She hoped he was all right.

Merrick remained where he was.

She squeezed his hand but there was no answering squeeze back. "Merrick?" She tugged on his hand but he continued to stare, unseeing. She looked down and found the journal clutched in his other hand.

Shouts erupted from inside the motel room. A loud crash and a thump of a body hitting the floor had Sydney jumping. She dropped Merrick's hand and grasped his arms to shake him.

This wasn't part of the plan. They needed Merrick to hold onto the journal so they could barter Joel's life with it. In this state anyone could walk up to Merrick and take it.

What was he thinking reading it at a time like this?

She shook him harder. "Come on, Merrick, snap out of it," she pleaded.

"I thought I smelled vanilla," a female voice drawled behind her.

Sydney froze. She dropped her hands and curled them into fists. She knew that voice. Regina.

She turned slowly, doing her best to block as much of Merrick as she could. She couldn't let Regina see the journal. She had no physical powers, but then again neither did Regina.

She had no one to help her this time and while that scared her, she wasn't going to back down. This was the woman who'd had her hands on Merrick during his captivity. She'd touched Sydney's man against his wishes. That alone was enough to have her seeing red.

She wouldn't let Regina get to Merrick. Now, like at the facility, he was helpless and she was all that stood in Regina's way.

"Is he trapped in a fantasy land again?" Regina tilted her head like a bird. "Did you distract him with your thoughts?" Her eyes roved over Merrick's face greedily. "You know he's most vulnerable when he's trapped in a vision, right?"

Sydney widened her stance and held her arms loosely out at her sides, ready for anything. She may not be a black belt but she'd watched Felix and Joel enough times to have some semi-confidence in how to throw a punch. "I'm not letting you take him. He's mine."

Regina smiled. A yell came from inside the room but she didn't so much as flinch.

"Merrick belongs with us. I laid claim to him long ago. While you were snuggled up to your man back in that room, I was caressing all the hard planes of Merrick's body."

Sydney ground her teeth.

"He's my pet and I let him off his leash to lead us to what we needed. His usefulness has ended and now it's time for him to go back into his cage. I've been given orders to collect you as well."

That sent a jolt of fear straight through Sydney. She'd known Vander liked to "collect" people with powers, but that was back when he would harvest their life energy to expand his own. Now that he was limiting himself to keep the appearance of age she'd thought his kidnapping days were over.

He'll never stop, she realized. *Once a monster, always a monster.*

And now he'd set his sights on them. They'd stepped on his toes for the last time.

Sydney swallowed her fear and lifted her chin. "You're not taking us."

Regina thrust out her hip and crossed her arms. "And you're going to stop me? A child sized woman with no remarkable powers whatsoever?" Her casualness disappeared in the next second and a feral gleam came to her eyes. "I'd like to see you try." Regina lunged.

Sydney's first instinct was to jump out of the way, but that would leave Merrick exposed. Instead she ducked down and shot forward with both hands fisted.

Regina's height ended up being her downfall.

Sydney was able to get under her and drive her fists into her gut, right beneath her sternum.

Regina cried out and stumbled back, hunched over. "You bitch," she wheezed.

Sydney didn't wait for her to get her bearings again.

If your opponent is injured and retreating, go on the offensive.

With no idea what to do, Sydney rushed her. She tackled Regina like a football player and together they flew into the motel room and landed with a crash.

Regina cushioned the fall. Her head snapped back, connected with the floor, and her eyes glazed over. Sydney shot to her feet but Regina didn't follow.

Sydney was breathing heavily. Adrenaline was rushing through her veins like fire and she stared down at Regina, unable to believe that she'd taken her out.

"Holy hell," she breathed, feeling invigorated. She wanted to jump and holler but refrained when her eyes caught on Joel. She cried out his name and ran to him.

"Syd?" He still had two black eyes and a busted lip. His arm was wrapped in a horrible excuse for a sling that hadn't been there before.

Tears burned the backs of her eyes. "Oh Joel, I'm so sorry." Her hands fluttered uselessly around his obviously broken arm.

He cupped her face, his thumb brushing against her cheek. "It's okay. I can't believe you're here. I can't believe you took out that bitch." Pride sparkled in his midnight blue eyes. "This wasn't exactly what I had in mind for today but happy three year anniversary anyway." He tried to smile and grimaced instead.

Sydney's heart ached and she couldn't hold the tears back anymore. "Happy three-year anniversary," she whispered back to him.

Arms grabbed her from behind.

Joel shouted.

Sydney kicked back blindly.

"I remember you," a voice hissed in her ear before pain tore through her body. She screamed.

"Sydney!" Merrick's roar echoed through the whole room.

The pain suddenly ceased and she dropped to the floor, limp. She blinked back the spots in her vision as she tried to get to her hands and knees.

Grunts came from behind her.

A hand appeared in her line of vision and she looked up into Joel's eyes. "We need to get out of here, quickly, while everyone is distracted."

She grasped his hand and he helped her to her feet. She swayed and turned around to see Felix battling it out with Vander and his guards while Cali helped an innocent woman in RN scrubs. Merrick was fighting off the man from San Francisco.

Her eyes dropped to the floor and she smirked in satisfaction as Regina still lay there.

Sirens sounded out in the distance.

Cali was at their side within seconds. The woman in her nurse's uniform tucked under her arm. "We need to get the hell out of here before the authorities arrive. Where's the journal?"

"Merrick still has it."

Cali nodded. "Looks like we didn't have to barter Joel's ass for it after all."

Joel looked too exhausted to comment. Sydney wrapped his arm around her shoulders and together they made their way to the door. Cali paused and shouted back at Felix as she launched a sound wave right at Vander.

He flew into the wall and Cali smiled viciously.

"Wait." Joel paused at the door.

"Why are you stopping?" asked Sydney. "We need to leave."

Joel refused to move. "Get everyone out and I'll Lock the rest inside until the authorities get here."

Sydney exchanged looks with Cali. Cali shrugged and bellowed into the room. "Felix, get your ass out here, now."

"Merrick," Sydney shouted. "Hurry."

Both men finished with their opponents before booking it out of the room. Merrick grasped the door, slammed it shut, and held it that way as Joel placed his hand on the rotten wood.

Sydney held him steady as he finished. He felt so weak and fragile. It frightened her. "We need to get you to a hospital," she said.

"Not yet," said Joel.

Felix's Hummer came screeching around the corner. Luke leaned across the seat and opened the passenger door for them.

Joel smiled at Luke. "Skywalker," he drawled. "They got you working as a driver now?"

"It's better than being used as a human shield."

Joel laughed but it turned into a cough.

Cali opened the back doors for them and Sydney ushered Joel inside as the sirens grew closer.

"Stay close by," Joel instructed once they were all packed into the Hummer. "I need to be able to keep the door Locked."

Luke nodded and steered the vehicle into the next driveway

over, which happened to be a 24-hour donut shop. "Anyone want donuts?" he called.

The only answer was the hysterical mumbling coming from the woman Cali had saved. Cali tried to keep her calm and even offered her a donut but she just kept repeating how they wanted her to heal Joel and how she couldn't and how they kept hurting him. "It's all my fault," the woman sobbed. She started to cry in earnest and Cali looked to Sydney, lost.

Sydney didn't know what to tell her. They needed to get that woman to a hospital just as much as Joel.

In the safety of the donut parking lot they watched as the police surrounded the motel and were led to the room in question. Joel was watching it carefully and at the precise moment the police went to open the door, he released his Lock. The door flew open as those inside tried to flee.

They all watched in silence as Regina, Vander, and his goons were all taken into custody.

"You think it's finally over?" asked Sydney.

Felix and Cali exchanged looks. "Truthfully?" said Cali. "Vander won't stop until he's dead. But I'd say this is a major setback."

"But there is the bonus that we didn't even have to give him the journal," said Felix optimistically.

"Journal?" Joel asked groggily as he slouched in his seat and rested his head against a window.

Sydney spent the car ride to the hospital filling him in on their adventure finding Kevin's journal and the significance behind why he wanted it. Of course, this was all shielded from the woman in the back, courtesy of Cali's powers.

There wasn't much talking once they reached the hospital. The woman disappeared as soon as they walked her into the emergency room. Joel was taken into the ER after waiting for three hours. Apparently a hysterical, sobbing woman came first as opposed to a man with a broken arm.

After he was tended to the doctors instructed him to get lots of bed rest.

"Niella will be waiting for us." Felix took over driving duties and drove them all to his house, and just as he'd predicted, Niella was waiting.

"It's good to see you in one piece," she said to Joel.

"I'm happy to be in one piece," Joel said.

Sydney escorted him back to the guest room where he passed out as soon as his head hit the pillow. She watched over him for a good hour until she was satisfied that he'd be all right. From the outside he didn't look too roughed up but that wasn't what worried Sydney. She feared what kind of scars were on the inside. Time in captivity with Vander, no matter how short, always left a mark.

She didn't want to think about what they could have done to him, especially with that man who caused the worst kind of pain imaginable with nothing but a touch. She shuddered and jerked when a blanket was carefully put over her shoulders. She grasped the fabric and turned to find Cali waiting there.

Cali's obsidian eyes moved from Sydney to Joel. "He'll be okay," she said. The sympathy on Cali's face was an oddity and it was a painful reminder of when she had been held captive by Vander for a week. "When are you going to tell him?" she asked after a few moments of silence.

Sydney could have pretended ignorance but she wouldn't do that to Joel. He needed to know that she'd found her Mirror Mate—that Merrick was it. Her heart ached. "I don't know," she answered truthfully. "Today is our three-year anniversary. Even with all the chaos going on around us, he took the time to tell me happy anniversary."

"I know today seems like the worst day to do it, but you can't go around pretending that everything's okay. This would be the worst day to do that to him. He wants to celebrate three years together. He thinks you're still in love with him and you're not. You have to bite the bullet and tell him about you and Merrick before he's really hurt."

"I know, but I'm not going to wake him up just to break his heart. That would be cruel."

"True. As soon as he wakes up then?"

Sydney nodded miserably. Why couldn't Joel have found his Mirror Mate at the same time so that their parting would have been a mutual agreement?

Because nothing works like it does in the movies.

"What should I say?" she asked Cali.

Cali combed her fingers through her hair a couple of times as she thought. "You know I'm not very good at that touchy feely shit, right? Under normal circumstances I'd say just tell him how it is. This, however…" She waved her arm to encompass his injured state. "This calls for a different kind of delicacy. Maybe ease into it? It's not like you hate his guts or something. Everyone can still see how much you care for him. It's not your fault that the love you felt turned into platonic love. Maybe explain that to him. As weird as this is going to sound, maybe tell him how happy you are with Merrick. Joel was always the kind of guy who'd rather chop off his own arm then see you upset or hurting. He'd do anything to help you—this time that just happens to include letting you go. He'll understand. Maybe not today or tomorrow, but eventually he'll realize that you have to be with your other half." She pulled her gaze from Joel to regard Sydney. "Speaking of which, have you guys bonded yet?"

Sydney studied the carpet. "No, and I'm not sure how. You said that we'll bond when there are no more barriers between us, right? I feel like I'm ready but what if Merrick's not open to this?"

"Have you ever thought that maybe it's your unfinished business with Joel that is holding you back? You may think you're ready to bond, that you're open as open can be, but even the smallest doubt can hold you back. It took me forever to learn I loved and trusted Felix with my life, that I'd do anything to keep him. It wasn't until I was being dragged away from him that the deep dark part of myself believed it too and cried out for him. I don't think it's something that can be forced." She placed her hand on Sydney's shoulder. "It'll come. You don't have to bond instantly, trust me. That was the one fear that Collette exploited when she was trying to break my spirit. It'll happen, just have faith."

Cali left the room.

A few minutes later Niella rolled in. "I can watch him for a while," she offered.

Sydney nodded and went out to find the others. They were all sitting around the TV. Cali was next to Luke on one sofa while Felix was in the kitchen cooking. Merrick sat alone and Sydney went to join him. His arm came around her shoulders and drew her near. Her body instantly relaxed into his but her mind continued to war with itself.

Shouldn't she feel guilty about being in Merrick's arms when Joel was lying injured in the next room?

The guilt she thought she'd overcome came back full force and she didn't know how to deal with it this time.

The moment was upon her, but it wasn't what she was expecting. It wasn't how she had planned it. Spontaneity was not her friend. She needed order. She needed Joel to be perfectly healthy in both mind and body, but now he was neither and she felt horrible for having to add to his pain.

Remember Cali's words, she reminded herself. Joel would do anything for her, he understood how amazing finding your Mirror Mate was and she didn't think he'd try to stand in her way.

I'm sorry, Joel, but it looks like our three-year anniversary marks our beginning and our end.

Chapter 26

Joel didn't surface into complete consciousness until two days after his rescue. Enough time for the guild to learn through Merrick that Vander had gotten out of police custody without a hitch.

Sydney sat at Joel's side, her jaw aching from how hard she'd been clenching it.

They'd never get that bastard.

Vander had slipped through the authority's fingers again without them even knowing it. His appearance had only played into his cover that he'd been kidnapped by Regina and her goons and beaten. The police had arrived and seen an old man at the mercy of young thugs.

Sydney had the sudden and surprising urge to hit something. She was also terrified that sometime during the night Vander would come for her. Or any one of her guild members.

After he'd been released Merrick had no way of tracking him. Vander had officially disappeared once more. She bet it was only a matter of time before he surfaced. The question was where would he pop up next.

Joel started to stir at her side. His eyes opened slowly and he stared at the ceiling for a few moments before he turned his head. "Hey."

Sydney offered him a watery smile.

"I look that bad, huh?" he asked.

She laughed. "I was just really worried about you." She brushed back some of his hair. It was getting shaggy again. Like always, Joel had forgotten to make a hair appointment. She remembered all the times she'd had to schedule haircuts for him and how most of the time he'd protest cutting his longer than average locks.

A small part of her ached at the thought of never doing that again, but there was a much bigger part waiting in anticipation to start making those kinds of memories with Merrick.

Would Merrick protest if she asked him to cut his hair now? It was down to his shoulders and fell around his head like a messy inkblot. Her heart tripped in her chest at the thought of those raven locks sliding through her fingers.

The ache in her chest was mild but she still felt Merrick's absence, even with him in the kitchen of Felix's home.

Fingers snapped right in front of her face. She jumped.

Joel laughed softly. "Are you with me? Maybe you need to get some sleep. How long have you been watching over me?"

Not as much as you're probably thinking.

"On and off," she answered evasively. "Niella, Cali, and Felix have been taking shifts. Even Luke and Merrick have been watching over you."

The second she said Merrick's name, something came over Joel's face. His expression shut down. A small difference, but one Sydney recognized instantly.

"He's a really nice guy, isn't he?" Joel said quietly.

Sydney swallowed past the lump in her throat. "He is," was all she managed to get out.

"You know I wanted to hate him for the way he looked at you. For the way you seemed to look at him instead of at me."

Her lungs constricted.

"But he helped save my life and that'd make me a real asshole if I begrudged him for it, wouldn't it?" His eyes, which had been downcast, rose up to meet hers.

When their gazes locked she felt no shiver in her soul, no answering yearning to reach out and touch him. With a finality that went all the way down to her bones, she realized that it was over with Joel and it was cruel to let him think anything else.

She grasped his uninjured hand in hers and inhaled. "Joel, I'm so sorry for what's been done to you. I know you're hurting and the last thing I want to do is add to that hurt but…to not say anything now, I think would hurt you even more."

She heard footsteps out in the hallway and was glad that she'd shut the door so no one would witness their private moment. Joel's face already told her that he had a feeling where she was taking this conversation and she felt the tears in the back of her throat. But she had to plow forward, she owed it to him.

"I always wished you were my Mirror Mate." She paused, wanting him to see the truth of that in her eyes. She heard a door slam in the distance. "But I don't get to decide that. I know now that what I feel for you isn't what you want or need. You deserve the truth, Joel, and the truth is that I've found my Mirror Mate and…" Her eyes started to cloud with tears. "And it's not you."

She couldn't stand the broken look on his face. Couldn't stand the fact that she was the one that gave it to him, but she refused to look away. This was her doing and she needed to face it. She'd take whatever lashing he decided to give her because she deserved it.

In her heart she hadn't felt as if she'd cheated on Joel because she'd already moved on, but in his eyes he'd see her affection toward Merrick as utter betrayal. He had every right to leave the guild, to never help them again and never speak to her again. The idea had her choking back a sob.

She didn't know what else to say. All the nice and pretty words she had picked out two days ago dried up, and her mind stuttered as she tried to tell Joel her feelings. In this moment all the preparation in the world wouldn't have helped her.

"I'm so sorry," she said at last.

Joel gently pulled his hand from hers. Sydney could feel him pulling away more than just physically and she had no idea what to do about it. She needed to let him pull away—it wasn't her job to comfort him like that anymore. She'd be glad to comfort him as a friend but she doubted he'd want that right now. It'd probably be a long time before she was given that luxury again.

"I had a feeling," said Joel. "Every time you entered a room your eyes sought him first. When I was injured you ran to him instead of me. I get it. I've been beaten enough times to realize that I'm not your man anymore."

A thick silence fell over them.

"Does he make you happy?"

Sydney barely heard him. She swallowed her tears at the emotion in his voice. "I think so." She didn't want to lie and say yes. The truth was she didn't know.

Joel looked up after she answered. There was a touch of anger in his eyes, but it wasn't directed at her.

She spoke up before he could threaten Merrick for something he'd never done. "The truth is, I haven't known him that long. My emotions have been in such a state of turmoil that I can't tell what I feel, but I know I feel lighter when he's around." She rubbed her chest, the ache more intense than it had been earlier. "I can't really describe what he makes me feel but if you want my honest answer then yes, I think he can and will make me happy."

She waited with bated breath for the statement to crush him but all he did was nod, as if that was the answer he wanted to hear.

"I'm sorry it couldn't be me," he said.

She reached out and placed her hand on his forearm, over one of his scars. She flinched at the sight. "You'll find yours. She's out there somewhere. I'll help you look. You know I will. I'm so afraid of losing you, Joel. Please don't leave the guild because of me."

He jerked in surprise. "Leave the guild? You thought I'd leave?"

"I thought for sure you wouldn't want to be around me anymore. I was terrified that you'd leave and never look back—that the guild would fracture and break apart. I know you don't want to hear this but I still love you, just not in the same way."

He grimaced. "You're right, I didn't want to hear that. But Syd,

I'm not going to leave the guild. I may need some time to myself for a bit, and I may not want to be around much when Merrick is, but I'm not going to leave. We're the Guild of Aletheia. What kind of guild would we be if we disbanded every time there was a complication within our group? We stick together and that's final."

She stared into his face. He was so brave, such a good guy. "You're going to make some woman very happy," she told him earnestly.

He blinked, caught off guard. He looked away but not fast enough. She saw the raw hurt and wanted to smack herself. She was acting as if they'd been broken up for three months and not three minutes.

She got to her feet. "I should let you rest some more. I'll come back later to check on you, if you want."

He gingerly touched his cast. "Maybe it'd be best for now to have someone else check on me."

His words were like a punch to the gut but she kept the smile on her face. "I'll have Niella or Luke come check on you then." With nothing else left to say she closed the door behind her and exhaled.

"How'd it go?"

Sydney nearly jumped out of her skin. "Would you stop doing that?" She whirled on Cali. "Do you do that to Felix?"

Cali uncrossed her arms and smiled. "All the time. One time I got him so good in the kitchen he sent cake dough flying straight into the ceiling."

Poor Felix.

"So, how'd it go?" she repeated.

Sydney shrugged and looked back at the door as if she'd be able to see Joel on the other side. "Not like I wanted, but better than expected, I guess."

Cali gave her a sympathetic pat on the arm. "At least it's over now and you can start afresh with Merrick. There'll be nothing hanging over your guys' heads."

"Thanks. By the way where is Merrick?" She stepped into the living room and found that everyone was accounted for except her Mirror Mate. Was that why her chest had ached worse while she was talking to Joel? He'd left? But why would he leave?

Cali shrugged. "I have no idea. He went down the hall I think to check on you and then he stormed out of the house a few seconds later."

Sydney's stomach sank. She thought back to the door slamming after she'd told Joel that she'd wished he'd been her Mirror Mate…

"Oh no." Sydney grasped Cali's arms, bringing her to an abrupt halt. "How long ago did he leave?"

"I don't know, five minutes ago maybe. What's wrong?"

Sydney dropped her hands and bolted for the door.

"Sydney?" Cali yelled after her but she didn't stop.

The streets in Felix's neighborhood were empty. She scanned the sidewalks but saw no sign of Merrick. Where could he have gone? She'd been his ride over here and she knew for a fact that he didn't have a cell phone yet so he couldn't have called a cab.

She cupped her hands around her mouth and shouted his name. There was no answer.

She raced back inside Felix's house and nearly collided with Felix. "Whoa." He caught her shoulders and held her. "What's going on? What's wrong?"

She jerked free of his hold. "I have to leave. I have to find Merrick." She snatched up her purse and keys.

Felix tailed her. "Did something happen to him? Do you need us to go with you?"

She waved him off as she climbed into her car. "I'm fine. I have to do this on my own. It's my fault he left."

*

Merrick stared out the bus window lost in thought as his surroundings passed him by. He didn't know where he was going. He didn't care. He'd been such an idiot.

Sydney'd told him she was going to break up with Joel. That she wanted him. And like a fool he'd gobbled it all up.

She never wanted me, he thought bleakly. All this time she'd wished Joel was her destined soul mate. *You can't fight destiny.*

He grunted and curled closer into himself when a man took the seat next to him. The back of his neck was prickling on and off again and he really didn't feel like seeing what was in anyone else's head. He didn't want to see how shitty everyone else's lives were or weren't. He just wanted to go back to what he'd been doing before Sydney entered his life: paying bills, finding missing persons, finding Alyssa.

Alyssa…

Sydney had promised to ask Niella about her.

He shook the thought away. That promise, like everything else she'd spoken, was nothing but a lie. He'd been a moron to trust anything she'd said.

He shoved his hands into his worn jean pockets and stopped when his fingers encountered a slick piece of paper. He pulled it out and stared down at the card Vander had given him. His gaze fell to the worn blue notebook nestled between his body and the bus wall. It had been in his possession ever since he took it from Greg's house. He'd refused to let it out of his sight.

If you give Vander the journal, you could find Alyssa.

He ran his finger over the phone number on the card. He had nothing to lose. Not anymore. No one to lose, no one to protect. Sydney had made her choice, she'd lied to him and deceived him. Him! The one that was able to read emotions and thoughts from objects. And like an idiot he'd never read anything of Sydney's purposely because he didn't want to violate her privacy. It had only been her shirt that one time.

Fuck privacy.

He knew better than to trust women. They were never what they seemed and this was the last time he was going to be kicked in the teeth. He rubbed at his chest in an attempt to quell the hollow feeling within. The action only angered him more.

He yanked the chord above his head and the bus pulled off at the next stop. He clutched Kevin's notebook to his chest as he maneuvered himself off the bus.

He scouted his surroundings until he found what he was looking for. He pulled some coins from his pockets and punched in Vander's number.

"Yes?"

"It's me." Merrick said without preamble.

"Mr. Haskell, can this really be you?" Vander oily voice slithered over the line.

"It is. Are you still in California or did you flee the state?"

"I'm still here. Just taking care of some investments is all. One of which I'm sure is going to be delighted to hear your voice."

Regina. Vander was getting her out of jail.

Merrick shuddered at the thought of her free once more. He'd worked months on end before to put women and men like her away.

But that was a different life.

"Do you still want Kevin's journal?" He cut the bullshit and got straight to the point.

Silence on the other end before, "You have it? The real one?"

So he'd realized the box he'd obtained was filled with nothing?

"I do, but I want your word—you're to help me find my sister. You said you could guarantee it."

"And I can, but I'm curious, what has caused the sudden change of heart?"

A change of heart, indeed.

He redirected his thoughts before they got away from him.

"Nothing that need concern you. I'm willing to trade the journal for access to your company's resources and a guarantee of finding my sister when Kevin wakes up. I will not work for you. Are we clear? This is a one time deal: the journal for my sister and anything related to my sister."

"That doesn't sound like a very fair trade, Mr. Haskell. You'll be getting all my resources but any help you could offer me you're refusing to give?"

"Take it or leave it, I don't care. I'll burn this journal right now if you don't take the deal, it's no matter to me."

"And what if there's nothing in it about my Mirror Mate?"

He clutched the notebook in his hand. "There is."

For the next few seconds he heard nothing but Vander's breathing. "You read it?"

"I did. Is that a problem?"

There was a thoughtful sound on the other end. "No, I guess not. Very well, Mr. Haskell. When and where would you like to exchange items?"

"Exchange items?"

"Yes, the journal for a laptop connected to any and all databanks to the Kratos Corporation. You won't have to deal with any pesky security codes. You'll have full access to anything, everything, and anyone. There will be a specific e-mail set up for you that will grant you access to numerous people in high places. Is that good enough for you?"

"What's the catch?"

"No catch, Mr. Haskell. The laptop for the journal. But I'd like to point out that I'm taking a lot on faith here that there will be useful information for me in this journal. If you've lied to me again, your death will be a slow and painful one, that I can guarantee."

"Your threats don't scare me, Vander. There's information you want in here. Swing by my apartment in two days' time and you'll get your trade. I trust you remember where I live."

"I do."

"Good. And by the way, Vander, her name is Deborah."

He hung up the phone and dug out the attached phone book for the closest hotel. There was no way he could return to his apartment. He couldn't trust Vander. He'd probably sic Jente on him in the middle of the night to slit his throat and take the journal. There'd be less hassle that way. That's what Merrick would do if he were an evil and power hungry millionaire.

Chapter 27

Merrick waved down the cab he'd called to take him to his apartment. As the taxi pulled up to the curb he got a good look at himself in the window. Dark circles under his eyes, pale skin, sunken cheeks. If possible he looked worse than he did when he'd first escaped Vander.

He blamed it on his horrible sleeping pattern. He'd barely been able to sleep for the past two days. His thoughts kept circling unbidden to Sydney. Every time he'd dreamed, it was of her face, her body…

He'd wake up with a raging hard-on and a fierce aching in his chest that refused to leave him.

Was this what he was to endure for the rest of his life?

He hoped Sydney was suffering as much as he was, but as soon as the thought left him he instantly regretted it. Even now he wanted no harm to come to her.

He swore under his breath and wrenched the car door open. He barked his address to the driver and sulked in the back, already feeling on edge. He'd thought finding his Mirror Mate would be a blessing, not a curse.

I guess that's what happens when your Mirror Mate doesn't want you.

And to think he thought himself in love with her.

His stomach twisted painfully. He rolled down the window to get some air.

"Are you all right?" the driver asked him. "You look a little green. Do you need me to pull over? I don't want you puking in my car."

"I'll be fine," Merrick growled at him. "Just drive."

He clutched the edges of his seat. No wonder this was so hard for him. He was in love with Sydney. The realization was worse than being kicked in the gut.

You're pathetic. Weak. The whole thing was an act and you went and fell in love with the woman. It serves you right.

He leaned forward in his seat and rested his head in his hands. He fisted his hair—wanted to pull it from his head. Damn her. Damn her whole guild for making him feel anything for them.

It was his time back at the station all over again.

Not for long, he thought darkly.

He straightened and glanced down at the journal next to him. In a few short minutes his mind would be occupied with finding Alyssa. He'd be back to what was really important in his life. He had no reason to be invested in stopping Vander. He wasn't a member of the Guild of Truth. He scoffed at the title. Truth… yeah, right. As long as he was left alone with the Kratos resources at his fingertips, he didn't care what the Guild of Truth did.

Yes you do. Don't lie to yourself. You're not that heartless of a person.

Yes he was.

If you were, then you would've given Vander the journal yesterday, not today when—

"We're here," the cab driver said bluntly.

Merrick snatched the journal and flung money at the driver, uncaring when he started shouting obscenities at him.

He didn't see any suspicious vehicles parked outside his apartment building but he could sense that he was being watched. "Come and get it, Vander," he mumbled and took his stairs two at a time.

There were no intruders inside his apartment and he hastily changed into a pair of clean clothes. As soon as he stepped out of his bedroom there came a knock on his door. Short and clipped. A business knock. Vander.

He tucked the journal into the back waistband of his pants and tugged his shirt to cover it.

Vander was waiting on the other side of the door, along with Regina, Dennis, and the nameless pain inflictor. Merrick didn't step back to let them in. "Those three stay out here," he told Vander plainly.

Vander inclined his head. "If that is what you wish."

Merrick stepped back.

Vander strolled into his home, a fancy cane held in one hand. There was a slight limp to his gait and Merrick smirked. He wondered if Felix or Cali had been the one to give it to him.

He slammed the door in Regina's face and turned to Vander. "Body's a little more fragile these days, huh?"

Vander leaned heavily on his cane. "I'm afraid old age just doesn't agree with me. Now, where is the journal?"

"Where's my laptop?" It hadn't escaped him that Vander wasn't carrying any kind of backpack.

Vander smiled and gave a careless shrug. "You'll get your laptop after you give me the journal. Regina has it out in the hall."

"Bullshit." Merrick ripped open his door.

Regina and her two partners still stood there in formation. Dennis handed her a black bag that she held up to him. It was the right size but when he went to reach for it she pulled it back.

"We had a deal, Mr. Haskell," Vander said from behind him.

He turned so neither party was at his back. "How do I know that bag has a laptop in it and not a collection of rocks?"

"Very paranoid, aren't you?" said Vander.

"I like to think of it as being careful."

Vander nodded to Regina and she zipped open the bag, exposing a shiny new laptop. Vander held his hand out and she carefully handed it over.

He limped back into Merrick's apartment.

Merrick slammed the door in Regina's face. He'd never get tired of that.

Vander set the bag on the coffee table and remained standing. "You have your prize, now where is mine?"

Merrick lifted up the tail end of his shirt and pulled out the notebook.

Vander smirked. "How very like a cop you are."

Merrick shrugged. "Some habits are hard to kick."

Vander came forward and gingerly took the journal. "I know the feeling," he said before latching on to Merrick's exposed forearm.

A mad gleam came to Vander's eye, a gleam that Merrick knew all too well, but it was too late. Pain ripped through him as Vander stole his life energy into himself. Vander moaned. Merrick's knees buckled and he fell to the floor.

*

Sydney brought her phone up to her ear.

"911, what's your emergency?"

"I-I'd like to report a break-in." She forced shakiness into her voice. A few seconds later she hung up and pulled her bag of goodies into her lap. She readied three syringes and slung the strap over her head as she made her way across the street to Merrick's apartment. For the past two days she'd been staked out. She'd refused to let him go without a fight, without explaining that what he'd heard had been out of context. After the first night, she'd seen Regina scouting out the place so she'd gone back to her clinic and picked up a few supplies. It was obvious that Vander was still after Merrick.

Now he was trapped in his apartment with Vander and the trio from San Francisco. She'd be damned if she let them get the better of Merrick. As she climbed the stairs to Merrick's apartment she pulled out a bottle of Felix's cologne and sprayed herself.

No need to give Regina a heads up.

She spied the backs of their legs first. She readied her syringes, her heartbeat hammering in her chest.

You can do this.

She crawled up the stairs slowly, hoping Regina wouldn't notice her smell coming up behind her. She'd only wanted to disguise her scent so Regina wouldn't identify her. She was tempted to use her powers but if she used her Shield then that would give her away faster than her scent.

Her plan was working as she reached the top of the stairs. Regina didn't even turn. A moan and a grunt came from inside and all her fear vanished as her concern for Merrick overtook her.

"Looks like Vander made his move." Regina went to open the door.

Sydney sprang. She got both men in the thigh and shoved the plunger down without mercy. Both men screamed like little girls.

Regina whirled, Merrick's apartment door swung open, forgotten. "You." Regina's eyes glittered with hate.

"Me." Sydney charged. She was out for blood.

Regina tried to duck but there was nowhere to go. Sydney crashed into her and they fell into Merrick's home, Sydney on top. She held her syringe in both hands, struggling to push it into Regina's chest.

Regina's face was bright red with exertion as she held Sydney off. Both their arms where quaking with the effort. "You bitch," Regina ground out. "If you inject that into my heart, you'll kill me."

"I'm a vet, you fucking moron. I know dosages—and how do you know I don't want you dead?"

For the first time Sydney saw true fear in Regina's eyes.

Sydney gained a few inches. She was so close.

Regina was starting to sweat.

Sydney could see her victory. She just had to find Merrick—

She looked up.

Big mistake.

Vander hovered over her Mirror Mate like a giant spider sucking the life out of its prey.

"Merrick!"

She threw up her Shield. Regina took advantage of her distraction and flipped Sydney over her head.

She landed with a grunt. Pain exploded in her chest as air was forcefully expelled from her lungs.

Numbly she flexed her fingers and found the syringe still within her grasp.

Regina lunged for her.

Sydney rolled. Not far enough.

Regina landed on her back and grasped her hair. She drove her face into the hard floor.

Sydney cried out. She threw her arm back and stabbed Regina right in her trapezius. She screamed.

Sydney shoved the plunger down. Regina threw her face back into the floor and Sydney lost her grip on the syringe. Her vision wavered in and out. The back of her neck tingled then stopped.

No. Must protect Merrick.

She forced her Shield back up and threw her head back with everything she had.

A sickening crunch met her ears and Regina groaned in pain.

Something hot and sticky drenched the back of Sydney's neck and shirt and copper tinged the air.

Blood.

Sydney rolled and Regina fell like a rag doll onto the floor next to her, the needle still sticking out near her neck.

Despite her dizziness, Sydney plucked the needle out and got to her feet. The world spun but she forced herself to focus. Vander was nowhere in sight.

Sydney ground her teeth but there was nothing else to be done. She ran to Merrick's side.

"Merrick." She cradled his head.

His eyelids fluttered open. "Syd?"

She kissed him. "Are you all right? Can you stand?"

She helped him into a sitting position and got him onto the couch. "I should be okay in a few minutes," he said. "That fucker tried to kill me."

"Vander has a nasty habit of doing that," she said dryly.

"Sydney, what the hell are you doing here?"

"You mean besides saving your life? I've been staking out your house for the past couple days. There's something I have to tell you, something I think you need to hear in proper context. But right now I have to take care of something." She left his side.

"Where are you going?"

She grasped Regina under the armpits and heaved. "I have to stage a break-in one floor down."

Despite Merrick being weakened by Vander he helped Sydney break into an unsuspecting neighbor's apartment where they threw Regina, Dennis, and their buddy inside.

Sydney could already hear the sirens and dashed back up the stairs with Merrick to hide in his room. "I need to shower in case they come asking questions," she said.

And ask questions the police did.

Dressed in nothing but a robe with wet hair, Sydney stood by Merrick's side in his doorway as they explained the commotion they'd heard downstairs.

"And you didn't report it?" the officer asked.

"No sir," said Merrick, his arm wrapped around Sydney's shoulders. To the officer it would look like a sign of affection but Sydney knew that if it weren't for her, Merrick would be swaying on his feet.

The officer made a few more notes. "And what happened to your face, miss?"

Sydney's hand instantly went to her face. It throbbed from Regina's abuse but she'd hoped the heat from the shower and the flush on her face would cover it up. But it looked like their officer was a little more perceptive than she'd anticipated. She quickly sought out an excuse.

"When I heard the sirens and then the pounding of footsteps downstairs, I was given quite the fright. I slipped in the shower and bashed my poor money maker into the tile." She used her best bubbly voice to convey that she was an accident prone bimbo.

It worked.

"Very well, thank you for your time."

Merrick shut the door and they turned around to both stare at the large blood stain on his floor.

"Good thing he didn't want to be invited in," Sydney said as she helped Merrick over to the couch. "I'll clean that up right away."

Merrick remained eerily silent the entire time she cleaned. By the time she finished her whole body was on edge. She could feel the tension building in the room.

She drained the last of the water down the sink and nearly jumped out of her skin when Merrick's voice spoke right in her ear. "What are you doing here, Sydney?"

The bucket clattered in the sink as she spun on him.

His face was dark and haggard. He looked horrible. Vander's attack on him didn't help either. Anger simmered in his ice blue eyes, but there was also a flicker of vulnerability. A spark of feeble hope.

Her heart lurched.

"Why did you leave Felix's that day?" She needed to know what he'd heard, what he was feeling, and deal with it accordingly.

He crossed his arms. "I had my reasons."

Sydney's temper sparked. He was going to pretend that he hadn't heard anything? Fine. Two could play at this game.

"So you just decided to leave us high and dry for no good reason? I thought you were better than that."

His jaw bulged.

"I don't know what made you want to leave," she continued, "but the least you could do is give us back the journal." She held her hand out.

If possible, his face grew darker. "I don't have it."

Her little act crumbled. "What? What do you mean you don't have it? You left with it!"

"I traded it to Vander for information on my sister."

Sydney's world spun. All she could think was that Greg had been right. They never should have taken the journal. "You idiot!" she exploded and shoved him. "What were you thinking?"

Merrick snapped. "I was thinking how stupid I was to fall for your lovey dovey act. That's what! You played me. You never wanted me as your Mirror Mate, you said as much to Joel. I heard you. All that time together you had me tagging after you like some whipped puppy! Why bother stringing me along? Huh? You wanted another man on the side, was that it?"

Sydney's hand flew before she knew what was happening. She punched him in the gut.

Merrick grunted and clutched his abdomen. He chuckled before speaking in a deadly voice. "Get out of my house."

She trembled.

Merrick would never hurt you.

"No." She raised her chin stubbornly. "You want to know why I've been staked outside your house? It's because I care about you. You said you overheard me telling Joel I didn't want you as my Mirror Mate, well, if you would have stuck around you would have heard me tell him that at one point in time I *used* to wish Joel was my destined soul mate. But not anymore. I broke things off with Joel. You would have learned this if you hadn't run off. I broke up with him just like I said I would because I don't love him anymore."

Merrick's brow furrowed.

She tried stepping closer to him but he backed away from her. "I don't want to hear your lies. Save them for someone more gullible than I because I'm done."

"I'm not lying, you jackass." She finally understood Cali's need to resort to name calling. Men just seemed to respond better that way.

Merrick blinked. "What did you call me?"

"You heard me. Now are you going to listen to me or not? I don't love Joel." She dug deep inside herself for courage and plowed onward. "I love you, Merrick."

His eyes wavered and right when she was sure he'd cave, he turned his back on her. "If you won't leave, then I will," he said gruffly.

Her heart shattered.

She watched him make his way toward the door. With a finality that made her want to cry, she knew that once he stepped through those doors he'd be gone from her life forever.

Please don't leave me, she whispered in the deepest part of her soul. Something fragile inside of her reached out. *Merrick…*

Merrick stopped dead with his hand on the knob of his door.

In the recesses of her mind she heard a tentative and hopeful, *Sydney?* before everything was enveloped in heat and whiteness.

Chapter 28

Merrick awoke to a fierce burning inside his chest. He blinked up at his ceiling before jackknifing into a sitting position.

How the hell had he gotten on the floor?

He rubbed at his chest absently. Heat blazed from within, like a mini fire. It filled him up—made him feel whole.

Sydney—

He spotted her a few feet away on the floor just like he'd been.

"Sydney." He rushed to her side and cradled her against his chest. With her in his arms, the heat in his chest turned into a deep warmth that seeped into every pore of his body. He stared down at her beautiful face in awe.

Could it be possible?

Had they…bonded?

He shook her gently. "Come on, Sydney, open those beautiful green eyes of yours. Even if all you do is glare at me, which I might add, I deserve. I was such an asshole. I should have believed you. I wanted to—I just—"

"You can quit babbling." She spoke without opening her eyes. A smile curled her lips. "I accept your apology."

He crushed her to his chest, vowing to never let her go.

"Merrick," Sydney squeaked. "Can't breathe."

He released her instantly and she inhaled deeply.

"I see you got your strength back."

He quickly took an assessment of his body and found that he felt great. Better than great. He was rejuvenated.

"How do I feel so fantastic?" He pulled back far enough to stare into her eyes.

Her emerald eyes shone up at him with such love it made his heart hurt. "Because we bonded." She placed one hand over his heart and the other over her own. "I've never felt anything like it before," she whispered.

He covered her hand with one of his. That oh-so-familiar jolt skittered through his body. His cock tightened and his eyes dipped down to take note that Sydney was clad in nothing but a bathrobe.

When his eyes wandered back to hers, he found stark desire flaring bright. "Have you ever been taken on the floor?" he asked her roughly.

She visibly shivered. She undid the belt of her robe and shook her head. "No," she said breathlessly.

Merrick hissed when the robe fell open, exposing her perky breasts. Her nipples were already hard and begging for his mouth.

Easy, he calmed himself.

He rolled onto his back and dragged Sydney atop him. There was no need for her to suffering being on the bottom. He hadn't cleaned the floor in a while and he didn't mind a little dirt and grit.

She straddled his waist and pulled his shirt up and over his head. He kept himself in check as her hands ghosted over his chest, light as a fairy. He cupped her breasts in his hands and gently kneaded.

He groaned when she raked her nails along his skin and he couldn't help but ground himself against her bottom.

He cursed his jeans. They were all that stood in his way of sliding deep inside Sydney.

As if sensing his distress she leaned down until her chest was flush with his and fused their lips together.

Merrick's control was slipping. He hadn't sampled her in so long and she tasted so good. He wrapped his hand in her hair and pressed her closer to deepen their kiss.

She slid herself against him wantonly.

Merrick forced his attention to their kiss, lest he come in his pants.

He forced his tongue past her lips and stroked deep into her mouth. She met him stroke for stroke, lick for lick. His body was driven to a fevered pitch. His cock strained against the fly of his jeans and he didn't know how much more he could take.

Sydney broke their kiss to trail her lips down his neck, her hands questing further south until she reached the waistband of his jeans.

Finally.

Merrick dropped his head back as she worked his pants down his thighs, just enough to free him.

She inhaled sharply, as if she'd forgotten how big he was.

Merrick smirked.

He pushed her robe the rest of the way off her body until she was blessedly naked atop him. The sight was erotic as hell.

They were both breathing heavily by the time she pushed herself down onto him. They both moaned and the heat inside Merrick felt near to bursting. He arched his back and slid deeper inside her.

Her fingers bit into his chest where she was using him like a balancing board. Slowly she started to rock, then she rose up on her knees to sink back down on him.

Merrick bit his tongue to keep from shouting. She was so wet and hot around him.

Eventually she found a rhythm that had him meeting her halfway. When she started to tire he grasped her hips and helped her, driving himself up into her over and over as she rode him.

He felt his climax building.

Sydney's inner muscles clenched around him and she came with a muffled cry.

Merrick drank in the sight of her: her head thrown back, her blonde hair a messy halo around her head. Her green eyes glittered with satisfaction and he'd been the one to give it to her.

"I love you," he told her right as he was thrown over the edge.

His hands tightened on her hips, pulling her close as he shoved up off the floor to empty himself inside her.

He must've temporarily blacked out because when next he blinked, Sydney's head was pillowed on his chest. She traced lazy circles along his biceps and from time to time he could feel her lips press delicate kisses to his flesh.

"I love you too," she whispered against him.

He ran his hand through her hair, down her spine, and cupped her bottom. "I'm so sorry I was an asshole to you earlier."

She picked her head up to rest her chin on her arm. "I'm sorry you heard what you did and thought I didn't love you."

He traced his finger down her cheek. "I should have never doubted you. I was hurt. Ever since my powers manifested I've never been able to trust another. I should have realized I could trust you, but I was too fucking stupid."

She kissed him tenderly. When she pulled back her eyes were filled with sadness. "Greg was right, we should have never taken Kevin's journal. Now Vander has it in his clutches."

And this was where Merrick felt like a real fucking moron. "I should have known he'd double cross me. My anger at you and the guild clouded my judgment. He took the laptop, the journal, and tried to kill me. Under normal circumstances I would have seen his deception a mile away."

She pressed her finger firmly against his lips. "Shh, we'll get it back."

He shook his head, dislodging her hand. "There's no need."

She gave him a puzzled look.

"While I might have been out of it, I wasn't a complete fool. I read the journal and I found the information Vander was after. I also kept the journal a day longer than necessary. Old habits die hard, and no matter how much I wanted to think I didn't care about Vander or your guild, I couldn't bring myself to completely sabotage all our hard work."

"What are you saying?"

He squeezed her bottom affectionately. "I'm saying that if Vander had gotten the journal a day earlier he would have found his Mirror Mate. Her name is Deborah and she was visiting from out of town and would have been at a certain location at a certain time. Yesterday. Today she's gone and the information Vander has at his fingertips is all but useless."

She pushed off his chest hard enough to make him grunt. "Are you serious?" She was grinning like an idiot.

He ran his hands up her back and returned her grin. "Very serious. If Vander wants to find his Mirror Mate now, he's going to have to wait until Kevin wakes up."

"That could take years," said Sydney.

"Let's hope longer."

He pulled her down for a kiss.

Epilogue

Two months later.

Merrick helped Luke center the Christmas tree in the corner of Sydney's clinic's lobby.

"You're still crooked." Niella tilted her head as she watched them from a distance.

"That's because your head is crooked," shot back Luke.

Merrick still had no idea how he'd gotten roped into this. Last night he'd been happily lying in bed after sex with Sydney, ready to drift off to sleep, when she'd asked him if he'd help decorate the clinic. He'd been too tired to do anything else but agree. Now, as he adjusted the tree for perhaps the millionth time, he realized Sydney had tricked him into this. She'd lured him in with sex until his defenses were down and his mind was fogged, then she'd sprung her trap.

He shook his head. The plan was brilliant, actually.

"Let's finish with everything else, then we can come back to the tree and mess with it some more." Merrick pulled out decorations that stuck to the exam room doors and handed some off to Niella.

Luke stepped up to take a share and stopped when Sydney's voice traveled from the back of the clinic. "Luke, I need some assistance here, please."

Luke smiled. "Duty calls." He cheerfully sprinted off.

Luke had started working for Sydney weeks ago after going through a crash course in being a veterinary assistant. It turned out that Luke had a real knack for working with animals. He looked a lot happier, though Merrick could still sense his unease every once in a while. It'd take Luke a long time before he felt comfortable enough to not have to check over his shoulder every five minutes.

Hell, Merrick even found himself still checking every dark corner of his life for Vander, half expecting him to come out of the shadows and kill him for ruining his only chance at finding his Mirror Mate. But so far he'd remained off the radar. A week ago they'd gotten a lead on some illegal activity at another Kratos location and had sent Felix and Cali. The two were due to return today, and they were all going to gather at Felix's for a welcome home/pre-Christmas dinner.

While it was a nice change to think of Vander as gone for good, Merrick knew he'd be back. Kevin and Collette were still waiting in their hospital room. Vander wouldn't leave that kind of treasure just sitting around. If Merrick had to guess, he'd say Jente was left behind to watch over Vander's prized Dreamer.

Merrick made his way toward the exam rooms to begin the decorating process when the phone started to ring.

Niella smirked at the excuse to stop helping with the decorations.

"Not you too," he said.

She gave Merrick a mock salute before quickly rolling behind the receptionist desk. "Duty calls," she parroted Luke's words and picked up the phone.

Merrick stared down at all the cheesy Christmas decorations in his hands. "Unbelievable."

*

"Can I talk to you for a minute?"

Merrick looked over his shoulder and started at the sight of Joel.

Dinner was over and everyone had sprawled out on the couches as Felix put on some ridiculous animated—claymation?—Christmas movie.

Merrick had been busy in the kitchen opening another bottle of wine when Joel had snuck up on him. He hadn't really seen much of Joel for the past two months. Not that he could blame him for wanting some space.

Tonight had been the first time they'd all really been together for a long period of time. Sydney had cut back on the public displays of affection and Merrick had had no problem with that. He didn't want to rub it in Joel's face. Joel had been doing a good job of keeping a fake smile plastered on his face, and Merrick had only caught a couple of wistful glances at Sydney the entire night.

Merrick cleared his throat and turned his attention back to the man in front of him. "Sure. What'd you need to talk to me about?"

Joel led him back to the guest room and gently shut the door once they were both inside. "It's not so much talking as I wanted to give you something—something for Sydney." He pulled out a velvet box from his pants and quickly gave it to Merrick as if he was afraid of losing his nerve.

Curious, Merrick opened the box. His eyes widened. "Joel, I can't give her this. It's too much." Inside the box was a beautifully crafted gold necklace with a pearlescent seashell charm.

When he tried to give it back to him, Joel pulled his hands back and held them out at his sides. "I can't give it to her. I don't have that right anymore, Merrick. Besides, the necklace screams Syd. She'll love it and I can't bring myself to return it. Just give it to her. She doesn't need to know it was ever from me."

Merrick stared down at the pendant. "Why are you giving it to me? You could have given it to anyone else in the guild."

Joel shrugged. "You make her happy. This'll make her happy and as long as she's happy, I can pretend that I am too."

Merrick's respect for Joel went up about ten notches. Under different circumstances he'd like to think they could've been the best of friends. But life didn't work that way, and so Merrick kept his distance. Maybe one day they'd be able to become friends. He didn't mind waiting.

He curled his hands around the necklace. "Thanks. Is there any specific date you'd like me to give it to her?"

"Tonight, if you want. I heard rumors that tonight was going to be a special night."

With that he left.

Merrick had no idea what Joel had meant until after the movie when Felix started to put on some seasonal music. Sydney pulled Merrick up to dance while Felix and Cali swayed around the floor. Out of nowhere a very non-Christmas song came on and Felix dropped down to one knee in front of Cali.

Sydney gasped as Felix took out a little black box and flipped it open to reveal a white gold band adorned with a black diamond.

"Cali Crazar." He stared up into Cali's wide obsidian eyes. "I'm already yours for the rest of time, but would you marry me anyway?" Felix flashed her a grin and Cali nearly tackled him to the ground.

"You pompous ass," Cali said. "You told me you were going into that jewelry store to gather intel."

"And you bought that?" Niella asked incredulously.

Cali glared at her good naturedly over Felix's shoulder.

"So is that a yes?" Felix asked.

Cali kissed him soundly on the mouth. "Of course it's a yes," she told him, then her lips moved but Merrick couldn't hear a word. It was as if he suddenly went deaf.

Felix's grin grew wider at whatever Cali said. It looked as if he had no trouble hearing her.

The alcohol really started flowing then. Merrick stole Sydney away before they had too much.

"What is it?" Sydney giggled as he closed the guest door behind her.

It looked like she'd already had a few good drinks.

"I wanted to give you something. I figured tonight was a good night." He pulled the box out and handed it to Sydney.

She instantly sobered. "Oh, Merrick…" She gingerly opened it and her breath caught. "It's beautiful. How'd you know I loved seashells?"

Merrick's smile was bittersweet. "Let's just say someone passed on the information."

Sydney beamed and threw her arms around his neck. "I love it. Will you put it on for me?"

When they went back to the living room everyone commented on Sydney's necklace. Cali and Sydney had fun comparing jewelry and as the night neared its end, Joel and Felix held up their beer bottles to gather attention.

"All right everyone, we have an announcement. We've official created a Title for Merrick."

They lifted their drinks in his direction.

"I know it's been a while," said Felix, "but you were a little tricky to figure out. So we've settled on…drum roll please…"

Joel pounded on the nearby coffee table.

"The Decoder," Felix said with a flourish.

Sydney's nose wrinkled. "Ew," she yelled. "You make him sound like a cereal box toy or something."

Joel and Felix opened their mouths to protest when Luke shot eagerly to his feet. "Hey guys, have you thought up a name for me yet?"

"Uh…" Joel looked to Felix.

"Sure," said Felix. "You're the…um…"

"The Generator," Joel shouted triumphantly as if the thought had just struck him.

Merrick stared down at his drink and realized with all the alcohol they'd consumed the name probably had just popped up to him.

Luke's face fell. "The Generator? That sounds too much like terminator."

Felix shoved Joel. "Yes! The Generator." He dropped his voice and adopted his best Arnold Schwarzenegger accent as he spoke the title. "I now dub it mandatory to say your name like this."

"What?" said Luke.

"Come on," Joel piped up. "Say it." Then he put on his own accent. "Luke the Generator."

Felix shook his head. "Mine was way better, man."

"I don't think so," argued Joel.

Merrick sat up a little straighter and put on the accent. "Luke the Generator, come with me if you want to live."

Joel and Felix both froze and stared at him. Then at the same time they burst.

"Holy shit!"

"That was awesome!"

Cali and Niella both cheered.

Sydney leaned into him with a grin. "I'm so proud," she teased him.

*

"So something has been bugging me. You mentioned before that everyone comes up with titles and terms for the guild." Merrick came to a stop at the light as he drove himself and Sydney home.

Sydney yawned. "Yeah. And?"

The light turned green.

"And I was wondering who made up the term Mirror Mates?" he asked.

"Felix. He was the first to find out about them so he named it."

"Is there any reasoning behind it?" He pulled into her designated parking spot and turned off the car.

"Felix believed that two souls that reflect one another are always destined to find each other. Or something."

Merrick turned in his chair and cupped her face. "He's right. And I've never been so glad that you found me."

Sydney's eyes sparkled with love and affection. She was his everything.

She leaned in and kissed him. "I'm glad I found you too."

About the Author

Mary K. Norris loves to travel the world and go on crazy, extreme adventures. Unfortunately, she can't do that all the time, so she creates crazy adventures for her characters in supernatural worlds from the comfort of her home in Southern California. She has a bachelor's degree in Kinesiology and when she's not reading or writing she's usually found doing some kind of physical activity, playing video games, or at Disneyland.

In the mood for more Crimson Romance? Check out *Once Upon a Couch* by Kristine Overbrook at *CrimsonRomance.com*.